Good
as
Gone

Good as Gone

DOUGLAS CORLEONE

Minotaur Books 🐾 New York

This is a work of fiction. All of the characters, organizations, and events portrayed in this novel are either products of the author's imagination or are used fictitiously.

www.minotaurbooks.com

Library of Congress Cataloging-in-Publication Data

Corleone, Douglas.
  Good as gone / Douglas Corleone. — First U.S. edition.
      pages cm
   ISBN 978-1-250-01720-8 (hardcover)
   ISBN 978-1-250-01721-5 (e-book)
   1. Private investigators—Fiction.   2. Missing children—Fiction.
3. Kidnapping—Fiction.   I. Title.
   PS3603.O763G84 2013
   813'.6—dc23

                                                        2013009828

Minotaur books may be purchased for educational, business, or promotional use. For information on bulk purchases, please contact Macmillan Corporate and Premium Sales Department at 1-800-221-7945 extension 5442 or write specialmarkets@macmillan.com.

First Edition: August 2013

10 9 8 7 6 5 4 3 2 1

FOR VINCENT ANTONIELLO

I think constantly of those who are gone; as my body continues on its journey, my thoughts keep coming back to bury themselves in days past.

—Gustave Flaubert (1849)

Part
One

THE THIEVES
OF PARIS

Chapter 1

I was resting in the rear of a taxi heading north out of the city on our way to Charles de Gaulle when I first heard the sirens. I opened my eyes and watched the red needle on the speedometer drop steadily as the driver turned the wheel to the right. In the rearview I glimpsed a half-dozen white Peugeots topped with flashing light bars bearing down on us. As we pulled to the shoulder, two of the cruisers skidded to a halt diagonally just in front of us, two boxed us in on the side, and the remaining vehicles screamed to a stop at our tail. I instinctively inventoried myself though I knew I wasn't carrying any contraband—nothing at all that would link me to the missing boy in Bordeaux.

The driver casually rolled down his window. One of the officers poked his head in, asked the driver in French where we were going.

"L'aéroport," the driver said.

The officer nodded, glanced at me, and switched to English, speaking to the driver as though I weren't there.

"I require your passenger to step out of the vehicle," he said. "Slowly, always showing me his hands."

Two younger officers stood outside the window to my right, hands on their sidearms. In the rearview I noticed several other officers taking cover behind their open car doors, their weapons already drawn.

With a sigh I slid over to the driver's side and gently opened the door. With my hands held out before me I stepped onto the road.

"Monsieur Fisk," the officer said as he sized me up. The rank insignia on his uniform jacket indicated he was a lieutenant, formerly known as an inspector. "I would like for you to accompany us back to Paris."

Cautiously, I lowered my hands.

"Sorry, Lieutenant. I have a plane to catch."

"You may return with us voluntarily or involuntarily," he said, "it makes no difference to me."

"Am I under arrest?"

The lieutenant made a show of gazing over my left shoulder at his officers with their drawn SIG SP 2022s.

"Does it appear to you that you are free to leave?"

I didn't give him the satisfaction of looking behind me. Instead I pictured the route back to National Police Headquarters. If memory served, we'd be heading to Ile de la Cité, which meant passing through several areas of heavy traffic. Assuming we wouldn't be blaring sirens all the way, we should be moving slowly enough to facilitate an escape. Perhaps on Rue du Faubourg Saint-Honoré near the Palais de l'Elysée, a short distance from the American embassy, and thus, safety.

"All right, then," I said. "Let's get on with it."

The lieutenant, whose nameplate read DAVIGNON, escorted me to the last cruiser, patted me down, and opened the rear door. He didn't cuff me, didn't push me roughly into the car while pretending to protect my skull. He just motioned to the inside and permitted me to seat myself. *Strange*, I thought. But then, I'd never been arrested in Paris. Tokyo, yes. Beijing, sure. Moscow, Oslo, Budapest. Mexico City, more than once. But never Paris. Until now.

"What about my luggage?" I said.

Davignon smirked and slammed the door.

Maybe the French police weren't so cordial after all.

No worries. Lieutenant Davignon had left me my hands, which were more than I needed. I'd planned to make do with only my feet. At the first congested intersection, I'd summon this morning's croissants and espresso and decorate their backseat. All I needed from them was to open my door; the rest would be up to me.

Davignon, who looked to be in his midforties, sat up front in the passenger seat. The moment we pulled off the shoulder, he turned forty-five degrees and began talking at me.

"Simon Fisk," he said in heavily accented English, "thirty-nine years old. Born: London, England, to Alden and Tatum Fisk. One sibling: a slightly older sister named Tuesday, who was actually born six minutes after midnight on a Wednesday morning. When you were five, your father, who possessed dual U.K. and U.S. citizenship, left London for Providence, Rhode Island, taking you with him and leaving your mother and sister behind. To my knowledge, you have not seen either of them since."

I set my jaw and glared at him through the wire.

"If you're attempting to get a rise out of me, Lieutenant, I suggest we stop off at the nearest pharmacy and pick up a bottle of Cialis. Otherwise, you're wasting your time."

Davignon ignored me. "At seventeen you left home to attend American University in Washington D.C., where you majored in Justice and minored in Law and Society. While at university, you met Tasha Lynn Dunne of Richmond, Virginia, and soon fell head over heels in love, as the Americans say. Both of you graduated American with honors and married a year later in a sizable ceremony in Norfolk. Your father, Alden, wasn't invited and didn't attend. From there you moved back to the District of Columbia, where you began serious study and conditioning to become a United States Marshal. You submitted a flawless application, excelled in interviews, and were invited into Basic Training at FLETC in Glynco,

Georgia. After seventeen and a half weeks of rigorous training, you were assigned to fugitive investigations in the D.C. field office, an assignment you yourself requested."

I stared out the window at the unfamiliar landscape blowing by. Wherever we were making for, it wasn't National Police Headquarters.

"After four months on the job," Davignon continued, "you announced to your immediate supervisor that your wife, Tasha, was pregnant. Another six months after that, your daughter, Hailey, was born."

"Enough," I finally snapped, angry at the direction in which both the conversation and the vehicle were heading. "Where are you taking me?"

Davignon finally turned fully in his seat to face me. It was only then that I noticed just how heavy and tired his eyes looked, how his five o'clock shadow reflected an additional twelve hours or so.

"To a very private place," he said. "Where you and I can have a long talk. And possibly come to some sort of an arrangement."

Chapter 2

Signs indicated that we were approximately forty kilometers north of Paris when we parked behind a quaint two-story cottage set off from its neighbors in a quiet, rural village called Saint-Maur-des-Fossés. Only one other cruiser had followed us into the village and it was now nowhere in sight. Thoughts of escape morphed into curiosity. Clearly, this wasn't an arrest, wasn't a hit. For the first time I wondered if this had anything at all to do with the boy in Bordeaux.

Davignon opened my door and I stepped out under the tired gray sky and headed for the dull peach-colored house. As I flattened the tall blades of grass underfoot, Davignon uttered some instructions to his partner in French. Glancing back, it appeared that he had told him to wait with the car.

The interior of the cottage was brighter than I had expected. Natural light poured in through large, uncovered windows, illuminating a well-appointed living room with a sofa, love seat, and several straight-back cushioned chairs that looked as though they belonged in a seventeenth-century castle. Davignon motioned for me to take a seat in the chair positioned kitty-corner to a tall, well-used fireplace. I sat, folded my arms, and crossed my right leg over my left.

"Something to drink?" Davignon said. What little hair remaining on the sides and back of his head was shaved down, nearly to the skin. He possessed a bulk that came free with age, and a casualness that conveyed confidence and authority. I could tell that he liked being in charge, that he'd do just about anything to maintain control of a situation.

"I'd rather we get to it, Lieutenant."

"Very well."

Davignon stepped out of the living room and returned a moment later with a thin manila folder. He dropped it in my lap and remained standing next to the sofa across from me. He didn't remove his jacket.

Inside the folder were several photographs of a female child, age five or six, with straight auburn hair that fell to her shoulders. Wide emerald-green eyes highlighted a perfectly symmetrical face and stole attention from her tiny smile, which revealed two rows of neatly aligned teeth. The image reminded me immediately of Hailey, though this little girl looked nothing like my daughter. It wasn't the shade of her hair or shape of her face, wasn't her flawless complexion or even the color of her eyes, but rather the sparkle of light afloat in each pupil—that distinctive sign of life—that made me flash on the past, on days spent sailing on Chesapeake Bay, on nights when Tasha and I watched little Hailey dance through the sprinklers from our lounge chairs on the back porch.

"Her name is Lindsay Sorkin," Davignon said, "six years old. Born: Santa Clara, California, to Vincent and Lori Sorkin. No siblings; however, Lori Sorkin is presently fifteen weeks pregnant." He cleared his throat. "The night before last, Lindsay Sorkin went missing from the family's room at Hotel d'Étonner in Champs-Elysées. The family was in Paris on holiday and claim to know no one else in France. They are, to put it mildly, devastated." He paused. "And they are desperate, Monsieur Fisk."

I closed the folder and set it on my lap, sighing deeply, truly regretting what I had to say.

"Since you know my history so well, Lieutenant, I'm assuming you also know what I do for a living."

"I do. You retrieve missing children."

"No," I said. "I retrieve children abducted by estranged parents who flee to countries that don't recognize U.S. custody decisions."

"Countries like France."

"The point is, Lieutenant, that I don't deal with 'stranger abductions,' only parental abductions—cases in which the kidnapper is known and related to the victim."

Davignon put his head down and clasped his hands behind his back.

"Given what you have been through as a husband and father, that is understandable."

My body tensed. In that moment I could have snapped Davignon's neck. Was he really using the abduction of my six-year-old daughter and the subsequent suicide of my wife to play on my emotions? Did he really think that would work? Or was he hoping I'd attack him, giving him the leverage he needed? I drew a deep breath, trying to think only of the Sorkins. Still, I had no intention of playing into his hands, regardless of how noble the cause.

"But the past is past, Simon," he said, "and at present there is a terrified young American couple who require your services in Paris."

I stood, tossed the folder onto the chair I'd just vacated.

"Fortunately," I said, "you have the resources of the National Police at your disposal. Roughly, what, a hundred and fifty thousand agents?"

Davignon nodded. "Roughly," he said. "But as I am sure your service with the United States Marshals has taught you, sometimes organization and cooperation within an agency of that size can prove difficult. Too many chefs, as they say, spoil the soup. And in these cases, time is of the essence. Each hour that passes makes it that much more unlikely that we will ever find Lindsay Sorkin alive."

"I'm sorry, Lieutenant," I said, moving past him, trying to disguise my emotions. "But as I said when you pulled over my taxi, I have a plane to catch. If your driver will take me to Charles de Gaulle, I still have a chance of making my flight."

"Or . . ."

I stopped, stared at the door, my pulse racing.

"Or you can spend the next several months in a French prison awaiting trial. As you may have read in *Newsweek,* our former president Nicolas Sarkozy left office with our prisons operating at a hundred and twenty-six percent capacity, far higher than the European average. The prisons are overcrowded, and frankly an embarrassment. But it's not my job to comment, only to enforce the law."

I turned back to see that Davignon's gun was drawn, aimed at the dead center of my chest.

"I am afraid, Simon, that without your cooperation, I would have to place you under arrest for the kidnapping of Jason Blanc from his mother in Bordeaux."

I stared at him, ignoring the weapon as best I could.

"And here I thought that you admired what I do, Lieutenant."

My statement was met with a mirthless smile.

"I do, Simon. It is why you are here and not at headquarters being booked. It is why I am offering you this opportunity."

Coincidentally, most of my referrals came from U.S. government officials who thought I could do more for the victimized parent than any government agency could. The father of Jason Blanc, for instance, was referred to me by a case officer at the U.S. Department of State. The case officer had been assigned the unfortunate task of informing Peter Blanc that his Massachusetts child-custody order could not be automatically enforced in France. Once he learned that he'd have to file for custody again in the French courts, Peter Blanc immediately began fearing for his son's life. Peter had won custody only after Jason's mother, Fanny, smacked the nine-year-old boy's left hand with a hammer, sending him to the emergency room at Mass General with three shattered fingers and a mouthful of lies.

Peter's caseworker at the State Department sympathized—her sister had been in a similar situation four years earlier and I'd helped. So, within twelve hours of opening the case, Jason's father received an anonymous e-mail with my phone number. Yesterday, after taking Peter's frantic call at five in the morning, I had dropped what I was doing, verified the information he gave me with his family lawyer in Boston, and been on a Delta flight to Charles de Gaulle three hours later.

Needless to say, all my referrals were very hush-hush, but none had been delivered under threat of arrest, none with a handgun pointed at my chest.

"You say the Sorkins are desperate, Lieutenant, yet you're the one leveling a semiautomatic pistol at my heart. Smacks a bit of desperation on your part, I'd say."

"You no doubt followed the disappearance of little Madeleine McCann, the three-year-old British girl who went missing in the resort area of Praia da Luz in the Algarve region of Portugal. The girl was never found. To this day, the Portuguese police are swallowing criticism from international media outlets accusing them of being slow and inept. Meanwhile, Portugal's own media have attacked the police for their massive effort, contending no other missing child in the history of the country ever received such attention. You see, Simon, in the case of a missing child, the police cannot win, nor can the country in which the child went missing, particularly when it is the child of foreign nationals from the U.K. or the U.S."

Davignon lowered his weapon so that it pointed at the floor, but continued to hold it in both hands, elbows slightly bent.

He said, "France and the National Police are in no condition to endure an international media circus that will not aid one iota in returning Lindsay Sorkin to her parents. The Sorkins have agreed to hold off speaking to the media, because I promised to deliver you. I have only until noon today. So yes, Simon, I am desperate to find that little girl. To save an innocent life, and to spare my department and my country from a deluge of unwanted attention."

I considered Davignon's plea. Frankly, I could not have cared less about the National Police or their image. Even the country itself, though welcoming, wasn't high on my list of priorities.

However, I had the grave feeling that if I didn't at least entertain Davignon's offer, he wouldn't let me leave France. At least not without a fight. Of course, my own well-being didn't rank much higher than French national pride; it hadn't for some time.

On the other hand, there was Lindsay Sorkin. This little girl—her image would remain burned into my mind at least until this crisis was over. As painful as it might be for me, I owed it to Lindsay to hear her parents out.

"I'll give you twenty-four hours of my time," I said. "If I have no leads by the close of that window, I'm returning home. Because if that's the case, my presence will make no difference. It'll mean the girl is gone."

Davignon hesitated, but finally he nodded.

"Fair enough." He holstered his weapon and removed the walkie-talkie from his belt. "Bring in the Sorkins," he said into it.

He held the walkie to his ear and listened before speaking again.

"*Oui*, Bertrand," he said. "Both of them. *Maintenant, s'il vous plait.*"

Chapter 3

Vince Sorkin appeared to be in his midthirties, the wear of the previous twenty-four hours already showing on his face in the form of a vacant gaze I knew too well. The same dead eyes often stared back at me from the mirror, causing me to question whether I was still among the living. Both of us continued breathing, both of our hearts continued beating, but both of our little girls were missing and it wouldn't matter how much time passed. Until and unless his daughter was found alive, Vince Sorkin's eyes would never burn with life again. Just like mine.

We'd moved into the dining room, with the Sorkins seated across a thick marble table from me and Lieutenant Davignon.

"Thank you for agreeing to meet with us, Mr. Fisk," Vince Sorkin said.

"You're welcome," I replied, though I thought thanks were hardly in order. "Now, first things first. Give me a complete description of Lindsay. Height, weight, birthmarks, scars, the works."

Vince said, "She's about three feet four inches tall. Approximately forty-two pounds. She has a large birthmark on her big left toe, and a small scar on her right knee from when she took a bad spill off the couch and onto our glass coffee table as a toddler."

"Blood type?" I said.

Vince glanced at his wife and frowned. "All we remember is that it's rare. We'd have to contact her pediatrician back in the States."

"We'll take care of that," Davignon said. "What's her doctor's name?"

"Richter," Vince said. "Keith Richter in San Jose."

Davignon took the name down and motioned for me to continue.

"Now," I said, "tell me everything that's happened since you arrived in Paris. Don't leave out any details."

Unfortunately, there wasn't much to tell. The family had arrived at Charles de Gaulle only forty-eight hours earlier and immediately took a taxi to their hotel. The driver wasn't overly friendly; in fact, he hadn't struck them at all. He was nondescript, spoke barely a dozen words during the entire transaction, all of which were uttered either at the beginning or end of their ride. In front of the hotel he halfheartedly thanked Vince for his generous tip and sped off.

"Did you catch his name?" I said. "It would have been posted somewhere inside the taxi."

Neither of them had. It had been a long day of air travel, fifteen hours from San Jose with connections in Seattle and Reykjavik, the capital of Iceland. They were exhausted and, understandably, Lindsay had been fussing.

"I have men at the airport, making inquiries," Davignon assured me. "We'll inform you as soon as we identify their driver."

"Which leads us to the hotel," I said.

Vince described Hotel d'Étonner as a six-story luxury hotel with rooms starting at six hundred euros a night. The nineteenth-century mansion was a brief walk from the bright lights of the Champs-Elysées and had been artfully restored to blend small-chateau charm with world-class appeal. They'd booked their stay online.

"How many people did you interact with when you arrived at the hotel?" I said.

Vince turned his smooth, aristocratic face toward the ceiling in thought.

"The desk clerk," he said, "who was a young female, a brunette, black hair with blue eyes. Her name was Avril, like the pop star. Then the bellhop, a young male, light hair. Seemed more German than French. He also brought our food when we ordered room service. Both he and the desk clerk were friendly enough, but neither seemed to take any particular interest in Lindsay." He shook his head and frowned. "No one else, at least not that I remember."

I turned to Lori, who had remained perfectly silent since she entered the cottage.

"Mrs. Sorkin?" I said gently.

Lori shrugged; it was a tired gesture befitting a woman twice her age. The flesh around her eyes was red and puffy from crying and lack of sleep. When she finally spoke, her voice sounded like she'd spent a lifetime smoking, though that probably wasn't the case.

"I can't remember speaking with anyone," she said. "I was preoccupied with Lindsay the entire time. She was upset that we'd left our Yorkie, Lucy, behind."

Upset, I thought. If so, it could be that she left on her own. Or at least not put up a struggle or screamed when she was taken. If someone overheard that bit about the dog, they could have used it to calm her or even lure her away.

Of course, that was if she had been taken by a complete stranger, which was rare. Far more often, children were abducted by people they already knew.

So I changed direction and said, "Any enemies, Vince?"

He seemed taken aback by the question.

"Enemies?" He shook his head. "No, no enemies. I mean . . ."

I tried to remain even-tempered. "Let's start with work. Tell me, Vince, what is it you do for a living?"

"I'm a software developer for Nepturn Technology."

"Nepturn Technology?"

"It's a Silicon Valley start-up."

I asked him to elaborate.

Vince Sorkin sighed, rubbed his eyes. "Typically, military contractors are funded by federal agencies, right? They use taxpayer money to build, test, and sell new weapons designs. Nepturn takes a different approach. We're funded by private investors. This cuts out the majority of the wait time and bureaucratic red tape."

"So you design weapons technology," I said.

Vince didn't respond, didn't need to. Instead, Davignon cut in with what he already knew.

"Monsieur Sorkin helped design a remote-controlled automaton that could potentially replace soldiers on the battlefield. It is two and a half feet in height, can travel up to fifteen miles per hour, and it has the ability to blow a one-foot hole through a steel door with perfect accuracy from a distance of five hundred meters."

In the span of less than a minute Sorkin and Davignon had changed the very nature of what we were dealing with. Chances were, this wasn't a random abduction perpetrated by an amateur pederast who lived alone or in his mother's basement. There was now a very good chance that we were playing with professionals. Which meant extortion, the exchange of life for information, quite possibly a ransom demand.

I tried to choose my words carefully. I wanted to do everything I could not to upset Lindsay's parents any further.

"I'm sorry," I said, "but this isn't my field. I want to help you find your daughter but, given the circumstances, I'm afraid I can't. You're much better off in the hands of the National Police."

Lori Sorkin, who bore an uncanny resemblance to my beloved Tasha, broke into tears.

"We know the statistics, Mr. Fisk," she said. "If you're wrong, if this has nothing to do with my husband's business, then we're running out of time. Please . . ."

I slowly pushed my chair out and stood.

"Mrs. Sorkin," I said gently, "if time is indeed of the essence, I can't help but think I'd be wasting yours, and I can't do that." I turned to Davignon. "Lieutenant, I promised you twenty-four hours. But given this new information, I think I'd only be hindering the investigation. . . ."

"I understand," Davignon said, his eyes locked on the marble table. "But there is nothing to indicate that Lindsay's abduction has anything to do with Monsieur Sorkin's employment. There has been no contact whatsoever with the kidnappers, which is rare in matters of extortion." He finally stood, stared me straight in the eyes. "I have only one more request, Simon. Visit the crime scene in Paris. Perhaps you will see something my men may have missed."

I shook my head. "Lieutenant, there may be no evidence Lindsay was taken for Mr. Sorkin's trade secrets, but there's also no indication she was chosen at random—"

"But there is," Davignon said quickly. He lowered his voice to a near whisper. "I am afraid that Lindsay is not the only young girl to be abducted in Paris this month."

I shuddered despite the warmth of the cottage. Children abducted by estranged parents was one thing; physical harm was seldom done to them. But victims of stranger abductions—the crimes often committed against them were unthinkable. And when more than one went missing from the same region in a short period of time, it eliminated a number of innocuous possibilities. Rarely did such stories conclude with the parents and child happily reunited. Indeed, the odds of recovering the missing in these situations were rather bleak. Tragic endings, from my experience, were almost inevitable.

I suddenly found myself in an impossible situation. The reason I didn't take on cases dealing with stranger abductions was simple: I couldn't bear to relive the days following Hailey's abduction. It didn't matter that Lindsay Sorkin wasn't my own daughter. I would see this case through Vince's eyes, watch Lori's heart tear a little more every moment there was no news. If I became involved to any significant extent and little Lindsay couldn't be located, I didn't think my body could make it through the next seven days. My stomach would never mend if this six-year-old girl was found dead. Since Hailey's abduction, I'd felt as though I was teetering along some imaginary line and I feared this search would finally push me over the edge.

But when I turned back to the Sorkins to apologize one last time, I fixed my eyes on Lori and saw total devastation, the same desolate shell I had faced ten years ago when I stared across the kitchen table at Tasha and tried to explain that there was nothing else we could do to bring Hailey home. *Isn't there, though?* she'd shouted. *Isn't there?* And that unfathomable weight—that absolute helplessness—that had been pressing down against my chest since the day my daughter disappeared finally caused my ribs to cave in and crush my lungs. In that moment I couldn't speak, couldn't breathe, and that same pressure was bearing down on me again now as I stared across the marble table, trying to blink away my light-headedness and explain to Lori Sorkin that there was nothing I could do to return her daughter.

Isn't there, though?

Those three words still held so much power over me.

As I looked into Lori's moist, pleading eyes, I thought, *What if I could do for her what I couldn't do for Tasha?*

And what if I walked? How could I go on, having failed her twice?

What could I possibly say? That I couldn't get involved? Like it or not, I was already involved and I had no right turning Lori Sorkin and her husband down. No right giving up on Lindsay without making a proper effort. Finding Lindsay alive wouldn't return Hailey, but at least it would mean there were two less parents in the world walking aimlessly through their own hell on earth. If there was a chance I could spare Vince and Lori Sorkin the burden of losing a child, I had to try, my own feelings be damned.

Chapter 4

In the case of a missing child, the parents are always suspects. Unfortunately, Vince and Lori Sorkin were no exception. Negligent death followed by a cover-up couldn't be ruled out. Nor could outright murder. But then, I'd been working with parents of abducted children going on eleven years now, and both Vince and Lori Sorkin played the role of frantic parents to a tee. I had a hard time imagining that either one of them was involved.

Entering the Hotel d'Étonner, one would never suspect that a small child had been abducted on the premises less than thirty-six hours earlier. All seemed perfectly normal. A pair of guests stood patiently at the front desk, apparently waiting to be checked in. Carrying luggage through the opulent lobby were two bellhops, neither of whom Vince Sorkin recognized. Of the desk clerks on duty, one was fair-haired and the other was male, so no Avril.

"We've questioned both the female clerk and the male bellhop," Davignon informed me, "and it seems highly unlikely that either of them was involved."

"You demanded my assistance for a reason," I told him, "so, with all due respect, Lieutenant, that's something I'd like to decide for myself."

Straightaway we went up to the Sorkins' hotel room, one of eight rooms located on the fifth floor. Actually, it was considered a junior suite, spacious and bright, with a view of the hotel's lavish patio. The suite consisted of three parts, including an entryway, a sitting room, and a capacious bedroom complete with its own master bath.

"This is where Lindsay slept," Vince said, pointing to a large roll-out bed in the sitting room.

I hesitated to touch anything but Davignon said that the room had already been gone over with a fine-tooth comb.

"This is more a matter of gaining your perspective," he said.

I knelt next to the roll-out. From where Lindsay was lying, she wouldn't have been able to see her parents' bed.

I looked up at the parents. "The door to your room was open, I assume?"

Lori shook her head. "Even though we were so exhausted from all the traveling, we made love, then fell asleep right away. I don't know if it was jet lag or being in a strange bed, but something woke me in the middle of the night. When I looked up I noticed our door was still closed. I got out of bed to open it and look in on Lindsay." She paused to regain her composure, then rushed through the final few words as though saying them aloud somehow made things worse. "But Lindsay wasn't there. She was gone."

"Wait here," I said, moving toward the bedroom. "When I close the door behind me, Mrs. Sorkin, I'd like you to say my name, Simon, six times, beginning in a conversational tone and increasing in volume with each repetition."

I stepped into the bedroom and closed the heavy wooden door. I waited thirty seconds but heard nothing, just as I'd suspected. I walked out of the room, shaking my head, then moved on to the front door.

"No sign of forced entry," Davignon said.

I opened the door. The lock and the dead bolt required a key, not the usual electronic cards you find in most hotels these days.

"Do either of you recall sliding the chain?" I said.

"I was pretty certain I did slide the chain after slipping our room-service trays out into the hall," Vince said. "But with Lindsay gone, I guess I couldn't have."

Don't be so sure, I thought. "What time was that?"

"After nine," Vince said. "Probably closer to ten."

I stood in the narrow entryway, examining the coat closet.

"You stored your jackets and stuff in here?"

"No," Vince said, "we hung them in the bedroom. That door was locked when we arrived."

"Did you call down to the front desk for the key?"

Vince shrugged. "Never got around to it. It didn't seem that important. There's more than enough closet space in the bedroom."

"It was still locked when we arrived," Davignon added. "The hotel manager opened it for us. He said it has a lock because of the hotel's wealthier clientele. Women customarily store furs and such in that closet."

"Did the manager inventory the keys?" I said.

Davignon nodded. "None were missing. We printed the two sets they kept downstairs. Both were clean."

"Clean? As in they'd been wiped?"

"All the keys receive a quick polish before they're hung back on the rack for the next guest, we were told. We checked just about every key they had down there and didn't find a single print."

I stepped inside the closet and examined the back wall, feeling around for seams. The closet was only two feet deep, barely enough room for a man to stand comfortably.

"Do you have a flashlight, Lieutenant?"

Davignon stepped to the doorway of the closet a moment later, holding out a miniature Maglite.

"That'll do," I said.

I twisted the flashlight on and studied the ceiling, then turned the narrow beam to the floor and ran it across the edges. Having spotted nothing, I got down on one knee and ran my finger along the floor, collecting nothing but dust. When I aimed the light on my finger, one lone white speck stood out against the gray-black dirt.

I stood and exited the closet, then walked into the sitting room.

"When room service arrived," I said, "did the server leave the door open behind him as he brought in the food?"

Vince peered down the entryway. "I don't know. I opened the door and the server followed me back to the sitting room. I didn't look behind me, and because of the long hallway, the door wouldn't have been in my line of vision if I had."

"Think," I said. "Do you recall *hearing* it close?"

He shook his head. "I honestly don't remember."

Lori said, "I was in the other room with Lindsay. It was late, I was getting her ready for bed."

I stared down at the white speck still on my right index finger.

Oh, what the hell, I thought. *It's not going to kill you.*

I placed the finger on my tongue.

Bitter. Could be MDMA.

"What have you found?" Davignon said, studying my face.

"Maybe nothing," I said. "But it seems there was a tiny piece of a tab of Ecstasy lying on the floor in that hall closet."

"Ecstasy?" Lori said.

"A club drug," I told her. "A pill that vastly improves the mood, makes you want to hug and dance."

Her voice caught. "You think they drugged my child?"

"No," I said. "At least not with this. It could be that someone snuck into that hall closet while your food was being delivered, someone with a key. For most people who slide the chain on a hotel-room door, it's pure habit, and I'm betting Vince did, just as he thinks. That means someone had to be lying in wait. If so, it's possible the perpetrator kept himself busy with drugs, either to boost his courage or to kill time until the two of you finished dinner and went to sleep." I paused. "Then again, this bit of Ecstasy could have been sitting in that closet for ages."

"So where does that take us?" Vince said.

"To the most viable route of escape."

I moved toward the entryway and told them to follow. When I exited the hotel room, I surveyed the edges of the hallway ceilings for cameras.

"CCTV is set up only in the elevators and the main lobby," Davignon said.

"Then our man would have taken the stairs," I said.

Davignon nodded. "Closest exit is to our left."

"Your men searched the stairwell, I assume," I said as we moved down the hall.

"Of course," he said. "It was clean."

When I entered the stairwell, I raised my arm against the flickering fluorescent lights. Like a vagrant, I assiduously searched the steps for cigarette butts, a dropped coin, something, anything that could connect me to the next dot. But the stairs leading to the fourth-floor landing were empty; those leading to the third, the same. On the fifth step down to the second floor, I found something.

"What is it?" Davignon said from the landing above me.

"Something your men evidently missed," I called up to him.

The pill was crushed to pieces and spread over two steps, but one taste told me it was the same chemical I'd discovered in the Sorkins' hall closet. An off-white tab of MDMA with a stamp on the face of it. Only it was in too many pieces to make out the stamp.

"Stay there," I said as Davignon and Vince started down. "I need the light."

I knelt on the second step and tried to piece the bits of the pill together like a puzzle. It was damn difficult, required more concentration than I thought I could muster in this dingy stairwell with the flickering lights.

The stamps on Ecstasy tabs were marketing tools, like the various brand names for heroin and marijuana. I'd seen Mitsubishi Turbos stamped with the car manufacturer's logo; dolphins; doves;

playboy bunnies; shamrocks; hearts, stars, and diamonds; crowns; peace signs; smiley faces. Some were even stamped FBI or DEA, though I'd never seen one marked for the U.S. Marshals.

This pill appeared to be stamped with letters. Or was it numbers?

"What have you got, Simon?" Davignon called down.

It *was* numbers. I continued to piece the top of the pill together as best I could. Three distinct numbers finally materialized before my eyes.

"Simon," Davignon called down again, unable to contain the impatience in his voice. "Tell us, what is it you've found?"

"Bond," I said under my breath. "James Bond."

Chapter 5

Following a long conversation with Davignon about Paris's present drug scene, I decided there was nothing much I could do until the sun went down. Dipping into the governmental coffers, Davignon provided me with enough money to get through the next few days in Paris. The first thing I did was grab a grilled ham-and-cheese sandwich at a nearby café, forgoing the espresso I was dying for because I knew I'd need to get some sleep before night came.

I hadn't promised Davignon that I would stay if I found a lead, only that I'd leave if I didn't, but I was never one to play with semantics, and the truth was, I wanted like hell to find Vince and Lori Sorkin's little girl. I knew what the Sorkins were going through, thoughts as black as night racing through their heads like an invading army. I knew they'd be unable to sleep, unable to eat, unable to make the slightest efforts to maintain their health, to preserve their bodies. They would age a year for every day Lindsay remained missing, until their hearts finally grew calluses that not even the sharpest blade could penetrate. Even then, they'd loathe themselves for allowing their little girl to go missing, regardless of whether they could have done anything to prevent it.

I was put up in a small hotel on a quiet cobblestone street a few blocks away. The room, which contained nothing but a wooden desk and a double bed, was quaint and cozy, with matching floral-patterned wallpaper and bedding that reminded me of Tasha's favorite bed-and-breakfast back in Newport, Rhode Island. I filled a plastic cup with tap water, then finally stripped out of the clothes I'd been wearing since I arrived in Paris.

The moment my head hit the pillow I was out. But before I reached my first dream there was a loud rap at my door. Bertrand, returning my luggage. I spent the next forty-five minutes fading in and out of sleep, then finally leaped from the bed, dressed, and headed to Rue François to buy whatever I'd need for the night.

When I returned to my room, I downed another cup of tap water and again tried to get some sleep. Although this attempt was met with substantially more success, the hours I spent in bed were plagued by familiar memories-turned-nightmares, and I woke several times in a cold and clammy sweat that had drenched the sheets.

When I finally woke for good I spent twenty minutes under a steaming-hot shower, trying to clear my head. The morning had stirred up the worst that lay on the floor of my subconscious, and I feared it would be weeks, maybe months, before these things settled at the bottom again. For the time being, all I could do was try to make sure these intruders didn't fully rise to the surface and cloud my thinking. I couldn't allow them to affect my judgment if I had any hope at all of finding Lindsay Sorkin.

Late that night, I went clubbing. And looking to score. By eleven, I had tried most of the trendy clubs—MadaM, Batofar, Le Gibus, Elysée Montmartre—but was unsuccessful in procuring any 007s. Pink Supermans seemed to be the "in" thing; mixed with a bit of ketamine and GHB, the combined effect was fittingly called an EKG. One dealer I found suggested I try one of Paris's most infamous after-parties, an underground late-night rave held nightly at an abandoned cathedral. Still, I hoped to draw a bead on James Bond well before four in the morning.

So next I visited some of Paris's more exclusive clubs: Le VIP,

Showcase, L'Etoile, Le World Place, and Le Cab. Fortunately, I'd dressed the part, looked like money. I'd spent a chunk of the afternoon at Francesco Smalto's, getting fitted for a sharp black suit that hung meticulously on my lean, muscular frame. Speaking English to bouncers at the door didn't hurt my chances of gaining entry. Neither did the few hundred euros I slipped those doormen who were staring down longer lines.

It was in the ultramodern club Le Cab, also known as Cabaret, where I met a slender, attractive man who immediately came on to me. Said I didn't give off the vibe but that I was hot enough that he had to give it a shot. I thanked him for the compliment but didn't hint either way about my sexual orientation. I let him buy me a diva martini and we talked.

"Know where I can get some E?" I said over the deafening house music. The club was packed. Not a face or a body in sight that couldn't pass for a model's.

"Of course," he said, his English nearly as good as his French.

He dipped into his pocket, pulled out a tab, and told me to stick out my tongue.

"What kind is it?" I said.

"Baby, you're in Paris. What does it matter?"

"I scored some 007s last night," I said, taking a pull off my martini, "and I was tripping balls till eleven this morning. Tonight, it's James Bond or nothing."

"Oh, I see," he said, popping the tab onto his tongue. "You're a drug snob." He put his index finger to his lips. "Don't tell anyone, but I am, too. Tell you what. I'll take you out for some 007s later, but how about some tina while we enjoy our drinks?"

"Crystal?" I said. "Never touch the stuff."

"Bad experience?"

"You could say that."

I didn't tell him about the meth-head father I'd recently tracked down in San Salvador. Bastard put a gun to his teenage boy's head.

Better dead than with his *puta* mother in New Mexico, he told me. When I dropped my gun, he turned his .22 on me and fired. The gun jammed. The kid ran. Then I beat the father to within an inch of his life. Told him if he ever went near the boy or his mother again, I'd finish the job. I'd never made a more truthful statement in my life. And the father believed me.

"Let's finish these martinis and get out of here," my new friend said. "By the way, what's your name?"

"Simon. Yours?"

"Claude." He polished off his drink and shot up off the cushy fuchsia seat. "Now let's go find ourselves a little Daniel Craig in pill form." He stared into my eyes as a pair of A-list celebrities brushed past us. "Or do you prefer Pierce Brosnan?"

"Actually, I prefer Sean Connery."

"Oh, he's like eightysomething," Claude said, making a face. "Well, to each his own, I guess."

Claude brought me to Le Queen on Champs-Elysées, a once-hot gay nightclub, he advised me, that had been shanghaied in recent years by heteros. We didn't go inside but rather loitered around the premises, Claude surreptitiously eyeing the crowd for someone he recognized. The air was as crisp as a new five-hundred-euro banknote, the City of Light lit well enough to live up to its name. I glanced at my new TAG Heuer, courtesy of the French police, courtesy of a coke kingpin they took down earlier in the week, and saw that it was closing in on one A.M. Forty-eight hours since Lindsay had been abducted. The little girl was fast running out of time.

"See the man you're looking for?" I asked Claude.

"No, but I think I see his flatmate. Over there." I followed his finger to a lanky lad who looked to be in his midtwenties. "Name's Geoffrey. Want me to call him over here?"

"Please do."

Claude whistled. Geoffrey and a few others looked our way. Claude motioned him over, and Geoffrey held up an index finger, then grudgingly peeled himself away from the Asian girl he'd been chatting with.

"Don't get any ideas," Claude warned me. "Geoffrey and his flatmate are both straight."

"Wouldn't think of it," I said.

Geoffrey couldn't speak English. Or wouldn't. So Claude translated. Told him I was an American looking to roll, but I'd only pop 007s. After some back-and-forth, Claude turned to me and said that Geoffrey's flatmate, Remy, was back at the flat with a woman and didn't want to be disturbed tonight.

"Tell him I won't be any bother. I just want to purchase the pills and run."

Geoffrey seemed to understand me. Instead of waiting for the translation, he replied to Claude in French.

Claude said to me, "Geoffrey says, 'Forget it. Not tonight.' But he can sell you something better. He has blue Batmans, green Christmas trees, and Mickey Ds. Any one of those can get you off longer than a 007."

I pulled a wad of euros from my pocket and spoke directly to Geoffrey in English.

"Listen," I said. "I'll pay your flatmate a hundred euros a pill for three pills, and throw in another two hundred for you in order to show my appreciation. Now what do you say?"

Geoffrey stared at the money. "I say you are either crazy or you are a cop. Maybe both."

"Maybe I'm just rich and used to getting what I want," I said. "Do you know anyone else in Paris who can sell me some 007s?"

Geoffrey shook his head. "Remy is the only one in the whole city. These 007s, they are not even in fashion."

"Well, I intend to bring them back into the limelight. So do we have a deal or not?"

Geoffrey pulled out his iPhone.

Chapter 6

Geoffrey and I took the Metro from George V to Saint-Michel in the Latin Quarter. From there we walked to Geoffrey's flat on Rue Galande. We didn't speak two words the entire way. I could tell the kid was nervous, his hands constantly twitching, eyes darting among passengers like a pinball machine. I'd told Claude to wait for me at Le Queen. If things turned messy, I didn't want to risk his getting involved or even hurt. He made me promise I'd return. I promised, knowing it was a promise I wouldn't keep. Luckily, all he was out was the price of one diva martini at Le Cab. Wouldn't take him very long to get over me. Not in Paris. Not at Le Queen.

The third-floor flat was exactly what you'd expect of an Old World apartment in Paris. A tight space, lots of strong, weathered wood. Solid furniture that didn't look like it came from IKEA. It was an impressive place for a couple of twentysomething bachelors. I stood in the living area, as instructed, and stared out the window at the dark, narrow cobblestone street as Geoffrey slipped down the hall to retrieve his flatmate.

Following a tap at his door, I heard Remy's voice. Sounded as though Remy didn't want to be disturbed, indeed. Too bad. I intended to disturb him.

Through the door, Geoffrey tried to reason with him. The word *euros* was used more than once. After a few minutes, I heard the creaking of door hinges.

"Merci," Geoffrey said, then the door slammed shut.

That wouldn't do at all. I met Geoffrey at the end of the hall. He was staring down at his palm, pushing pills around with his finger. He was startled to see me.

"I told you to wait near the sofa," he said.

I immediately grabbed Geoffrey by the shoulders and spun him around.

"I need to have a brief talk with Remy," I said.

Geoffrey began to protest in French, but I slapped a hand over his mouth and told him to calm down and remain silent. I flung open Remy's door without knocking, holding Geoffrey in front of me in case Remy had a piece.

On the bed a naked young woman screamed.

"Geoffrey, tell her to keep quiet and put something on."

Panting, Geoffrey said, "She understood you."

"Good," I said. "I'm not here to hurt anyone, but, Remy, I'm going to need a few answers from you. You speak English?"

"Who the fuck are you?" Remy shouted.

"I'll take that as a resounding yes," I said.

I grabbed Geoffrey's wrist and twisted it behind his back till he howled in pain. This was the problem with going private and not carrying a badge or a gun. You always had to display *something* to assert your authority, and brutality was often all you had.

"Remy," I said, "grab that pen over on the nightstand and start me a list of everyone you sold 007s to in the past ten days."

"Why should I do that?"

"Because if you do, I'll go away. If you don't, I'll stay. And take my word, Remy, you don't want me to stay. I get bored very easily, and when I get bored, I tend to break things. Your flatmate's arm, for example: it's all but begging to be fractured. And that's just a start."

Remy reached for the nightstand and snatched the pen. As he did, I inched closer to the bed.

"I have no paper," he said.

"Get creative."

Remy reached to the nightstand again. This time he opened the drawer. Slowly and just enough for his hand to fit through. I noticed his wrist tense, as though his fingers were closing around something. I glanced at his bare chest; his breathing was growing more rapid.

At that moment, I threw Geoffrey hard into the wall, reached under the sheets, and gripped Remy by the ankles. The girl screamed again. I pulled with everything I had. Remy hung on to the edge of the drawer, pulled it out of the nightstand, its contents crashing onto the floor. Remy's naked body flew off the bed like a kid's at the end of a water slide. Only Remy's body didn't hit pool water; his back hit the hardwood with a harsh thud.

I glanced at the spilled contents of the drawer on the side of the bed. A bunch of pill bottles, a few vials, a number of one-inch glassine bags. And a .38 Special snub-nosed revolver.

"That was a mistake," I said, grabbing Remy by his thick, curly hair. I dragged him across the wooden floor, past his fallen friend, toward the spilled drawer. I knelt and picked up the gun, felt its weight in my hand. It was loaded. I stood, pushed Remy facedown onto the bed. Cocked the hammer.

"All right, you want to do this the hard way?" I said. "Fine by me. The first bullet goes into your Achilles tendon. Never seen it done before, but I imagine it hurts like hell."

"*Non, s'il vous plait,*" Remy muttered. "Please, I'll do anything."

"Now there's the French spirit. Tell me, Remy: in the past ten days, how many individuals did you sell 007s to? Lie to me, and I'll put a bullet in you."

"About six, maybe seven people." He was already short of breath.

"How many of those were women?"

"Three."

"And the men, what were their names?"

Remy hesitated. I pressed the gun into the back of his skull to help him along.

"My friend Andre," he rasped, "and his cousin Louis. The two others, I don't know their names."

"Your friend Andre, where can I find him?"

"He and Louis left on holiday to London last week. That is why he wanted the pills."

"And the other two," I said, "how did you meet them?"

Deep breaths. "I met them at a pub in the Marais."

"What did they look like? Where were they from? Were they residents or tourists?"

"Business," Remy said. "They told me they were here on business. I don't know where they were from; they spoke French very well. They were light-skinned. Maybe German or Austrian, I don't know."

"Were they staying in the Marais?"

"They didn't say. Our conversation, it was very short. I was drunk. I made the sale and left the pub. They stayed. That is all I can tell you, I swear."

I released his hair. The girl was crying. Geoffrey was trembling in the corner. I slowly backed away, out of the room.

"The pills, Geoffrey, where are they?"

Geoffrey stared at me as though he'd forgotten why I was there. The three pills were scattered on the floor next to him. He collected them, stood, and handed them to me.

"Thank you," I said, unloading the revolver. "I'm going to let you keep the gun. But I'm afraid the bullets are coming with me. Any objections?"

No objections were raised.

Chapter 7

Early the next morning, all hell was unleashed. The media caught wind of the missing girl due to a leak in the French police department. The AP picked up the story, and before you could say *vultures*, photographs of Lindsay Sorkin splashed onto the BBC, followed instantly by the twenty-four-hour horror networks back in the States. National Police Headquarters received a barrage of phone calls from the producers of Nancy Grace, Greta Van Susteren, and a host of other clowns too numerous to count. Journalists spilled into the lobby of the Hotel Claridge, where Vince and Lori Sorkin were now staying. A carefully controlled investigation had erupted into total chaos.

"That's it," I said quietly to Davignon. "Now the bad guys go to ground."

We were standing outside a small café on Champs-Elysées, not far from the Hotel d'Étonner, as a drizzling rain bounced off our hard faces. It was only a few hours since I had left Remy's, and although I hadn't gotten any sleep, I felt wired. Unfortunately, however, that energy was quickly devolving into anxiety.

Davignon punched a button and put his phone to his ear. "Any sign, Bertrand?"

I finished my espresso as Davignon cursed and placed his cell in his coat pocket.

I said, "Nothing yet, I assume. Means our boy is more than forty minutes late. He's gone, Lieutenant."

We had been waiting for the bellhop Johan Fleischer to show up for work at the hotel. From the information I had gleaned from Remy the night before, Johan was now our link to finding Lindsay. There was little doubt that he was somehow involved. Too many coincidences otherwise. Remy had sold 007s to two German guys in Paris on business at a pub in the Marais, the same neighborhood where Johan Fleischer, a German national himself, was known to live. Only when Davignon's men showed up at his flat at six in the morning to have another chat with him, Johan was nowhere to be found. He was due at the hotel for work at eight A.M. and still hadn't shown. Johan Fleischer had vanished into the ether.

"Where do we go from here?" Davignon said tentatively without looking at me.

Davignon's men had found me the Sorkins' taxi driver and I'd chatted with him for half an hour this morning. The driver was a family man. Had two daughters of his own. Seemed sincere when he said he sympathized with the Sorkins. He had noticed little Lindsay. Adorable. Made a lot of noise, gave him a splitting headache, but adorable all the same. I believed him. He was clean.

So was Avril Severin, the desk clerk who had checked the Sorkins in. She was studying literature at Paris-Sorbonne University and would graduate next year. During my talk with her at the hotel this morning, she broke into tears. Not about the girl necessarily—she'd caught only a glimpse of Lindsay in her mother's arms—but about the state of the world and how nothing seemed to make sense to her anymore now that she understood so much. I felt for her, and let her go after just twenty minutes.

I looked at Davignon. "Tell me more about the other little girls that went missing here in Paris this month."

"Two others," he said. "As I mentioned, not tourists. Both French citizens, both Arabic. Both from the Latin Quarter. The families did not know one another."

"And the media?" I said. "Not quite as interested in missing Arabic girls?"

Davignon bowed his head, wiped a bit of rain off his face. "Not so much, no."

"I'm not entirely convinced their disappearances are connected to Lindsay Sorkin's."

"Maybe, maybe not."

"But I'd still like a look at your reports," I told him.

"Of course."

The dilemma in my mind was how to approach this from the other side. My experience was in handling parental abductions. I was accustomed to knowing who I was looking for and why they'd committed the crime. But stranger abductions were a different animal entirely—an animal I wasn't sure I was qualified to track. What if I took this investigation too far in the wrong direction? What if I missed an angle? What if my own incompetence became the reason why Vince and Lori Sorkin never saw their child again?

I couldn't allow that to happen. I'd need to remain sharp, keep one eye on the details and the other on the big picture. I couldn't let anything slip past. I'd need to examine the facts from every imaginable perspective.

The possibility that Lindsay Sorkin had been taken because of her father's sensitive work was too compelling to dismiss. The problem lay in assigning the motive. Were we dealing with a state? A terrorist group? Mercenaries? Competitors? A professional crew seeking a big score? And if any of this was true, why hadn't Vince Sorkin heard from the kidnappers before the involvement of the media, which complicated matters exponentially on all sides? It could be that they hadn't yet gotten her someplace safe, somewhere from which they could communicate without worrying that the National Police would be beating down their door the moment they hung up the phone or logged off the Internet. The only other reason I could fathom was that something had gone wrong. Something unthinkable. In that case, we'd be searching for a tiny corpse. And, of course, the men responsible.

"So," Davignon said, a beseeching look on his face, his voice barely audible over the sounds of city traffic, "with Johan Fleischer on the run, where do we go from here? With respect to your involvement, I mean."

Whether Davignon intended to arrest me for retrieving the boy in Bordeaux and putting him on a plane back to the States was now irrelevant. Lindsay needed to be found, and I was in this for the long haul. Finding Lindsay wouldn't mend the hole in me that had opened the day Hailey was taken. Finding her wouldn't bring back Tasha, or numb me enough to prevent a single sleepless night. But I knew that leaving France without trying to retrieve her would be the end of me. And I wasn't ready for the end quite yet.

Chapter 8

I took the Metro to the Bastille and from there walked in the rain to Rue Keller, where Johan Fleischer leased a studio apartment. Two plainclothes officers who were watching the block looked the other way when I walked by. The downstairs door was left unlocked, so I entered Fleischer's building and bounded up a creaky wooden staircase to his flat. I didn't bother to knock, didn't waste my time picking the lock, just took a deep breath, lifted my right leg, aimed inches below the knob, and kicked in Fleischer's door.

The studio apartment was dingy and as tight as a prison cell. A large black futon ate up most of the space. A stainless steel sink and minifridge to its immediate left made up the entire kitchen. In the rear I saw a gray-tiled bathroom with a scummy washbasin, shower, and toilet. The shower curtain was so cruddy, you wouldn't wrap a dead body in it. I nearly dry heaved from the smell.

"So much for German discipline," I muttered.

I went to work, digging through the few plastic drawers, checking the cabinets beneath the sink, opening the minifridge, poking around under the futon that served as his bed. Fleischer possessed a whole lot of nothing. In a corner of the room, a few electrical components were piled one atop the other. A portable boom box that played cassettes, a VHS player, an old-school printer with a tractor feed. But no computer.

I spotted a small plastic trash can and dumped the contents onto the floor. No question, this was where the rank odor was emanating from. I kicked aside the foodstuff and found some balled-up pieces of paper. Old-fashioned computer paper, unmistakable with those tiny holes on each side. The pages were wet, sticky, covered in what I assumed was maple syrup. I unrolled one at a time, flattening each against the floor, trying not to retch.

The first page was the printout of a Wikipedia entry for some band I'd never heard of, the second what appeared to be an abandoned attempt at poetry. On the third, I hit pay dirt. An e-mail from someone named Sandrine. *"Je t'aime,"* it read. *"À bientôt."*

I love you. See you soon.

Below the e-mail was an electronic signature, complete with the sender's full name, position, place of business, business address, telephone, and fax number.

Sandrine Bettencourt, human resources at Le Bon Marché, a department store located in the Left Bank.

I tore off the signature, folded the scrap of paper, stuffed it into my pocket, shot down the stairs and out into the rain, and made for the Metro at the Bastille.

The southern bank of the river Seine had inspired artists the likes of Pablo Picasso and Henri Matisse, writers such as Hemingway and F. Scott Fitzgerald, the poets Arthur Rimbaud and Paul Verlaine, not to mention the philosopher John-Paul Sartre. The area had also inspired the first department store in the world, Le Bon Marché, designed by Gustave Eiffel. Inside, Le Bon Marché was awe-inspiring, even for me, a widower who considered shopping slightly less desirable than dusting the furniture. Compared to finding your way around Le Bon Marché, finding your way around Paris was easy. Soon as I entered the monstrosity I became lost.

"Looking for human resources," I said, just as some overzealous clerk attempted to spritz me.

"Top floor," he said. "Sure I cannot interest you in some Guerlain to go with that splendid suit?"

"Never been so sure of anything in my life," I said, suddenly wondering if I reeked of Fleischer's rotting garbage.

I jumped onto the escalator. Given the wide berth fellow shoppers granted me, I figured I probably still smelled of rubbish. Of course, I hadn't slept or showered, and I was wearing the clothes I'd worn to the clubs the evening before. Figured there would be plenty of time for bathing once little Lindsay was found.

When I passed the children's department my mind flashed on Hailey. If my daughter were still alive we'd have recently celebrated her sweet sixteen. Sixteen. Nearing the end of high school, preparing for prom, visiting colleges, arguing over her borrowing the Volvo, things like that. She'd be dating. Looking for someone so unlike me you'd think we were a different species. But still Daddy's little girl, Daddy's little darling. If she were still alive. She could be. And that's what really sent me over the edge on nights so dark I couldn't burn them away with a million candles. Those were the nights I'd sit on the floor next to my bed, arms wrapped around my knees like a child sitting on the carpet of a library at storytime. Listening for her screams as though I could hear her no matter where in the world she was. Sitting. Listening. Rocking back and forth like an octogenarian passing time until death arrived. Sitting. Rocking. Thinking. Always thinking.

She could still be alive. It was that possibility that tore at me. Alive but not. Alive but trapped, held prisoner like Jaycee Lee Dugard or the daughter of that sick, sadistic prick Josef Fritzl over in Austria. Hailey in some shed, in some dungeon. Some monster laying his hands on her. What would *she* be thinking? What had she been told? That her parents were dead? Or worse, that they'd completely given up hope and stopped looking for her? That they'd moved on? Had another child, another little girl to replace her? Had she been brainwashed like Elizabeth Smart? Told the same damn lies again and again until she believed them? Was she tortured? If she were alive today would she loathe me? Would she even remember me? These were the thoughts that constantly clawed at my insides. And this was why I didn't—why I *couldn't*—take cases like Lindsay Sorkin's. Like Madeleine McCann's. Like—

"*Excusez-moi, monsieur.*"

"Sorry," I said to the female clerk I'd bumped into. "Know where I can find human resources?"

She pointed. "Right back that way. I just left there. Actually, the girls are on their way to lunch. You may want to try back after one o'clock."

"I'm looking for Miss Bettencourt."

"Sandrine," she said, smiling. She pointed across the floor to a tall brunette in a light blouse and dark skirt. "That's her there, heading for the elevator."

"*Merci,*" I said, and moved away from her, watching the lights above the elevator. The door opened. Of course they were going down. Hopefully, to the ground floor. I hopped back on the escalator.

The women beat me to the street level, but I made it in time to see Sandrine walk out the front door by herself. I hurried after her, trying not to look too conspicuous. Easy to get away with in any big city like New York or London or Paris. Everyone's always in a hurry. Only those who moved slowly appeared suspicious.

I stepped back into the rain to find that a sea of umbrellas had risen. *Damn,* I thought. *Now I've lost her.*

But I hadn't. I caught her lovely profile as she crossed the boulevard.

I followed. Running was no longer a problem. I was a man in a four-figure suit caught in the rain without an umbrella. What nutter wouldn't run?

———

Ten minutes later we were aboard the Metro. I rode in the car just behind Sandrine's so that I could see her without her seeing me. We stepped off at the next stop, on Rue du Bac. Just as I'd hoped, it appeared she was heading for her flat.

I waited until I thought she was upstairs, then climbed the steps to the door outside her small lobby. I searched the yellowed strips of tape for the name Bettencourt. Second floor, apartment B. I stabbed at the buzzer. If she didn't answer I figured there was a good chance her boyfriend, Johan, was there. I waited thirty seconds, then descended the concrete steps. The rain was coming down harder. I rounded the corner and found the fire escape. It was creaking under the weight of a man carefully climbing down. A young man with light hair, who evidently had just stepped out of the second-floor window, where Sandrine stood, watching him nervously.

She turned her head and spotted me. Her eyes went wide, then she screamed out, "Johan!"

Fleischer spun around and saw me. He gauged the distance from his step to the ground and decided to jump. He landed on his feet, but barely. I'd already taken off in a sprint in his direction and I liked my chances of catching him, even if he did have the edge in age and knowing the territory. This was hardly my first footrace.

He turned right at the first corner and I bolted after him, my dress shoes now pounding cobblestone rather than grass, beating my soles into pulp. I kept going but I wasn't gaining ground; on the contrary, I seemed to be losing it. Fleischer was faster than I had anticipated. And, as I'd expected, he knew his way, winding around corners and darting down narrow alleys like a ferret. I kept pace, tried to keep him in sight. I had to have an advantage in endurance. Long as I made this a marathon, I was in good shape. My training would pay off. All that cardio wasn't just for my health, after all. It was for the chase.

Fleischer seemed to know it, too. He adopted a different strategy by breaking out of the maze. If he couldn't outrun me, he'd put obstacles in my way. Moving obstacles. Two-ton chunks of metal and glass barreling down the pavement at forty to fifty miles per hour.

He was already across the street by the time I dodged my first Volkswagen. I spun and just missed being clipped by a Renault. Tried to regain my balance. Nearly fell flat in front of a black Audi A4. A Mercedes screamed to a halt just in front of me. I bounced off the hood and kept moving.

Luckily, a wave of pedestrians slowed Johan Fleischer down on the far sidewalk. I accelerated enough to catch up, then grabbed the back of his jacket just as he tried to hurdle a small gate protecting the tables in front of a busy café. Our momentum took us both over the rail and we crashed into a table with a pair of empty chairs, knocking over a tray of water glasses and beer bottles in the process. People screamed. Most reached for their cell phones. Some to make calls, others to shoot pictures or video.

I lifted Fleischer off the concrete and hurried him out of the area before the police arrived. There was no time for explanations.

"Where are we going?" he shouted as I pushed him in front of me. He struggled every step of the way.

I worried he'd slip out of his jacket and lead me on another chase, so I grabbed hold of his left ear and twisted it until he yelped in pain.

Chapter 9

For such a romantic city, it's not easy to find any privacy on the streets of Paris. So I ducked into a pub, warning Fleischer that I had a gun and wasn't afraid to use it.

"Straight back to the toilets," I said in his ear.

He went for the men's room but I shoved him into the ladies'.

"Why in here?" he said.

"Because I saw plenty of gentlemen out there but not a single lady. If memory serves me, males are much more likely to be day drinkers."

I spun him around, lifted him by the lapels of his jacket, and threw him into the last stall. Perfect landing, ass on the toilet. I took a second to catch my breath.

"Who are you?" he said.

"You're the man on the can," I said, "so I ask the questions." I pushed some of the rain water out of my face. "Why didn't you show up at work today?"

"'Cause I was sick."

His answer stung like a slap to my face. I pictured him rolling the food-service cart into the Sorkins' room with a grin, knowing a thief was about to sneak in behind him and hide in a hall closet to snatch a little girl. Something like heat filled my stomach and my shoulders tensed. I gripped him by the jacket again, lifted him off the toilet.

"Wrong answer," I told him.

He spit in my face and the last twenty-four hours suddenly caught up with me, adrenaline flooding my system as though a dam had been torn down by his single drop of saliva. My vision blurred to the point where I saw two of him and my head became heavy with fog. Gritting my teeth, I spun him around, dropped him to his knees, and forced his head into the bowl. When he tried to scream, I pushed his face into the toilet.

He vomited. I drew a deep breath through my mouth and pulled him up to allow the toilet to flush.

"Okay, okay," he cried. "No more lies, I swear it."

"That's the ticket, blondie. Let me tell you what I know and you're going to fill in the blanks for me. Unless you want to drown face-down in a women's toilet."

"No, no."

I thought about all the hours he had let slip away this morning, hours that could've brought us that much closer to Lindsay. I gave him another quick taste of toilet water so that he'd remember it.

"All right, then," I said. "A little girl named Lindsay Sorkin was snatched from her parents' room at Hotel d'Étonner on the night you carried their luggage and delivered their room service. While you wheeled in their tray, you intentionally left the door open behind you. Someone snuck in, opened the coat closet with a key, and hid in there until Vince and Lori Sorkin went to bed. Give me that someone's name, or we switch stalls to that first one with the log in it."

"No, no. Okay." He spoke faster than a cokehead in the middle of a talking jag. "He called himself Hugh, but I don't think that's his real name."

"How do you know him?"

"I don't really, I just met him once before that night."

"Where?"

"At a pizza parlor near the Bastille. There were two of them. Look, man, I had no idea they were going to take that girl. They said the lady owned a bunch of expensive jewelry and they wanted to grab it, the price of gold being what it is. I swear. I never would have gotten involved if I knew they were kidnappers, man. You've got to believe me."

"What did they give you for your cooperation?"

"Five hundred euros up-front. They were supposed to give me another five hundred after they moved the jewelry, but I never saw them again, I swear."

"Where are they from?"

"They didn't say, but they spoke German to me. From their accent, I would guess the metro area."

"Where were they staying while they were in Paris?"

"I have no idea, man, I swear it." He continued to sound panicked.

Behind us, someone opened the door to the ladies' room.

"Occupied," I shouted.

The door squeaked closed.

"All right," I said. "You and I are going to do one last thing together. We're going to take a taxi to the Bastille to find that pizza parlor you met these two gents at, and we're going to see if anyone recognizes you and can identify the men you were with."

"Please, I just want to go home."

"It's the Bastille or National Police Headquarters, blondie. What's your decision?"

"Fine, man, I'll go with you."

I lifted his head out of the toilet, feeling sick to my stomach. I derived no pleasure from this whatsoever. On the contrary, I'd have much preferred to turn him over to Davignon and have the lieutenant sweat Fleischer under the hot lights. But there was no time.

As I turned I noticed some graffiti on the stall wall.

It read: FLUSH HARD. IT'S A LONG WAY TO THE STATES.

Chapter 10

The waitress at the pizza parlor in the Bastille was a shapely Algerian girl who spoke little English. But she recognized Johan Fleischer straightaway. Said she remembered the two men he was with a few days back, as well. How could she forget? The two Germans had been dining there every afternoon and evening for a week. Ordering pizza and hitting on her. Getting drunk on Kronenbourg and inviting her back to their room—their room at the Hotel Lyon Bastille on Rue Parrot.

I kept Fleischer's passport but let Fleischer himself scurry down into the Metro. He'd served his purpose and seemed on the verge of passing out. I was confident I'd extracted all the information he had. Bringing him to justice for his role in Lindsay's disappearance wasn't my job. The French police could handle that. Without his passport, it was unlikely that Johan Fleischer was going anywhere outside the EU anytime soon.

I held off calling Davignon and headed on foot for the Hotel Lyon.

The hotel lobby was bright and airy, colorful, but I wasn't there to admire the decor. I went straight to the front desk and spoke to a short young man wearing glasses.

"Excuse me," I said. "I'm looking for a couple of friends of mine. German fellows. Hope I'm not too late. They may have checked out a couple of days ago."

"What are their names, monsieur?"

I shrugged as though it were the most ridiculous question in the world. "That I don't know. Met them at the pub. We made plans to get together, but then I spent the last couple of nights with a young Norwegian model I met at Le Cab." I ran my hand down my stubble to show I hadn't shaved the past couple of days.

The young man seemed impressed. He smiled and said, "I understand, yes. Please, wait just one minute, I will check."

I reached into my pocket, ready to pull out my wad of euros, if necessary. In my job, I spent more money on information than most people spent on food, clothing, and shelter combined. And it was worth every damn penny.

After checking his computer, the young man picked up the phone and dialed three digits I couldn't see. I tried to draw his attention but he wasn't looking my way. Seemed as though he was avoiding my gaze. After sixty seconds he hung up the phone and turned back to me.

"Interesting," he said. "I do remember your friends, but I have not seen them the past couple of days. I checked the computer and it shows that they are still registered guests. I called their room, but there was no answer."

"What's their room number, so I can call again later?"

He hesitated. "That I am not permitted to say."

I smiled. "Understandably. Well then, what are their names?"

He tilted his head to the side. "I am afraid I am not supposed to divulge that information either."

"Come on," I said, still smiling. "I'm staying all the way over on the other side of the city at the Four Seasons. Don't make me trek all the way back here this evening, only to find that my friends aren't here again." I leaned in on the desk, hoping like hell I didn't still stink of Fleischer's rubbish. "Besides, I'm going to look like a complete ass if I don't remember their names. These are the guys that introduced me to Liv, that Norwegian model I told you about. Just, please, do me a quick favor and pull up your copies of their passports. I'd really appreciate it."

The young man sighed. "Really, monsieur, I cannot."

My read was that money wouldn't persuade this guy. Besides, there were too many cameras hanging over our heads.

"Listen," I said. "Liv's got a younger sister named Elle. Maybe the four of us could go out for a drink tonight."

His cheeks glowed red. "You are very persistent," he said. "One more moment, please."

He turned and opened a drawer, plucked out a file. He opened it just enough that I could see two color copies of German passports. I couldn't read the names but tried like hell to burn their passport photos into my brain. He closed the folder and stuffed it back into the drawer.

"Their first names are Dietrich and Karl," he said.

"And the last?"

"Sorry, monsieur."

"But if I call later—"

"If you give me your name, I will leave a note for the evening staff to connect you."

"Simon," I said. "And thank you." I turned to leave, but spun back around. "Would you mind ringing their room one last time before I leave? Maybe someone was in the shower when you called the first time."

The young man appeared irritated, but swallowed hard and said, "Of course."

I watched him dial. It looked as though his fingers punched the numbers 506. He held the phone to his ear and waited. After sixty seconds he hung up and shook his head.

I walked away, a little angry.

Oh, how I hated people who always played it straight.

Chapter 11

Instead of heading for the doors, I waited until the desk clerk turned away, then made straight for the elevator. I punched the button for the fifth floor. When I stepped off, I checked both ends of the hall. A maid's cart was standing a few doors down to my left. I headed for it. From a few feet away I saw a set of keys on a ring, with an electronic card dangling from the end.

Hell, I thought, *at least some things have to be easy.*

I heard the maid whistling from the far end of the room she was in. I snatched the key ring, held it tight so that the keys wouldn't jingle, and moved quickly up the hall to 506. There was a Do Not Disturb sign hanging from the door handle. Too bad. I intended to disturb them. I slid the key in, waited for the red light to blink off and the green to blink on, then I turned the handle.

I shoved the keys into my pocket and let the door shut behind me.

The room was a mess, hadn't been cleaned since they had fled. Crushed cans of 1664 were everywhere and the room stank of beer. Cigarette butts peppered the floor, and they'd ashed on every single piece of furniture, including the two double beds. I doubted they'd brought Lindsay here, but I was hoping to find something that would give me an idea about where they'd taken her.

I emptied the wastebaskets first, sorted through the aluminum cans and paper scraps. Nothing of use. I searched the desk. Room-service menus, entertainment brochures, television guides, but nothing that Dietrich and Karl had left behind. Same with the nightstands. I opened the drawers, all of them. Nothing but a Bible and more cigarette butts.

I got onto my knees and checked under the bed. More beer cans. The closets were empty except for the hotel hangers. They'd probably stolen the bathrobes. I flipped the light on in the bathroom. Shaving cream on the mirror, tiny hairs stuck to the sink. Toothpaste on the faucet, more cigarette butts in the toilet. Where had I gotten it into my head that all Germans were neat?

Piss on the floor. But also something I needed. A Rail Europe train schedule. I unraveled a bit of toilet paper and wadded it up. Bent over and lifted the schedule. It was from the week before. Two trips were circled. The first was 4:04 A.M., Berlin to Mannheim. The second was 9:41 A.M., Mannheim to Paris.

I let fly a little sigh of relief. If Berlin was where Dietrich and Karl had come from, chances were, that was the city to which they'd returned.

And that was where we'd find Lindsay Sorkin.

L et me try to understand this," Davignon said. "You are going to Berlin to find two blond-haired blue-eyed German men named Dietrich and Karl."

"That's right," I said.

"You may as well search for two specific rats in the Paris sewer system. You have nothing to go on."

"I have an idea what they look like," I said. "I saw their passport photos."

"From more than *three meters away.*"

"Have you got a better idea, Lieutenant?"

We were standing over espressos at a tall table in a tiny café near the Eiffel Tower. The café was owned by Davignon's brother. His brother had closed up for the next few hours so that we could use the café as a base. The Sorkins were waiting in the backroom. Ever since the media arrived, Davignon had been shuffling them around in disguise or under cover of darkness.

"And this Johan Fleischer, you let him get away?"

I reached into my suit pocket and pulled out Fleischer's passport. Slid it across the table.

"He's still in Paris," I said. "Your men can pick him up if they want. Or not. Doesn't matter. I got everything there was to get from the guy. Fleischer thought he was setting the Sorkins up to lose some jewelry, not their daughter."

"But the timing of all this tells us that the Germans were here specifically for Lindsay Sorkin."

"That it does."

"Then why no ransom demand? Why no demand for information? What in the hell is their endgame?"

"We can't rule out the possibility that something went wrong," I said. "That the girl is dead."

"Merde," he mumbled.

"Either way," I said, "my guess is that our answers are in Berlin, and that's where I'm going."

"Very well. Let's move to the back room and speak with the Sorkins."

Lori Sorkin was almost unrecognizable. Her eyes remained vacant, her neck hung loosely at an odd angle, her jaw had gone slack. She appeared heavily medicated. She had the same stare Tasha had when I returned home from Romania to find that Hailey had gone missing. Tasha had blamed me, of course. For being in Bucharest hunting a fugitive when Hailey was taken. In time, Tasha would come to blame herself a whole hell of a lot more. Enough to take her own life with prescription pills.

The coroner had ruled Tasha's death accidental. But I knew otherwise.

"It'll be seventy-two hours tonight," Vince said.

"If we're dealing with professionals, as the evidence now seems to suggest, then we may have a wider window than we originally thought," I said. "That doesn't mean we can slow down, but it does give us reason to maintain hope."

Vince nodded. "Lieutenant Davignon says you're leaving for Berlin. I want to come with you."

I shook my head. "That wouldn't be wise. First, you'd be bringing the media along with you, and that puts Lindsay at risk. It destroys the element of surprise. Secondly, I'm a professional, and I work alone. No offense, Vince, but you'll only get in the way."

Lori said softly, "What will you do if you find these two men?"

"*When* I find them, I will do whatever is necessary to make them lead me to Lindsay. Let's leave it at that."

Vince reached into his jacket and removed a thick envelope. "You'll need money," he said, holding the envelope out to me. "I've withdrawn ten thousand euros from my bank. If you need more, please call me."

I took the envelope. "All right."

"You will also require some new clothes," Davignon said. "I have taken the liberty of calling Francesco Smalto's. They have prepared several suits using the measurements they took yesterday. Bertrand is picking them up now."

From the corner of my eye I caught Lori dabbing at fresh tears with a ball of tissues. It reminded me of what our home looked like in the days following Hailey's disappearance. Tissues everywhere. On tables and counters, on carpets and hardwood floors. Tasha had carried a box of tissues around as though it were a life preserver.

Carried the box around even more often than the phone. A couple of nights after Hailey went missing, she'd placed the box of tissues in the middle of our bed. At first I was angry that she wouldn't let me comfort her anymore. Then I realized how much I needed *her* to comfort me. That night I experienced a second loss and it continued to eat at me even now. All it had taken was a box of tissues to keep me and my wife from holding each other while we waited out life's most brutal storm.

"You'll need each other to get through this," I said to the Sorkins. "At times you'll want to pull away. After you get tired of blaming yourself, you'll want to blame each other and that's fine. Have it out. Fight like hell, but never stop loving each other. Never think that it would be better if you were each on your own. Until we bring Lindsay home, there's no one in the world who will fully understand what you're going through except the two of you. Your shared history, your shared love of Lindsay, that's what will get you through. It may sound trite, but it's true."

Although the words were unsolicited, Vince wrapped a long arm around Lori and pulled her to him. She set the ball of tissues down on her lap and nestled her head on his chest while stroking his arm. Silently, she mouthed the words *thank you.*

I turned back to Davignon. "I'll also need transportation when I arrive in Berlin."

Davignon nodded. "An automobile?"

"No, something I can really maneuver. A motorcycle. And since I'm heading to Germany, best make it a BMW."

"It will be arranged," he said. "Anything else?"

"Yes, Lieutenant. I'll need a gun."

Chapter 12

I arrived at Tegel Airport early the next morning, following a two-hour Lufthansa flight from Charles de Gaulle. I picked up the silver BMW K 1600 GTL at a rental agency and drove straight to Tiergarten, where Kurt Ostermann now maintained his office. I hadn't seen Ostermann in ages. Eight years earlier the private investigator had aided me in tracking down a twelve-year-old girl and her father. When we found them, the father gave himself up straightaway. The girl, on the other hand, ran. Ostermann and I chased after her through the slush-covered streets of Berlin. The chase ended with the girl darting out in front of a night bus. The girl lived. But the matter nearly became an international incident. Ostermann, a former member of the parliamentary police, used his considerable influence with the Ministry of the Interior to keep the matter under wraps.

Ostermann's new office was located in a rather utilitarian building that resembled some federal holding facilities back in the States. The building looked as though it had been carved out of a single slab of concrete. The entire structure was cold, uninviting. I had half a mind to phone Ostermann and ask him to meet me outside. But then, Ostermann didn't know I was coming. Given our history, I thought it better that I request his assistance face-to-face.

I stepped into the building and stopped at the security desk. I was wearing one of the new suits procured for me by the French police. I hoped it was enough for me to gain entry. Only this wasn't a nightclub; it was a place where important business was conducted.

"*Identifikation,*" the guard said.

"Sorry," I said, emphasizing my British accent. "I am afraid I'm not carrying any. I'm here to see Herr Ostermann."

As a child I'd clung to my English accent as though it were a life preserver. Drove my father crazy, and the more it did, the thicker my accent became. It was the cause of a few ass-kickings, both at home and in the schoolyard, but by the time I reached college I'd realized it didn't hurt with the American girls, so I did nothing to dilute it. By the time I married Tasha, it was like a stubborn rash, impossible to get rid of. Now that I spent more time in Europe and Asia than I did stateside, it served me well. Especially in countries that didn't particularly care for American foreign policy during the W years.

"Is Herr Ostermann expecting you?"

"Of course."

"Name?"

I couldn't exactly throw the name Simon Fisk around Germany since the incident with the girl.

"Bateman," I said. "Patrick Bateman." It was the cover I had used last time Ostermann and I worked together. After he'd dubbed me an American psycho.

"One moment, Herr Bateman." The guard called upstairs, announced me as a visitor, took some instructions, then hung up the phone. To me, he said, "Fifth floor, Herr Bateman."

I made for the elevators. Rode one to the fifth floor. A sign indicated Ostermann's office was at the end of the hall.

"*Guten Tag,* Magda," I said when I entered the small reception area. I was surprised to see Magda Gerhardt still working for Ostermann. Eight years ago Ostermann had started getting it on with the fetching brunette, and he'd told me her husband was already suspicious. I checked Magda's finger for a ring and saw none.

"Herr Fisk," she said. Seemed she was even more surprised to see me. Not pleasantly, from the look on her face. "Excuse me. I will go and get Kurt."

"Danke," I said.

Magda remained in Ostermann's office longer than it would take to announce me. I was becoming anxious, pacing around reception, picking up and flipping through old copies of *Der Spiegel.* Finally, Ostermann showed his face. He'd aged well. In his midforties, he maintained a fit physique and his hair was every bit as blond as the day I'd met him. His ice-blue eyes bore into me like a laser. I noticed Magda had remained behind in his office.

"Simon," he said, without extending his hand. "This is unexpected. What brings you to Berlin?"

"A missing girl."

Ostermann smirked, regarded me silently for a few moments as though he thought I might be joking.

Finally, he said, "Yes, well. Last time did not end with champagne and balloons."

"No, it certainly didn't," I said. "But this time is different."

Ostermann took a step back and appraised me. "Why? Because you've learned how to dress?"

I watched for a smile but none was forthcoming. I was beginning to sense some hostility and I told him so.

"Well, at least you have *some* sense," he said, raising his voice.

"I'm not sure I understand."

"Well, Simon, you certainly did not show any sense by arriving in my office after eight years."

"Are you asking me to leave?" I said.

"Asking you to leave?" he shouted. "You are lucky I do not cut off your balls, *schwanzlutscher.*"

The door to his inner office opened and Magda poked her head out. Ostermann barked a command at her in German, then turned back to me as she disappeared.

"You have *one minute*, Simon," he said as his stern, pale cheeks turned crimson. "You have *one minute* to explain to me what the hell you are doing in Berlin."

I narrowed my eyes, then glanced at the door to the hall. I wanted like all hell to use it. But this wasn't about me and Kurt Ostermann and the events that had transpired nearly a decade ago. It was about a child. And I knew damn well that I needed his help to find her.

"This little girl I'm looking for, she wasn't abducted by one of her parents," I said evenly. "She was taken in the middle of the night from her hotel room in Paris."

Ostermann's Adam's apple bobbed in his throat. "The American girl?"

"Lindsay Sorkin, yes."

He remained silent for a moment, then stuffed his hands into his pockets and said quietly, "I stayed at home watching the coverage all of yesterday. Magda and I, we have a boy, Jakob. He's around Lindsay's age." His eyes dropped to the floor, then suddenly rose to meet mine. "But I heard nothing about this girl being in Berlin."

"The media have no idea," I said. "And I intend to keep it that way."

Standing in his reception area, I briefed Ostermann on the events of the previous forty-eight hours. Being pulled over by the French police, then hauled by Davignon to an empty cottage in a rural suburb forty kilometers north of Paris. Facing threats of arrest for retrieving the boy in Bordeaux. Meeting Vince and Lori Sorkin and agreeing to inspect their suite at Hotel d'Étonner. Finding the crushed tab of Ecstasy, locating the dealer Remy, and learning whom he'd sold 007s to over the past ten days. Linking the buyers to the bellhop Johan Fleischer, tracking Fleischer's girlfriend, Sandrine, then chasing Fleischer himself through the streets of the Left Bank. Dragging him back to a pizza parlor in the Bastille after he confessed to his role with his head in a women's toilet. The Algerian waitress's positive identification. Eliciting the names Dietrich and

Karl from the desk clerk at Hotel Lyon. Sneaking up to the kidnappers' room and finding the piss-covered train schedule.

"Which brings me here," I said.

"In Berlin," Ostermann said in apparent disbelief, "searching for two blond-haired, blue-eyed men named Dietrich and Karl."

"It's more than I had when Davignon brought me up to the Sorkins' hotel room in Paris," I said.

"I suppose it is." Ostermann paced about without looking at me. His right thumbnail found its way between his teeth and he bit into it. These nervous tics seemed entirely out of character. For as long as I'd known him, Ostermann had always been as cool as the North Sea.

"Simon," he said finally, "we must—"

The phone on Magda's desk began to ring. Ostermann held a finger up to me and lifted the receiver. He spoke quickly in German, hung up the phone, and turned back to me.

"That was the security desk downstairs," he said. "The police have arrived."

"The police?"

"I am sorry, Simon. I ordered Magda to call them a few minutes ago. Before I knew why you were here." He shrugged and forced a smile. "You would have known if you had brushed up on your German." He set aside the smile and raised a reassuring hand. "But it is all right. I just explained to security that the police must take the elevator and move all their men to the rear, because I do not want any media attention. We can take the stairs and exit through the front doors. You have a vehicle?"

"Yes," I said. "But why are the police after me?"

Ostermann glared at me as though I should know.

"The twelve-year-old girl Elise Huber," he said. "From eight years ago."

"Eight years ago," I said. "But surely Germany has a statute of limitations—"

"Not for murder, Simon."

"Murder?"

"Yes," he said calmly. "The girl died from her injuries." Ostermann grabbed my arm and pulled me to the door. "Now hurry, Simon. We do not have much time."

Chapter 13

The police didn't exactly follow Ostermann's instructions. As soon as we entered the stairwell we heard a bevy of boots tramping up the steps.

"*Scheiße*," Ostermann said.

I stood in the stairwell, listening to the echoes of their footfalls, and suddenly found myself frozen with shock. Elise Huber was dead. I'd made plenty of mistakes in my post-marshal career but nothing on par with this. This was exactly what I had spent the past ten years of my life trying to prevent—a parent from losing her child. Elise Huber's mother, Heidi, had been my client. She'd paid me and paid me well. I'd spoken to her just after the accident and she'd told me she would immediately fly to Berlin. Had she made it in time to see her daughter? Had she been by her daughter's side when she died? Why hadn't I ever heard from Heidi again?

Of course, she would have had no reason to call me. *I* should've called *her.* Why hadn't I phoned her to ask after Elise? Was it guilt? It had been an accident; as bad as I felt about the girl landing in the hospital, I'd never felt it was my fault. Or had I?

I'd been chasing people my entire adult life, first with the marshals and since on my own. Running down fugitives and then child thieves, from country to country, all around the world. But was I running after them? Or was I really running away? At what point had my objective changed? After Hailey's abduction, when I went out on my own? Had I been running these past ten years from what happened? Or had I begun this long before Hailey was gone?

Maybe Tasha had been right to blame me. Maybe I had no business being in Bucharest when Hailey was taken. I'd begun my career with the marshals at the D.C. field office. Less than a year later, Hailey was born. It was around that time that I requested to be put on international investigations, tracking down wanted fugitives in foreign countries, bringing them back to the U.S. for prosecution. Had I pursued that position in order to flee from Tasha and Hailey? Had I abandoned my wife and daughter the same as my father had done to my mother and Tuesday when we left London all those years ago?

After all I'd done to distance myself from him, was I no better than Alden Fisk?

"*Simon,*" Ostermann was shouting in my ear. "Snap *out* of it. Up the stairs. *Hurry.*"

We bounded past the door to the fifth floor and made for the roof.

Ostermann burst through the steel door and suddenly we were outside in the frigid Berlin air. Only we were six stories too high. I didn't care for heights. My father used to tell me that we came from a family of distinguished mountaineers. Said climbing was in our blood, tried to take me to the White Mountains in New Hampshire more than once. I refused to get out of the car. Told him to piss off. If he wanted to die at six thousand feet he was more than welcome to do so. Just be sure to leave me the keys to the house.

"We jump to the next roof," Ostermann said.

"Are you *kidding* me?"

"I have done it before," he said. "Seven years ago, when Magda's husband finally found out about us."

"You jumped to the next *roof*?"

"What was I to do? The psycho had a gun."

"I can't do it in these shoes."

"Nonsense," he said. "I did it naked. Try leaping across buildings with your dick swinging through the air."

There was no more talk on the subject. Ostermann simply took off in a sprint to the edge of the building. Reluctantly, I followed, my heart pounding harder than it did during a chase. As I neared the edge I felt a surge of nausea, but it was too late. My momentum would take me over the side and drop me six stories if I tried to stop. Adrenaline pumping, I jumped just as the door to the roof burst open. It felt as though I were suspended in midair for minutes on end. Then my feet hit something solid. I braced my body and let myself tumble. When I finally came to a stop, I stayed down, just as Ostermann had. I glanced over at him. We were both badly out of breath. The gap between the buildings had to be eight or nine feet, at least.

"What now?" I whispered, fearing they'd seen me leap.

Ostermann put a finger to his lips. "We wait."

We waited several minutes. Apparently, the police hadn't caught sight of me. We listened to the troops march around the roof, then back down the stairs. When we heard the steel door close, we surmised that the police had cleared the roof. Slowly, we rose to our feet.

"Let's go," Ostermann said, moving toward this roof's steel door. "I have friends in this building. They will help us wait out the storm."

I brushed myself off and walked alongside him.

"Sorry about the suit," Ostermann said, pointing from the torn elbow to the torn knee.

"It's all right," I told him. "I have six others just like it."

Ostermann had Magda check us in to the Ritz-Carlton right in Tiergarten. From the outside the Ritz looked an awful lot like New York's Rockefeller Center. Inside, I marveled at the marble columns and gold leaf as we swiftly crossed the lobby. Ostermann and I went straight to our suite on the eighth floor, an ultracomfortable, well-appointed space with a Prussian Neo-Classicist design. Once we had safely locked ourselves inside the suite, we crashed on opposite ends of the uncompromising sofa situated in the middle of the sitting room. Ostermann didn't bother to explain what Magda had told the police when they arrived at his office, and I didn't ask. What he did do was apologize again.

"But why call them in the first place?" I said, still trying to comprehend the goings-on of the past two hours.

Ostermann sighed, glared at me as he had back at his office. "You cost me years of headaches with the police and politicians here in Berlin," he said. "You fled Germany and left me holding the bag, Simon."

"I didn't know the girl died," I said.

"To be perfectly honest, that thought never crossed my mind. How could you be so inconsiderate as not to check?"

"I was devastated," I said, thinking back, trying to assuage this sudden sense of guilt. "Just by the fact that the girl had been injured at all. I couldn't sleep for weeks. But then I received a call from another desperate mother in San Diego. Her infant son had been stolen by his father and smuggled across the Mexican border. The mother was afraid that her ex-husband was involved with the cartels. She was sure her baby boy's life was in danger. I immediately left for Tijuana."

"But there is the Internet," Ostermann said. "You could have googled Elise Huber and discovered that she was dead. You could have made a single phone call, Simon. That is all it would have taken."

He was right, of course. I had no excuse. None, other than my damn obsession with every case I'd ever taken since leaving the marshals. My relationship with Ostermann had preceded the Elise Huber case. I'd met him a couple of years before, while tracking down a fugitive in Hannover. He'd come to my aid in a bar fight that erupted while I was trying to elicit information on my target. At the time he intervened, the business end of a broken bottle was being pressed against my throat. Fact is, Ostermann probably saved my life that night.

Now we stared silently at each other for a while, neither of us knowing quite what to say.

Finally, I realized it was my turn to apologize. Something that had never come easily for me. It was something my father had demanded from me almost daily, for even the slightest transgression. Now, whenever I had to utter the words *I'm sorry,* it felt as though I was being pressured and I instinctively fought to pull back. When the words finally came, they fell out of my mouth with a stiffness that undermined my sincerity. And there's nothing worse than a disingenuous apology. It's an admission and a surrender and a deception all tucked tightly into one overly used phrase.

Christ, I thought. Had I even apologized to Elise Huber's mother? Our first conversation after the incident was brief, just a rambling recitation of the facts. There was never a second conversation. Was that why? Because I couldn't bring myself to apologize? Was that why I had never called?

Ostermann solemnly acknowledged my apology, then reached over and roughed up my arm as though we were old friends, which I suppose, in a way, we were.

"It's all right, Simon," he assured me. "So, tell me. Did you ever remarry?"

"No," I said.

He leaned back, shook his head. "Neither did I."

"You and Magda haven't tied the knot?"

"Of course not," he said. "She's an adulterer. How could I ever trust her?"

I waited for him to laugh but he never got there.

After a moment, he said, "So, Simon, did you come to Berlin with a plan?"

"Yes," I told him. "But it didn't involve dodging the German police."

He grinned. "That should not prove so difficult. The places we would likely find your Dietrich and Karl, the police do not frequent them."

"And where might that be?"

"I suggest we start in Kreuzberg," he said. "But I don't advise bringing the BMW. Or, for that matter, the TAG Heuer around your wrist."

"How the hell will I know what time it is?"

Chapter 14

During the Cold War, Kreuzberg, known also as X-berg, was closed in by the Berlin Wall on three sides. After the wall fell, the area found itself in the heart of a major European city again. Twentysome years later, it's still struggling to find its identity. Currently, among other things, Kreuzberg is widely known for its large number of Turkish immigrants.

"The Germans complain that the Turks refuse to integrate into our society," Ostermann said as we made our way to the U-Bahn station. "But it's not so. The criminals have integrated just fine. The law-abiding Turks could learn a lesson from them."

Night had fallen hours ago. I'd spent the downtime taking advantage of the Ritz-Carlton's ridiculously comfortable bed, while Ostermann watched two pay-per-view Reese Witherspoon romantic comedies on the flat-screen television in the next room.

"Really?" I'd said. "Reese Witherspoon?"

"I never get to watch anything like this at home," he said. "You know how it is when you have kids. Unless it's some bloody Pixar movie it's not finding its way into the Blu-Ray player. And forget asking Jakob to sit in his room and watch it alone so that Magda and I can watch something we'd like."

Soon as he said it, Ostermann turned to me and whispered, "I'm so sorry, Simon."

I grinned at him. "People all over the world have children. And I love hearing about every one of them."

And it was true. Growing up in Providence without my mother had made me more curious about the mother-son dynamic than just about anything else as a child. I learned as much as I could from the few friends I had at school, and accepted every kid's invitation home to meet his parents. Even if I didn't particularly like the kid, chances were I could learn something from his mother.

It amazed me to observe how affectionate mothers could be with their sons, how generous and how forgiving. In the Fisk home, the prominent emotions were anger and occasional sadness. To witness these other, brighter emotions made me realize what I was missing. But by the time I hit high school, being around other kids' families made me uncomfortable. I felt like an intruder no matter how much they professed to wanting me there. Just wasn't my place, I told myself. I didn't belong there.

"Many young Germans have gone to work for Turkish organized crime," Ostermann continued. "The Turks specialize in narcotics trafficking, predominantly heroin. See, strategically, Turkey is in a perfect position for the heroin trade. The country serves as a gateway from Asia to Europe, and has access to opium from Afghanistan and Pakistan. Here in Germany, Kreuzberg acts much like a retail store, with young Turkish immigrants as its sales force."

"And the girl?"

He sighed, shrugged his shoulders. "When the world economy collapsed, Simon, most groups decided to diversify. Many drug traffickers began trafficking in humans."

"But an American girl of six, snatched from a hotel room in Paris? Surely that doesn't fit any MO you've ever heard of."

"No," Ostermann conceded, "it doesn't. But then, you must consider that Turkey lies next to Syria, Iraq, and Iran. If these two thugs, Dietrich and Karl, brought the girl here to Berlin, chances are this is just a stopping-off point." He paused but continued walking. "That the girl's father designs innovative weaponry not sanctioned by the U.S. government does not seem incidental to me. It is possible the girl was taken to lure the father. Perhaps this is Iran's sordid way of extending Vince Sorkin an offer of employment."

It was nearing 11:00 P.M. when we entered the underground station. We stopped at an electronic ticket machine and purchased two one-day travel cards, then waited ten minutes on a platform with a smattering of other people until a mustard-yellow train arrived right on time. The train itself smelled of skunked beer, and looking around it was easy to see why. Of the dozen passengers nine were teenage boys, each with a large brown paper bag sitting between his thighs.

We got off the U-Bahn at Gneisenaustrasse after a brief ride, the Glock that Davignon had provided me weighing heavily in the holster against the side of my chest as we ascended the cement steps back to the street.

From there, Ostermann led us straight to Tunnelbar, a relatively well-lit establishment with a young, energetic crowd. Not at all what I had expected.

"You taking us to pick up women or look for criminal sorts?" I asked him.

"Patience, Simon," Ostermann said. "This is where I usually find my favorite informant."

We moved slowly through several loud, crowded rooms before stepping into a lounge-type area with a relaxed vibe. In the far corner two dark men reclined on a couch, while a third sat comfortably in an oversize chair, sipping from a dark red drink.

"Alim," Ostermann said, "how nice to see you."

Alim didn't appear quite as pleased. He motioned for the two other men to leave the room and grudgingly offered us the couch. As his friends left, Alim called out, "Another Wodka Gorbatschow and cranberry." He turned to us. "Would you gentlemen like anything to drink?"

"We're fine," Ostermann said. "You've been watching the news lately, Alim?"

The young Turk shrugged. "What do I care about news, unless it involves me."

Ostermann nodded. "Well, allow me to update you, then. A few days ago, a six-year-old American girl was taken from her parents' hotel room in Paris. My friend here, who is not a policeman but works privately like me, has obtained evidence that the girl was brought here to Berlin by two German men named Dietrich and Karl."

Alim smiled smugly. "I know at least two dozen Dietrichs and twice as many Karls, Herr Ostermann. Tell your friend he should return to Paris and collect more evidence."

Ostermann looked around the room at the young, mellow faces. The speakers in the lounge were turned low and everyone was seated, a drink in one hand, one leg folded over the other. Ostermann leaned toward Alim and said, "For the time being, this is all we have to go on. So tell me where I can find these two dozen Dietrichs and four dozen Karls, and my friend and I will be on our way."

The Turk smirked and turned away from us. When he spoke, he raised his voice so that anyone in the room could hear.

"You know better than to come to me with this shit, Ostermann. I know nothing of what you are talking about. Now get the fuck out of my face."

In one smooth move, Ostermann leaped from his seat, snatched the rocks glass from Alim's hand, and smashed it against the Turk's forehead. Alim cried out and dropped to the floor as blood spilled into his eyes.

I stood and tried to play it cool, gave a cursory glance around the room. Everyone had turned his head but no one else was rising from his seat. One look at Ostermann standing over the bloody Alim and no one wanted to get involved.

"Talk to me again like that, Alim," Ostermann said, "and I will see that you die an old man in prison."

"Easy," I said in Ostermann's ear. "Remember, if the police show, I'm not leaving Germany."

As I said it, one of Alim's friends returned with the vodka and cranberry. He took one look at Alim, bloodied on the floor, and turned to leave. I grabbed him, brought him roughly over to the couch, and seated him, while stealing another glimpse around the lounge, eyeing down the one guy who'd taken out his smartphone. I took a single step toward him and he stashed the phone back in his jacket.

Ostermann said, "So, Alim, think hard. Do you know any thugs named Dietrich and Karl who are friends or confederates? Anyone who recently took a business trip to Paris?"

Alim remained on the floor, sobbing. Ostermann lifted his foot and stamped on the Turk's right hand. Alim screamed out as his friend popped off the couch and cried, "I do, Herr Ostermann. Please do not hurt him anymore."

Relieved, I turned to the friend.

"What is your name?" Ostermann asked him.

"Sidika."

"And you know of a Dietrich and Karl who recently returned from Paris?"

"I have not seen them since they returned," Sidika said. "But there were two men who called each other Karl and Dietrich, bragging about going on a holiday to Barcelona last week."

"How do you know this? You were listening in?"

"No, I do business with their friend, Hans. Hans was supposed to go on the trip as well, but he backed out at the last moment for a reason he wouldn't say."

"Where can we find this Dietrich and Karl?" Ostermann said.

"That I do not know. But I can give you Hans's address here in X-berg."

Chapter 15

From the opposite side of the street we saw lights on in the flat. Ostermann wanted to go in right away, but I suggested we hold back.

"It's not even midnight," I said. "What are the odds this guy's staying home tonight?"

"What do you suggest?"

"We wait an hour. If he exits the building, we tail him. Maybe he leads us directly to Dietrich and Karl."

Ostermann frowned. "And if he doesn't leave the building in the next hour?"

"Then we go in and put a gun to his head."

We waited for approximately forty minutes, I with my hands in my pockets, Ostermann puffing on Haus Bergmann cigarettes. We didn't speak. The wind made it feel like twenty below. And to think, I used to love the cold. Probably because my father hated it. Constantly threatened to move us to South Florida. I'd told him I'd rather die.

"There," I said as lights began to blink out in Hans's flat. "Stamp out that lung dart and get ready to move."

Ostermann flicked the butt into the street as Hans came bounding down the steps. The streets were fairly dead, which made tailing Hans a bit of a trick. Fortunately, he didn't go very far, only to Obentrautstrasse, to the famous nightclub SO36.

"You know, Iggy Pop used to come here," Ostermann said as we waited in line to get in.

"Is that right?"

"Back in the seventies, Berlin was home to the punk-rock movement."

I looked at him. "You're not going to tell me that *you* were a punk back then, are you?"

Ostermann smiled. "To the bone, Simon. To the fucking bone."

Tonight was metal night. A live band with painted faces played on stage in front of an ape-shit-crazy mosh pit. I'd never thought I'd find myself missing the techno music at Le Cab back in Paris.

Hans edged around the crowd and we followed at a safe distance. First he went to the bar, ordered a shot of Jägermeister and chased it with a Monster Energy Drink. Then he roamed by himself for a good half hour, stopping off at the bar for a shot of Jäger every ten minutes or so.

"Great, he's a loner," I said to Ostermann. "We're wasting valuable time."

"Give it another fifteen minutes," he said over the metal. "It's early yet for Kreuzberg."

We waited. Watched Hans circle the club another two, three times, not bothering to speak to anyone. He did another shot, chased it with another energy drink. After twenty minutes I was ready to approach him, but Ostermann held me back. And sure enough, ten minutes later, Hans met up with a number of friends who had just entered the club.

"Recognize any of them?" Ostermann said.

I couldn't be sure. But of the five, only two had light hair. So, if Dietrich and Karl were among them, those were our men.

"Only one way to find out," I said. "We'll wait for one of them to go to the pisser. You'll watch the door while I go in and have a chat with him."

"I can do you one better than that," Ostermann said. "See those girls over there in the corner? They're working girls. This is their off night. But for the right price, they'll take our friends into the back alley and give 'em a wank."

I wasn't exactly comfortable with Ostermann's suggestion. Still, a little girl's life hung in the balance. I pulled some euros from my pocket and handed them to him. "Will this cover it?"

He glanced down at the notes. "Are you kidding? This should cover every bloke in the club. Be right back."

I watched Ostermann go up to the skinny, young girls and slip them some money. He turned slightly and motioned to Hans's group with his sharp chin. Then he strolled back to me.

I said, "You sure these posers are going to believe these girls just picked them out of the crowd and want to take them out back for sex?"

Ostermann smiled at me. "Welcome to Europe, my friend."

Ten minutes later, Ostermann and I stepped into the narrow back alley. Ostermann raised his SIG P226 as I removed the Glock from inside my jacket.

"Now which of you ladies is Dietrich and which is Karl?" Ostermann said.

The girls quickly came off their haunches. One of the two screamed. The other threw her hands over her mouth.

"Quiet, girls," Ostermann said. "Go on your way. Tell anyone what you saw and we'll find you before you can say, '*Ich bin eine Hure.*'"

The emaciated girls took off down the alley. The men zipped up their flies, buttoned their denims, buckled their belts. If they were afraid, they didn't show it.

"Now answer his goddamn question," I said.

"I am Dietrich," said the taller of the two in a heavy German accent. He was wearing a pair of lightly tinted glasses with large black frames, a Rammstein T-shirt stretched across a broad chest.

The air was cold enough that I could see his breath.

I stepped up to Dietrich. Removed his glasses and studied his face. Close enough to the passport photo to make me think we had the right men. I took a step back, elbows bent, ready to raise the gun if I needed to.

"What were you two doing in Paris earlier this week?" I said.

"We weren't in Paris," Dietrich replied evenly. "We were in Barcelona. On holiday."

"Wrong," I said. "You were checked in to room 506 at the Hotel Lyon."

Calmly, he said, "I am afraid you have us mistaken for someone else. We were in Barcelona. On holiday."

"Lie to me again," I said, "and this is going to turn out bad for both of you. Now, what were you doing in Paris?"

"We weren't in Paris," Dietrich repeated in that same damn robotic voice. "We were in Barcelona. On holiday."

Before I could utter another word, Ostermann smashed Dietrich in the face with the butt of his gun. The blow broke the German's nose, blood spilling down his mouth and chin like a macabre waterfall.

The man who must have been Karl sprang forward, tried to grab Ostermann's gun, but he was too slow. Ostermann caught him with a right elbow to the jaw, threw him hard against the brick wall. Stuck his SIG P226 into Karl's mouth.

I straightened Dietrich up, eyed Ostermann with contempt, hoping he wouldn't make another move with the gun. Particularly not one that could earn us a few decades in prison.

"The next lie earns you a dislocated kneecap," Ostermann said to Dietrich. "And your friend here loses the left side of his face."

"We don't know what the fuck you're going on about!" Dietrich tried.

Ostermann cocked the hammer of his gun. Karl began emitting nervous sounds from deep in his throat, his lips still wrapped tightly around the barrel of Ostermann's pistol.

"I think your friend Karl here is trying to tell us otherwise," Ostermann said.

"We weren't in Paris!" Dietrich shouted. "We were in Barcelona! On holiday!"

Ostermann maneuvered the gun so that the barrel could be seen inside Karl's left cheek. He moved his finger to the trigger.

Christ, I thought. *Now who's the psycho?*

"Take the gun out of his mouth," I ordered Ostermann, sweat dripping from my hairline despite the bitter temps. He didn't even look my way.

"All right, Dietrich," Ostermann said without moving a muscle. "Start talking or it's Karl's funeral. If you remain quiet after that, you're not even going to be around to be a pallbearer."

I glanced down at Karl's legs. His blue jeans were turning black as he pissed himself.

"All right, all right," Dietrich said, finally in a genuine panic. "We were in Paris, Karl and I. We were given a job to do."

"What was that job?" I said, trying to remain focused, hoping Ostermann's finger didn't become too itchy.

"T-to take a child," Dietrich stammered. "An American girl named Lindsay Sorkin."

"Where did you take her?"

"Only as far as Hauptbahnof."

Hauptbahnof was Berlin's central railway station, a modern monstrosity with two sky-scraping glass-and-steel office towers and a massive main hall that doubled as a shopping mall with a couple of dozen restaurants.

"Be more specific. *Where* in Hauptbahnof?"

"The lower basement, near the Karlstadt grocery. Our instructions were to leave her in the third stall of a men's room that was closed for repair. Someone else would take her from there. We do not know who."

"Who hired you?" I said.

"His name is..." Dietrich swallowed hard, tried to catch his breath. "His name is Talik. I do not know his surname. He arrived here from Istanbul only a few days ago. I was introduced to him by his nephew."

"His nephew?"

"Alim. Alim Sari. He's a heroin dealer. Lives somewhere on Mehringdamm here in X-berg."

"Son of a *bitch*," Ostermann shouted.

"*Your* Alim?" I said.

Ostermann nodded.

I turned back to Dietrich. Drool dripped down his chin, and blood continued to flow from his nose.

"Where can we find this Talik?" I said.

"I do not know. We met him at Viktoriapark, near where Alim lives."

"All right," I said. "Give us Alim's address."

"It is in my wallet," Dietrich said.

"Remove your wallet," I told him. "Slowly."

He did. With trembling fingers, Dietrich opened his wallet, flipped through some cards, and gave us the address.

I was about to demand that Dietrich turn over his phone when Ostermann suddenly took the butt of his gun and knocked Karl out cold. Soon as he did, Dietrich broke into a run. Ostermann dashed after him, caught him just before he could escape the alley.

I hurried to them, but before I could intercede, Ostermann had Dietrich on the ground and was kicking him mercilessly. I grabbed Ostermann and, with all my strength, dragged him away from the fallen kidnapper. As I did, I looked back to make sure Dietrich was still breathing.

Chapter 16

What the hell's wrong with you?" I said once we neared the end of Mehringdamm.

I was angry. Livid, really. I wasn't in the torture business. Never had been. These two hadn't needed guns in their mouths to make them talk. And they sure as hell hadn't needed concussions after they'd already spilled their guts.

"What choice did I have?" Ostermann said. "They would have warned Alim we were coming. Besides, it was fun. Did you see the one named Karl piss himself?"

"*I* nearly pissed myself."

"Well, you'd still have five suits left," he said with a chuckle.

I didn't even smile, just looked away.

After Ostermann knocked them out cold, we checked the men for identification. The unconscious kidnappers were named Dietrich Braun and Karl Finster. Nothing else on their persons was of any use.

"Eight years ago, you called me a psycho just for *carrying* a gun," I said. "Now you're running around like you're Clint Eastwood."

"I am a different man now, Simon. I have a son. Rest assured, my beating two child kidnappers in a back alley of a Berlin nightclub will not cost me a single hour of sleep."

I grabbed hold of his arm, freezing him under the yellow glow of a streetlamp.

"Well, maybe it should," I growled.

"You're serious?" he said with that piercing blue stare of his. "This Dietrich and Karl, they kidnapped a six-year-old girl, Simon. We have no idea what has been done to her. But you, *you* know what has already been done to her family. You really think these two men deserved something better? We should have killed them, if you ask me."

I released his arm. "I'm here in Berlin to find this little girl, not to execute the men responsible."

"We executed no one," he said flatly. "I merely knocked them out. And I would do it again and again and again and *again*." Ostermann clutched me by the shoulders. "Tell me, Simon. What if instead of Lindsay Sorkin, these men had taken Hailey Fisk? What then? Would you have let them live?"

I didn't have an answer to that. Didn't feel I needed one, either. Hypothetical questions were for lawyers and storytellers, not for people like me. These men hadn't taken Hailey, and we had no business killing them. Period. No business busting their skulls, either.

"It's done," I said finally. "Let's leave it alone."

We continued walking. A few minutes later, Ostermann came to a halt and motioned across the street.

"There," he said. "That's the address for Alim."

According to Dietrich, Alim's apartment took up the left half of the second floor. From our vantage point, it appeared the entire floor was dark. We crossed the street.

As we walked up the steps to his building, a middle-aged Turkish woman was stepping outside with a black plastic garbage bag filled to the hilt but apparently not very heavy. She held the door for us.

"Excuse me," Ostermann said to her. "Do you know Alim Sari?"

She hesitated. "Are you the police?"

"Of course not," he said. "We're customers of his."

She didn't look convinced. But she didn't look like she much cared, either. "Yes, I know him. Second floor." She started down the concrete stairs.

"How about his uncle?" I said. "Do you know his uncle Talik?"

"I have met him once," she said. "He is staying with Alim these past few days."

I thanked her, but she was already on her way.

"That's convenient," Ostermann said once she'd left.

We entered the old building and walked quietly up the stairs to the second floor.

"Let's find a way in without damaging the door," I said.

Ostermann tried the handle. "It's unlocked." He didn't look too happy about it.

We both drew our weapons.

"On *drei*," he said before opening the door. *"Eins, zwei . . . drei!"*

We moved in, aiming our pistols in the darkness. For a moment, the only sound in the room was the pounding of my heart. Then Ostermann found a switch and the flat was illuminated. The place looked as though it had been hit by a tornado.

"They've gone already," I said, training my weapon on the bedroom door. I kicked it open as Ostermann examined the other end of the flat.

"Christ," I said, a sizable lump forming in my throat.

I took a tentative step forward and squinted, hoping my eyes had deceived me. But no. Facedown on the queen-size bed lay a naked body, the head and pillow covered in blood.

"What is it?" Ostermann called out.

I heard his footsteps approaching the bedroom.

"It's a corpse," I said.

He stood in the doorframe, a sick look on his face. "Is it Alim?"

I moved up close to the bed and knelt beside it, careful not to get blood on my suit. I surveyed the features of the dead man's face.

"No," I said. "It's not Alim. It's his friend Sidika."

———

Our search of the flat yielded nothing of use. Alim Sari and his uncle Talik had left in haste but had been thorough. Not a scrap of paper or business card, no train or flight schedules, not a single road map. Nothing to provide us any hint of where they were heading. Or, more important, where the girl had been taken. We had hit a wall.

"I am sorry, Simon," Ostermann said, once we'd gone over every square foot of the apartment.

Hands on my hips, I stared at each of the four walls, tempted to tear them down. Since they were bare, the electrical sockets stood out. As I paced the length of the living room, I noticed a phone jack. I pointed at it.

"Did you see any phone?" I said.

"Just an ancient thing with a cord wrapped around it in the closet of the second bedroom," Ostermann said.

"Get it, would you?"

Ostermann brought the phone to me and I unwrapped the cord, plugged it into the jack. I ran a finger along the receiver for dust but it was fairly clean. Which meant it had been used recently. I swallowed hard and put the receiver to my ear.

"Is there a dial tone?" Ostermann said.

I nodded, studied the handset. "This word here," I said, pointing to a button. "What does it mean?"

"Mute."

"And this one?"

"Redial."

I punched the Redial button. As the phone dialed, I handed the receiver to Ostermann.

"Here," I said. "I won't understand if someone picks up in German."

Ostermann listened. After a full minute he set the receiver back on its base.

"Well?" I asked.

"It's a law office," he said, pulling his Android from his pocket. "But it's not German. It's Polish."

His thumb worked the buttons as he entered the name of the firm in his browser.

"Have you found it?" I said after a minute.

"Yes, Simon, I've found it."

"Well, where is it located?"

He looked up at me.

"It's in Warsaw," he said.

Chapter 17

How far is it from here to Warsaw?" I asked.

Ostermann shrugged. "Not far. Just over five hundred kilometers."

We were seated in the rear of a taxi on our way back to Tiergarten. A flurry of snow fell from the sky.

"I'm going to take the motorcycle," I said. "I'll jump on the autobahn. Should make it in less than six hours. I'll get there shortly after nine A.M. and head straight for the lawyer's office."

"You understand, Simon, that I cannot go with you. After last night, I must stay and protect Magda and Jakob."

"I understand," I said.

He leaned back against the torn vinyl seat. "Perhaps we will go on a holiday of our own for a while. Magda is always asking me to take her to Portugal."

I thought of poor little Madeleine McCann. Of my daughter, Hailey. Of Lindsay Sorkin.

"I would like you to do me a favor once I leave," I said.

"Of course, Simon."

"Go to Hauptbahnhof Station and visit the men's room that's under repair. In the lower basement, near the Karlstadt. Check the third stall, all the stalls, the trash, everything. Then head to security and ask to see the CCTV tapes from yesterday morning, but do it quietly. Be discreet. On the tapes, look for Dietrich and Karl and the little girl. See who took her once they left the men's room, if you can. If you find anything, call me straightaway."

"Of course, Simon."

I took out my BlackBerry and called Davignon's cell phone, expecting to leave a message. But he picked up on the first ring. It didn't sound as though I had woken him.

"Simon," he said urgently, "are you still in Berlin?"

"For the time being," I told him.

"Any news on the girl?"

"I found Dietrich and Karl," I said.

"Are they in custody?"

"No," I said.

"They got away?"

"I don't have time to explain, Lieutenant. But I did reach them and they led me to a Turk named Talik and his nephew Alim Sari. They're involved in the heroin trade here in Germany. Part of the Turkish mob."

"Can you get to them?" Davignon said.

"I was too late. They're gone. But I think I've drawn a bead on them. Their last phone call was to a lawyer's office in Warsaw. That's where I'm headed."

"Simon, that sounds like a fool's errand. You do not know if that is where they went. Perhaps they remained in Germany."

"No," I said, "I was getting too close. They fled. If you can do so quietly, alert Interpol. I'd like to keep them off the trains and on the ground if I can."

"How about you? How will you get to Warsaw?"

"I'm taking the motorcycle. With any luck, I'll pass them on the road."

Davignon remained silent for a moment, then said, "I am staying in the Sorkins' new hotel suite, in case the kidnappers call. I promised Lori Sorkin that I would wake her if you phoned. She would like to speak to you."

"I'd rather not, Lieutenant. Not until I have the girl."

"Please, Simon. Hearing your voice will reassure her."

I hesitated. "All right," I said. "Go fetch her."

While I waited, I turned to Ostermann. "Am I leaving you holding the bag again?"

Ostermann shook his head. "No, I think we can agree that tonight was all my doing. If there is any heat, I will deal with it."

Before I could say another word, Lori Sorkin's sleepy voice came on the line. "Simon?"

"This is Simon."

Hearing her voice, I felt like I was speaking to Tasha all over again. Felt as though I were just returning home from Bucharest having captured Dumitru Antonescu, who would eventually be acquitted after a federal trial back in the States.

"Lieutenant Davignon says you're on your way to Poland."

"That's right."

She followed a long silence with, "I don't know what I'll do without her, Simon."

I took a deep breath. "That's not something you're going to have to worry about, Lori. Because I'm going to bring Lindsay back to Paris."

"You don't know that," she said, breaking down. "How, Simon? How are you going to get her back?"

I thought about Ostermann pushing the barrel of his handgun into Karl's mouth.

"By doing whatever it takes, Lori. Whatever it takes."

The taxi dropped us around the corner from Ostermann's office building, in case the police still had the place under surveillance.

I had parked the BMW in the lot less than twenty-four hours earlier, though I felt as if I had been in Berlin a month.

Once Ostermann assured me it was clear, we walked across the lot toward my bike.

"Thank you," I said to him.

"It was my pleasure, Simon. Just please, do me one favor, as well."

"What is it?"

"If you find Alim, *when* you find Alim, do not kill him." He paused. "Please. Leave that for me."

I said nothing.

Ostermann said, "You have my mobile number, Simon? If I can be of any further assistance, do not hesitate to call me."

"Of course."

We stopped at my bike. It was a beautiful machine.

Ostermann said, "You all right to drive?"

"I got plenty of sleep at the Ritz while you were spending quality time with Reese Witherspoon."

He smiled. "I hope like hell that you find that little girl, Simon. I hope you find her and bring her home."

"Oh, I'll find her," I said, climbing onto the motorcycle. "I'll find her." I placed the helmet on my head and opened the visor. "I just hope it's not too late when I do."

Part Two

THE LAWYERS OF WARSAW

Chapter 18

The lawyer's name was Mikolaj Dabrowski. His office was located in the city center, not far from Warsaw University. I arrived shortly after ten A.M., checked on the suits I'd stuffed into the side and top storage cases on the bike—not bad, considering—and made for the entrance.

The building was modern. Just entering, one might think the building was located in New York or Los Angeles. There was nothing Old World about it.

At the security desk, I gave my real name and told them I was a prospective client. There was no fuss at all. Security here was far more lax than at Ostermann's office in Berlin. I was given a sticker to put on my lapel and told to head straight up to the ninth floor.

"*Dzien dobry,*" I said to the receptionist when I stepped through the double glass doors and into the office. "I am here to see Pan Dabrowski."

The receptionist smiled with a tilt of her head. "I am afraid Pan Dabrowski is not in today. Perhaps another lawyer can assist you?"

"I suppose it's possible," I said, trying not to deflate in front of her. I gave her my name.

"Please, have a seat, Pan Fisk. It will be only a few minutes."

I sat and tried to busy myself with the morning's copy of the *Warsaw Business Journal.* I didn't understand a word the paper said, of course, but I wanted to hide my wilting head. I was exhausted from the morning's drive. And I hadn't slept since yesterday afternoon in Berlin.

As I sat there, waiting for some lawyer who wasn't Dabrowski, I wondered what the hell the young Simon Fisk had been thinking when he decided to go into law enforcement. I didn't remember ever making the decision, but at some point I must have. Maybe it was to piss off my father, who had all but insisted I follow in his footsteps and become a doctor. Maybe it was to prove something to him. Maybe it was to prove something to myself. What that was, I'd never known. What I did know was that if I hadn't been a U.S. Marshal, I would never have gone to Romania, and my daughter, Hailey, might still be alive. She was taken on a Saturday. If I'd been home, I would have been there to protect her. In fact, we wouldn't have been living in D.C. in the first place. If I'd gone to medical school after American University, I probably would have moved back to New England, and Tasha would have come with me. We were that in love. And, of course, if Hailey hadn't been taken, Tasha would still be alive. We would be Dr. and Mrs. Fisk of Boston, Massachusetts, or Narragansett, Rhode Island, or . . .

"Pan Fisk?"

I lowered the paper and saw two of the brightest green eyes in existence.

"Yes. Simon," I said.

"Pleased to meet you, Simon. My name is Anastazja Staszak, and I am Mikolaj Dabrowski's associate. Shall we move to the conference room?"

"Of course," I said, setting the paper down and pushing myself out of the chair.

I followed her, my eyes locked on the back of her head, her curly red-brown hair. She smelled of fresh strawberries, the genuine deal, nothing fake, nothing too chemical or sweet. And when we entered the conference room, I saw why. A bowl of fresh strawberries sat in the middle of the long rectangular table.

"Please," she said with a thick, appealing accent, "have a seat."

I was hungry. I must have been staring at the strawberries.

"Please," she said, pulling the bowl to us. "Help yourself."

"Thank you." I bit into one; it was the best damn strawberry I'd ever tasted.

"So," she said, "have you been charged with a crime?"

"A crime? You're a criminal lawyer?"

"Yes, of course. You did not know this? We are a small firm. Only three lawyers. We handle only criminal matters."

I finished off the first strawberry and took another.

"Where's Dabrowski?" I said.

"Pan Dabrowski is not in today. Was he expecting you?"

"Will he be back later in the day?"

She smiled uncomfortably. "I am sorry. But I do not know what this is about. Do you have personal business with Pan Dabrowski?"

"I don't know yet if it's personal." I stuffed another strawberry into my mouth. "I just know that I need to see him as soon as possible."

"Are you British?"

"I'm American."

"You do not sound American."

"I get that a lot," I said. "Especially in America."

She nodded amicably. "If you are in need of a criminal lawyer, Pan Fisk, I am happy to help you, if only until Pan Dabrowski returns. But if you need to speak with him personally, I am afraid you will have to wait. He is not expected back until next week."

"I can't wait that long. Where is he?"

"I am afraid I am not at liberty—"

"Is he in the country?" I said.

"What is this in regards to?"

"One of his clients."

"You are a witness?"

"You could say that. But I'm not here to supply information, I'm here to obtain it."

"Surely, Pan Fisk, you realize that a lawyer cannot divulge information about his client."

"He can if his client is involved in the commission of a major crime."

She froze for a moment. "May I ask which client you are referring to?"

"A man named Talik. Possibly his nephew Alim Sari."

"I have never heard of either of these men."

"They're Turks living in Germany. One of them called here recently."

She said, "If they are Mikolaj's clients, I would not know. He is the head of the firm. He does not share information about his clients with us unless he requires our assistance."

"But the names would be in your office database, correct?"

"It does not matter," she said. "I would not be able to access them if they were. And even if I could, I would not dare."

"Look, Miss Staszak—"

"You may call me Ana."

"All right, Ana, let me level with you. Ordinarily, at this point, I'd thank you for your time and stand up and leave. I would wait until your office closed. Then I'd break in, poke through your files, take what I need. But you seem like the sort I can reason with, and frankly, I can't afford the extra eight to ten hours. I'm running out of time as it is."

"Pan Fisk—"

"Simon. Call me Simon."

"Okay, Simon. I have no idea what you are speaking about, but you are frightening me. I would like you to leave now, or else I will have to call security."

Ana began to stand. I gently took hold of her wrist and lowered her back into the chair.

"Please, Ana, hear me out. If at the end of my explanation you want no part of this, I promise you, I will leave."

She looked at me for a long moment, then settled in her seat, crossed her long, lithe legs. "You have five minutes, Simon."

"That's three more than I need," I said, leaning toward her. "No doubt you have heard the name Lindsay Sorkin over the past few days."

"Relentlessly," she said. "The American girl who went missing in Paris."

"Abducted," I corrected her. "She didn't go missing. She was taken from her parents' hotel room in the middle of the night while they slept."

"I see. But what does this have to do with Mikolaj? Or with you, for that matter?"

"I'm getting there, Ana." I bit into another strawberry. "The French police asked for my assistance in finding the girl."

"And why would they do that?"

"Because that's what I do. I recover abducted children."

"You are with what organization? The FBI? CIA? Interpol?"

"None of the above," I said. "I'm a former U.S. Marshal, but now I work privately. I hunt down estranged parents who have abducted their children and fled overseas to countries that don't recognize U.S. custody decisions."

"But that is not what happened to this little girl."

"No, this little girl was abducted by strangers. Two German men named Dietrich Braun and Karl Finster. I followed them to Berlin. They were hired to do the job by the man I mentioned before—Talik. It's likely his nephew Alim Sari is involved. A call was recently placed to this office from their flat in Kreuzberg. It's all I have to go on. It is why I *must* speak to Dabrowski immediately."

Ana shook her head, her curly locks swaying from side to side. "But there must be some mistake. A misdialed number perhaps. Mikolaj cannot possibly be involved."

"Either way," I said, "I need to find out. And to do that, I need to know where he is."

She gave it considerable thought, then rose from her chair and said, "There is something I have to check out first."

I watched through the windowed conference room as Ana strolled down the hall to the office marked MIKOLAJ DABROWSKI. She looked back at me to let me know she wasn't concealing what she was about to do. To prove, I think, to me and to herself that she wasn't ashamed of it. She pulled a key ring from her pocket and opened the door.

The shades were drawn in Dabrowski's office, but I imagined her sorting through his files, looking for this fellow Talik, or Alim Sari. She was in there quite a long while. When she finally stepped out, she had a serious look on her face.

"All right," she said as she reentered the conference room. "I will tell you where he is, under one condition."

"What's that?"

"I am coming with you to speak to him."

"Forget it," I said. "I work alone."

"Then you will have to wait until he returns, as I said before."

"You found something in his office," I said. "What did you find?"

"His appointment book. Tomorrow morning is marked with the initials T.Y. It is not enough to convince me, but as long as I am with you we have an excuse for being together."

"An excuse?"

"I can tell him you are my lover."

Last time I tried to win an argument with a lawyer it went bad for me. Last time I tried to win an argument with a woman it turned out downright ugly. From the moment I first laid eyes on her, it struck me that Anastazja Staszak was adept at being both. So what choice did I have?

"All right, then," I said. "You're coming with me."

Maybe a mistake. Probably a mistake. Thing about mistakes is, you don't usually realize they're mistakes until well after you made them. I knew this was probably a mistake going in.

"Now," I said, "tell me where we're going."

"Krakow. Mikolaj keeps a home there near his parents."

I pushed out my chair and stood. "Are you okay riding on a motorcycle?"

"Are you kidding?" she said. "I drive one to work every day."

Chapter 19

The three-hour drive from Warsaw to Krakow was pretty much a straight shot. Ana and I stopped once in a small café in Kielce and sat across from each other, sipping espressos.

"So," I said softly, "the T.Y. on Dabrowski's appointment book was enough to convince you to bring me to him."

The left side of her lip turned up in a smile, revealing a dimple on her left cheek. "There was one other thing. Maybe it is something, maybe it is nothing."

"What is it?" I said.

"When I first went into Mikolaj's office I dialed his mobile number, hoping to get in touch with him to sort this out."

"And?"

"And I heard a ringing in his desk drawer. I opened the drawer and found his mobile sitting atop his files."

I raised my eyebrows. "So?"

"So, Simon, we always tell our clients, if you are up to something nefarious, do not bring your mobile."

I nodded. "GPS, cellular towers, and all that. Led me to more than a few targets over the years."

"Exactly. These wireless records are used all the time by police and prosecutors to place defendants at or near the scene of the crime at precisely the right time."

"So you think Dabrowski left his phone behind on purpose."

Ana shook her head. "That I cannot say. But I think it is worth inquiring."

"What exactly is your relationship with this Dabrowski?"

"It is complicated," she said, her eyes darting away from mine. "I have worked for him since I became a lawyer. Ten years now."

That was all she'd say on the matter, though I suspected there was significantly more history. I decided not to push the issue, though. At least not yet.

"I've been thinking," I said. "The best plan is to locate Dabrowski tonight and watch him tomorrow morning. There is nothing to be gained by making him aware of our presence."

Ana shook her head adamantly. "No, I refuse to spy on him. Not without further evidence. We will go to him today. I have brought his mobile phone. I will deliver it to him. It makes sense. He is never without it. I will say I heard it ringing as I was passing by his office and was sure he needed it. The office has no other way of getting in touch with him in Krakow."

"And then?"

"Then I will ask him what his plans are tomorrow. If he lies to me, if he fails to mention a meeting or something involving a T.Y., then we will watch him."

Krakow, of course, was victim to a brutal past. The city had served as capital of Germany's General Government following the Nazi invasion of Poland at the start of World War II. Krakow's Jewish population was herded into a walled zone known as the Krakow Ghetto. From there Jews were transported to a network of nearby concentration camps known as Auschwitz, where they were systematically executed. Hitler's "Final Solution of the Jewish Question." Those spared the gas chamber were killed by firing squad, or died of starvation, forced labor, disease, or medical experiments.

Mikolaj Dabrowski's flat was located on Grodzka in the Old Quarter near Market Square. We parked the bike and walked, hand in hand, at Ana's insistence.

"Mikolaj would not believe that I drove all this way alone just to give him his mobile phone. Better we say that you are my boyfriend. We met at Paparazzi; it is a posh cocktail bar in Warsaw. I told you the situation and you suggested we take a road trip, because you have never seen Krakow." She looked me up and down as we walked. "You are a criminal lawyer, too. Only white-collar crimes. You work on Madison Avenue in New York City."

I stopped her. "If I didn't know any better, I'd say you were trying to make this Dabrowski fellow jealous."

Ana looked me in the eyes. "You want to take me to Los Angeles because I told you I have always been dying to see Hollywood."

I stared into those emerald eyes and grinned, genuinely amused for the first time in days.

Chapter 20

Dabrowski's flat was larger than I had expected. It was elegantly furnished, full of light and warmth. Dabrowski appeared surprised to see Ana, but not overly so. He did, however, seem quite stunned to see me.

Once Ana introduced me, Dabrowski quickly asked, "So, what brings you two to Krakow?"

Ana reached into her handbag and plucked out Dabrowski's phone. I watched his reaction. Or nonreaction, that is. He certainly didn't look grateful.

"You drove all the way here to give me this?" Dabrowski tried a smile but it didn't work well.

"Well, not only for that," Ana said. "It was Simon's idea, actually. He has never seen Krakow and he suggested a trip."

"I want to take her to Los Angeles, too," I said. "She's been dying to see Hollywood."

Dabrowski nodded. "So she has told me. Many times."

"Simon and I are staying in Krakow tonight," Ana said. "I thought maybe the three of us could have lunch tomorrow."

"Oh, I wish I could," Dabrowski said. He still had not invited us to sit down. "But it would be impossible tomorrow. I am spending the day at Jagiellonian University. Professor Levitsky requested I speak to his class about the practice of criminal law."

"That is too bad," Ana said with the slightest hesitation. "Well, maybe once you return to Warsaw, we can all have dinner. Simon will not be leaving until next week."

"That sounds wonderful," Dabrowski said, finally smiling. He was handsome when he smiled, his round face contrasting nicely with sharp features and dark eyes that seemed they could pierce through flesh. "Something I will look forward to."

Dabrowski shook my hand, firm and steady, and we said our goodbyes.

Once we were outside, Ana said, "So, first thing tomorrow, we stake out his flat, and when he leaves, we follow him."

"I take it he didn't convince you he was speaking at the university tomorrow," I said.

"Not particularly, no."

She kept walking, fast. As though she wanted to get as far away from Dabrowski's apartment as possible.

"Is it that there's no possible link between Professor Levitsky and the T.Y. you found in Dabrowski's planner?"

"No," she said, lowering her brows. "It is that Professor Levitsky retired from the university last semester."

I shrugged. "Isn't it possible that Levitsky is covering for another professor, or visiting an old class, or even serving as an adjunct?"

"None of that is possible." Her voice was suddenly full of sharp edges.

"Why not?"

"Because two months after Professor Levitsky retired, he suffered a stroke and dropped dead."

I stopped, pulled her back to me. "Are you certain, Ana?"

She turned and stared up at me, her bright green eyes watering. "Quite certain," she said. "I spoke at Levitsky's funeral."

Chapter 21

We checked into a thirteenth-century guesthouse on To-masza, a few blocks from the main square. It wasn't my first choice for accommodations, but Ana suggested I live less like a tourist and more like a world traveler. We took two rooms on the third floor, one right next to the other. There were only six rooms in the entire guesthouse, and the other four were vacant. After I showered and changed suits, I met Ana downstairs and she asked if I was hungry. I told her I was starved. I had set my sights on Aqua e Vino, a trendy Italian restaurant on Wiślna, but Ana rolled her eyes at the mere mention of it.

"You can have Italian food anywhere in the world, Simon. It would be silly to eat it here in Poland."

My stomach didn't think so. "All right then, where?"

She insisted on Pierogarnia, an informal eatery on Sławkowska. So we went there, sat across from each other on old wooden benches, hovering over an old wooden table. I ordered a bottle of Zywiec, one of the more popular Polish beers, and stared at the limited menu.

"You look anxious," Ana said.

"All they have are pierogi," I said. It was true. More than twenty distinct dishes, all pierogi.

How many different things can you stuff into a bloody dumpling? I thought.

"What is wrong with pierogi?" she said.

"Nothing, it's just I've never had one, and—"

She reached over the table and smacked me. She was genuinely angry.

"How can you never have pierogi?" she said. "You have been to Poland before, yes?"

I shrugged. "A few times. Mostly up north, near either the German or Russian border, for work."

She reached over the table and smacked me again. "And you never tried pierogi?"

"No," I said. "What's the big deal? And stop hitting me, by the way."

"It is a sin to come to Poland and not try pierogi." There was a dead-serious look on her face, a fierceness in those green eyes.

I stared down at the menu. "Well, I guess I have no choice tonight, do I?"

"What do you mean, you have no choice? You can have them stuffed with meat, sauerkraut, mushrooms, fruit, cheese, anything you want. How can someone not like pierogi?" She was genuinely puzzled.

"All right," I said. "You've made your point. You're preaching to the converted. I'll have mine stuffed with cheese and pretend I'm eating a ravioli."

I could see she wanted to reach over the table and smack me again, but my look caused her to hold back.

"You must start with *barszcz*," she said.

"Now what is that?"

"Beetroot soup with lemon and garlic."

"Great," I said. "My fantasy dish."

The waitress came over and took our orders. Ana sipped her wine as I contemplated a table for one at Aqua e Vino.

"So, are you an only child, Simon?" Ana said a few minutes after the waitress took off.

"Why do you ask?"

"Because you seem to need to get your way all the time."

I stared at her in disbelief. "Are you out of your head? Projecting a little, maybe? We're staying in a goddamn haunted house and I'm eating dumplings for dinner when I haven't eaten a proper meal in over a week. How am I getting my way?"

"I did not say that you *get* your way," she said with indignation. "I said only that you *need* to. So, am I right? *Are* you an only child?"

"I had a sister," I said.

"Had?"

I lowered my voice. "My father and I moved to the States when I was five, left my mother and sister behind in London."

"Why?"

"Because my father's a shit," I said.

"Well, what about your mother and sister? When is the last time you saw them?"

"I just told you. When I was five."

Her eyes widened. "You have not contacted them since you grew up?"

"Why should I?" I said. "They never reached out to me."

"This is terrible," she said, shaking her head. "It makes me very sad."

"Don't be too sad," I told her, watching our waitress step out of the kitchen. "Here come our pierogi."

Well?" Ana said as I took my last bite. "What do you think? Delicious, yes?"

They were, but I refused to give her the satisfaction. "They were all right."

She was every bit as offended as if she'd made them herself. "Well, maybe we can find you a discarded hot dog lying in the street on the way back to the hotel."

"Guesthouse," I corrected her. "So, Ana, tell me. Were *you* an only child?"

"Of course not. I have an older brother named Marek. He is a politician in Warsaw."

The waitress came by and asked if we'd like dessert. We both declined. Then we fought over the check. I eventually won, but it was a struggle—a struggle made worse when I told her it wasn't my money but Vince Sorkin's.

"The father of the missing girl?" She snatched the check out of my hand for the third time. "He cannot pay for our pierogi! The poor man."

"It's okay," I assured her. "We eat pierogi, he gets his daughter back. It's a fair deal."

It was the first comment I'd made about pierogi that actually made her smile instead of reaching over the table and smacking me.

"Now that you've had some wine," I said, "care to tell me about your relationship with Mikolaj Dabrowski?"

The smile vanished from her face. "I told you, it is compli—"

"Complicated, yes, I know. But I'm pretty sure I'll be able to get my mind around it, and we certainly have the time to kill."

Ana sighed, swept her curly hair behind her sizable ears but the locks didn't stay in place. "You are going to think I am this silly girl who has jumped into bed with every boss she has ever had since she was sixteen years old."

"Well, have you?"

That earned me a dirty look, her eyes blazing in the candlelight. "No."

"Then why in the world would I think that?"

"Because I jumped into bed with Mikolaj. I was a stupid girl, just out of university. I was eager to begin a life. But for an entire decade I stayed in this job, going to bed with him a few times every year and always hoping there will be something more." She shook her head. "Still, I am stupid, I guess."

I didn't say anything.

Ana gave it a moment. "So you are not going to say anything?" she said, displaying that raw anger again.

I thought about my choices. Went with, "Sometimes it's difficult to move on."

She carefully considered my words, nodded. "And you? You are not married?"

"Widowed," I said.

"I am so sorry. May I ask you what happened?"

"Suicide," I said.

"Your wife, she was depressed?"

"Not always," I said.

"Something happened to make her sad?"

"Our daughter was taken," I said.

Ana drew a deep breath. I knew she was afraid to ask more questions. Most people were, once they heard those words. But she'd think about it. They all did. And I didn't want that hanging over the rest of the evening. And I sure as hell didn't want her thinking about it tomorrow morning when it was time to follow Dabrowski. So I told her.

"I was in Bucharest," I said slowly, "to apprehend a fugitive. My wife, Tasha, and I were living in D.C. with our six-year-old daughter, Hailey. Beautiful girl, my daughter. Well, both of them were. Beautiful, I mean. Hailey looked just like her mother. Anyway, we lived in a house in Georgetown. A nice house, as nice as the one my father owned in Rhode Island, the likes of which I never expected to be living in again. Not as long as I was in law enforcement. But Tasha's family had money. Real money. Old money. They insisted on buying us the house as our wedding present. I refused, but Tasha wanted it and she wouldn't relent. So it was ours.

"My daughter was taken on a Saturday. I was in Bucharest Otopeni International at the time, waiting to board my flight out of Romania. Now the airport's known as Henri Coanda, but back then it was called Otopeni. I had a brief layover in Frankfurt, but never bothered checking my phone. I didn't learn a thing until I landed at Dulles.

"A friend met me as soon as I got off the plane in D.C. Told me Hailey was missing. I went weak in the knees. Almost fainted, saw white all around the edges of my vision. My friend got me some water, kept me moving. Drove me to Georgetown, to our house, that huge goddamn house, which was now surrounded by vehicles from the Metropolitan PD.

"Tasha, poor Tasha was a mess, her hair all frazzled, her eyes looking as though they'd been dipped in a pot of chlorine. There was snot all down her face, vomit on her chin. She couldn't even stand on her own; one of the cops had to hold her to keep her on her feet.

"Tasha couldn't really articulate what had happened. But she never once used the word *missing*, always *taken*. At first it made me think she knew more than she was telling the police, but as time went on, I started thinking the same thing. If Hailey had just wandered off she would have been found. Even if someone had found her dead, lying in the middle of the road, struck by a Metro bus, someone would have spotted her. But after a few hours, a day, two days, you know you're not dealing with a lost child. How far can a six-year-old girl go on her own?

"Once we realized it was an abduction, we waited for the ransom call. You figure we live in a huge house, people think we have money. Maybe that's why they grabbed her. You *hope* it's why they grabbed her. For money. For money, not sex, not . . .

"Anyway, the ransom call never came. After a few days, you stop looking at the phone because the damn thing makes you sick just by keeping silent. By then, Tasha couldn't leave the bed. Not even to go to the bathroom. I had to get her a bedpan from Walgreens. Her doctor put her on tranquilizers and sedatives. Painkillers and muscle relaxers, too, because the back of her neck was knotted into a gargantuan fist. She slept all the time. When she wasn't sleeping she was dosing herself, dying to fall asleep again.

"One afternoon, a few weeks after Hailey went missing, she just didn't wake up. She'd left a few pills in each bottle to hide what she'd really done. And whether the coroner fell for it, or her parents intervened, her death was ruled an accidental overdose, as opposed to what it really was—a suicide. Not that it mattered much how she died. She was dead. And I knew so was Hailey.

"There was never so much as a true lead, let alone a suspect. Our family and friends and neighbors all turned up clean. Whoever it was, it was a stranger abduction. Like Lindsay's."

I caught tears at the corners of Ana's eyes, and I suddenly had a strong urge to reach across the table to comfort *her*, to assure *her* everything would be all right.

"Have you ever thought that maybe your daughter could still be alive?"

I felt my lower lip tremble.

"I lost hope that she was alive long ago, and I'd never want that hope back. Not in a million years. Not for one second. But I will forever be looking. In every shop, every café, every open home window in every city or town in every country on every continent. I can't help myself. I want to know what happened to her and why. And I want to know who took her."

I shook my head and swallowed hard as I thought about Ostermann knocking Dietrich Braun and Karl Finster out cold in the alley behind SO36 back in Kreuzberg.

"The violence I would do to that man, Ana, it can't be put into words."

Chapter 22

After dinner, Ana and I took a long, silent walk around Old Town. I was exhausted but knew I wouldn't be able to sleep. It was cold and there weren't many people on the streets. We began our stroll on the outer belt, along the poorly lit Planty gardens, then moved in toward the main square. From the corner of my eye I'd caught a band of skinheads loitering near the Straszewski Obelisk and kept my guard up until we were safely back at the guesthouse on Tomasza.

Inside, I followed Ana up the stairs to our floor. We stopped at her door. I leaned in to kiss her good night on her cheek. Her face was round and soft, as smooth as an ice sculpture and just as cold; yet, the brief contact warmed me to the core.

She looked me in the eyes and said, "You may stay with me if you like."

I was tempted. Beyond, really. But I gave thought to the next morning. For the past four days I'd been operating solely on instinct with little food and less sleep. My hunger, my exhaustion, my frustration—all my desires combined—seemed to fuel me. They kept me alert, on edge. There was a certain comfort in remaining uncomfortable. When there's nothing to lose, it's far easier, far more *sensible,* to put yourself at risk for the sake of someone else.

But what if I woke at dawn with a full stomach in a comfortable bed, my well-rested body pressed against Ana's warm flesh? It could make me soft, diffident. It could cause me to hesitate in a situation that didn't allow for hesitation. Could I pull a gun on Talik just hours later? Would I be able to kill if I had to?

I couldn't chance it.

"Good night, Ana," I said warmly.

"Good night, then, Simon."

I was just in the next room over. As I removed my suit I heard Ana's shower turn on. My face flushed even though the room was cool, so I pulled back the curtains and opened the window, breathed in the chill. I visited what had happened in Georgetown almost nightly in my sleep, but not often while I was awake. I pushed that house away whenever I could with whatever I could, usually my work. It was why my cases became such obsessions and probably why I was so successful at retrieving children like Jason Blanc, the boy in Bordeaux. Rarely did I visit Georgetown with my words; the retelling of the story was just too damn painful. And it wasn't a pain I could simply drink away. It was a pain that burrowed its way into every bone, carved out a home in every organ. A pain that couldn't be relieved with narcotics or removed surgically, a pain that would cease only with my death. In times like this, even all these years later, I could almost comprehend Tasha's reasoning for leaving, even if I couldn't condone it.

As I turned from the window, I heard footfalls out in the hall. Heavy steps, made by more than one set of feet. Nothing to concern yourself over in a large hotel. But this was a six-room guesthouse, and the desk clerk had said that the four rooms not occupied by Ana and me were vacant.

I stepped back into my pants and grabbed the Glock. Glanced at the door but there was no peephole. Next door, the shower was still running. I pressed my ear against the wall.

I didn't need to. Clear as a bell, I heard a key turning in the lock to Ana's room.

I made for my door, swung out into the hall with my gun raised. Just in time to see Ana's door close, immediately followed by the click of the lock, the slide of the chain.

I raced back through my room to the window. Stuck my head out and measured the ledge. Barely enough room for my bare feet. I'd need to hold on, so I stuck the gun into the back of my pants. Shirtless, I climbed out onto the ledge in the cold. Looked down three stories and remembered how damn much I hated heights.

I moved as quick as I could along the ledge. Ana's window was slightly ajar, which meant that it wasn't locked. The curtains were drawn. I couldn't see in but at least I couldn't be seen. Overall, it was to my advantage; I knew that someone was in there, but that someone sure as hell didn't know I was out here. I bent and raised the window, slowly so as not to make noise.

I heard the shower turn off and decided it was time to move.

I gripped the ledge just above the window, drew a breath, and swung my legs through first. I landed on my feet. Saw a thin skinhead with a blade spin around in surprise. I caught him hard in the temple with a right hook. The bathroom door swung open just as he crumpled. Ana stood in the doorway, dressed in a crisp white towel, and stared down at the fallen skinhead in shock.

Before I could say a word, a much larger skinhead came at us from the front of the room, swinging his knife like a sword. I turned and kicked at his knee and his large body blew by me like a bull blows by a matador. He shrieked in pain, his leg having snapped like a matchstick. Soon as he hit the floor, I stamped on the hand holding the knife and he dropped it.

I snatched the knife and gripped his bare head as he reached for his broken leg. As he cried out, I twisted his body, and held the blade to his throat. Over the next thirty seconds, his screams faded into whimpers.

Ana leaned over and recovered the skinny skinhead's knife while he remained on the floor, apparently unconscious.

"I'm going to ask you two questions," I said to the bull. "Lie about the first one and I'll remove an ear. Lie about the second and I'll cut your throat."

He didn't say anything, but I felt the warmth of tears rolling down my bare arm.

"First question," I said. "Who hired you?"

"A l-lawyer," he spit out with a thick Polish accent. "A lawyer named Dabrowski. He defended me on drug charges a few years ago."

"Second question," I said. "When and where are you supposed to meet Dabrowski to collect your money for the job you were about to do on us?"

"He p-paid . . . he paid us half up-front. The rest we were supposed to pick up outside Bunkier Sztuki at five A.M."

I stared up at Ana. "Bunkier Sztuki?"

"Bunker of Art," she said. "I know where it is."

I nodded to her, then leaned in and whispered in the skinhead's ear, "Congratulations, fat boy. You did good. For a minute there I was pretty damn sure you had eaten your last pierogi."

Chapter 23

I filled the bull full of Ana's Tylenol PM and waited till he fell asleep. The skinny one remained out cold. He'd wake with one hell of a headache, but at least both his legs were intact. The same couldn't be said for the bull.

"Dabrowski will be watching the hotel," I said, checking the skinheads for identification. "If he doesn't see these bastards come out he won't show at the rendezvous point. And he sure as hell won't meet with Talik in a few hours."

"I am sorry," she said. "I blew our opportunity by bringing you to his flat."

"Neither of us expected him to speak to Talik before the meeting," I said, pocketing their driver's licenses along with their knives and leaving the rest of their crap on the floor. "And we had no reason to think Talik knew I was in Poland."

She shuddered. "I still do not understand why Mikolaj would have a child kidnapped. It makes no sense."

"Ana, Dabrowski is nothing but a middleman, a broker. What he did, he did for money." I took her gently by the shoulders. "Right now Dabrowski is the wall between Talik and whoever ordered Lindsay Sorkin taken."

"You mean, even if you got to Talik in Berlin—"

"Even if I got him to talk, he would have only led me to Dabrowski. I'm sure of it. Talik and his nephew Alim Sari don't know who's on the other side of the wall, and they have no reason to want to find out."

"So we must find Mikolaj," she said. "That should not be so difficult. He will not leave his law practice, and I am sure he will not leave Poland."

"You're right, Ana. Finding him shouldn't prove too difficult. But now that he knows that I'm here—that *we're* here, working together—he'll be gunning for us, just as he did tonight. Only he won't continue to rely on amateurs like these two skinheads. Next time he comes at us, he'll come with professionals. So the trick isn't finding him. It's staying alive until we do."

"Then we must find him fast. How do we do that?"

"I don't know," I conceded.

"What do you mean you do not know?" There was that anger again. "You hunted fugitives, it was your job. How can you not know how to find one lawyer in Poland?"

"The U.S. Marshals don't find fugitives in a day, Ana. And they have resources. Manpower. They hang up photos and offer rewards to the locals. They use phone taps. They have access to credit card transactions and cell phone activity. What do I have?"

"You have me," she said. "Before credit cards and cell phones, what did they do, your marshals? How did they find fugitives?"

"By knowing who they were chasing," I said.

"And I know Mikolaj. I know him very well. What do you need to know?"

"All right," I said, pacing the length of the room, adrenaline from the confrontation still pumping. "Let's start with his relatives. You said his parents live around here. Who else? Are there any restaurants or bars he frequents? What does he like to eat? What does he drink? What kind of a hotel would he stay at? Is he an outdoors man? Could he fend for himself in the wild? Besides skinheads, who else does he represent?"

Ana's face went white. She bit hard on her lower lip to keep it from trembling.

"What is it?" I said.

"*Gowno.*"

"What is it, Ana?"

"It's Mikolaj: he represents some very dangerous men, Simon. Members of the Pruszkow mob, the Polish mafia. Recently, Mikolaj tried the case of one of Poland's most notorious gangsters—Kazmer Chudzik. Chudzik was acquitted. After the trial, Chudzik said in a statement to the press that Mikolaj Dabrowski was like a brother to him."

"Christ," I said.

I knew organized crime had increased in Poland in the late eighties and early nineties with the fall of communism and the rise of capitalism. The sea change in the country had also resulted in the diminishment of the power of the police, which allowed the Pruszkow mob and its offshoot, the Wołomin mafia, to thrive. Polish gangsters were known as much for their relentlessness as their ruthlessness. When given a job, their soldiers and assassins got the job done.

"Wait, wait, wait," Ana said suddenly. "I am so silly. I should have thought of this before. You need resources, manpower. You need police."

I shook my head. "We can't afford the attention, Ana. If the media catches wind, Dabrowski, Talik, Alim Sari, all of them will go to ground, and we'll never find Lindsay."

"Then you need police you can trust."

I smirked. "Right, Ana. Happen to know some?"

"No," she said. "But my brother, Marek, does."

Have you found the lawyer?" Davignon asked as soon as he answered his cell.

"I found him," I said. "But then I lost him. He sent a pair of skin-heads to my guesthouse to get rid of me."

Davignon sighed deeply. "If the lawyer disappears . . ."

"I know," I said. "But he won't. I made friends with one of his associates, a smart lawyer named Anastazja. Her brother, Marek Staszak, is a politician in Warsaw. He's alerted the *policja* to be on the lookout for Dabrowski, but to be discreet. Marek also put me in contact with a chief inspector who has his men working on credit card transactions, cell phone activity, and wiretaps. Dabrowski is a criminal lawyer; he's not exactly loved by the Polish police."

"What if the lawyer crosses the border into the Czech Republic or Slovakia or Ukraine?" Davignon asked.

"If Dabrowski tries, he'll have a tough time at it. Our politician also contacted the *Straz Graniczna*."

"The Polish Border Guard."

"Right." In the background I heard Lori Sorkin sobbing. "We'll find him, Lieutenant," I said. "And soon."

Davignon lowered his voice. "For the mother's sake, Simon, please do."

Once I hung up with Davignon, I called Ostermann's cell. On the third ring, Magda answered. From her voice, I knew right away that something was wrong.

"Hello, Magda," I said. "Is Ostermann around?"

"No," she said. "He is not." She could barely contain her sobbing. "Kurt was arrested at Hauptbahnhof Station this morning. He has been questioned by the police all day."

"What happened?" I said.

"I do not know. All I know is that two men who appeared on the closed-circuit television for the time period he requested were found dead last night behind a nightclub in Kreuzberg. The police suspect it has something to do with the missing girl."

"Damn," I muttered under my breath. After Talik and Alim took care of Sidika, they must have gone after Dietrich and Karl, either personally or, more likely, through one of their men. Ostermann's knocking the Germans out cold must have done them in after all. He hadn't pulled the trigger but he might very well be charged with their murders. Ostermann and I had been seen in the club. And if the Berlin police discovered the prostitutes Ostermann had hired, their testimony would all but seal his conviction. The girls had not only seen us, they had seen our guns.

"The media has arrived from Paris," Magda said. "They have surrounded the train station and our office. It is just a matter of time before they find our home."

"I'm sorry, Magda."

"Sorry is not enough, Simon. You must return to Berlin and confess to killing those two men."

Of course, I couldn't tell Magda over the phone what had really happened, that Ostermann had roughed up the dead men but hadn't killed them. It was quite possible that Ostermann's cell was already tapped. The police would be listening in.

"Listen, Magda. As soon as I find Lindsay Sorkin, I'll return to Berlin and help Ostermann in any way that I can, I promise."

Her voice rose in anger. "Every time you step into our lives you bring nightmares, Simon. Kurt has a family now. You can no longer do this to him."

"Magda, it isn't what you think," I said. "Now please answer one question. Did Ostermann tell you who he saw take the girl from the men's room stall on the closed-circuit television?"

I waited, but Magda didn't answer. The line was dead. She'd hung up on me.

Chapter 24

Four hours later Ana and I were back in Warsaw, at a small office in a private building, to meet with Chief Inspector Aleksander Gasowski. In sensitive matters, Gasowski didn't trust the probing eyes of the men and women in his department. Particularly where Kazmer Chudzik and the Pruszkow mob were concerned.

Gasowski, a hulk of a man with a round face and little hair, leaned back in his chair behind a black metal desk and smiled grimly.

"This morning alone," he said, "Pan Dabrowski's credit cards have made purchases in Katowice, Opole, Wroclaw, and Zielona Gora."

Ana leaned forward, excited. "So Mikolaj is heading west, toward the German border."

Gasowski shook his head. "All the purchases were made within thirty-five minutes of each other."

I wasn't surprised. The lawyer knew how the police worked, knew Ana had connections. He was smart. He was playing us.

"What about his mobile phone?" Ana said.

"Still transmitting a signal," Gasowski replied. "Apparently from a train heading to Rzeszow. The train was stopped and searched. Pan Dabrowski was not on board, and his mobile could not be found."

I said, "Do we dare ask about his automobile?"

Gasowski smirked. "Pan Dabrowski's vehicle was stopped at the Slovakia border. It was being driven by a young skinhead, who possessed all the proper paperwork. He stated that the auto belonged to his lawyer and that he was borrowing it to see his girlfriend in Bratislava. My men took the skinhead into custody on suspicion of grand theft, but the kid is not talking and we cannot hold him much longer."

"So much for resources and manpower," I said.

"But why would Mikolaj go through all this trouble?" Ana said. "He could simply not use these things and we would be no better off in finding him."

"Because he wanted us to show our hand," I said. "Now that he knows we're using the police, he can take the necessary precautions."

"Dabrowski has always been a slick son of a bitch," Gasowski said with disgust.

Ana bowed her head, defeated. "So, what do we do now?"

"For all his subterfuge," I said, "Dabrowski will still go where he feels safe."

"And where is that?"

"Where he will be under the protection of this Kazmer Chudzik."

"Pruszkow?"

"Pruszkow," I said. "My guess is, that is the only place in Poland he'll feel secure enough to hold his meeting with Talik."

Gasowski said nothing.

"So we are going to Pruszkow," she said.

"*I* am going to Pruszkow," I told her. "You are going to visit with your brother, Marek, until all this blows over."

"You are crazy, Simon, if you think—"

"Listen to Pan Fisk," Gasowski finally piped in. "I have spoken with your brother. We have arranged for the Biuro Ochrony Rzadu to protect you."

"I do not need protection," she hissed at us. "Not from the Government Protection Bureau and not from either of you."

She rose from her chair and exited the room, slamming the door behind her.

I thanked Gasowski and promised I'd get Ana to her brother. Then I followed her outside.

I called out to her as she made for my bike. "Ana, wait!"

She spun on me. "I am coming with you to confront Mikolaj, Simon. And to retrieve that little girl."

"Not a chance," I said. "I've told you. I work alone."

"*You* came to *me*, Simon. Not the other way around. You have already involved me, and you cannot discard me like a piece of trash. Either we go to Pruszkow together or we go separately. But either way, I *am* going."

I looked in her eyes and had no doubt she'd follow through with her threat to go to Pruszkow alone. She intended to leave me no choice but to take her.

Chapter 25

A half hour later, we rolled into Pruszkow, one of Mazovia's largest industrial centers.

"How will we know where to find these people?" Ana yelled over the roar of the BMW's engine as soon as we stopped at a light.

I turned my head back to her, lifted my visor. "I'd imagine most people in town would know where the mobsters hang out."

"They will be scared," she said. "Everyone will be too frightened to talk to us."

"Not everyone," I said. "There's one group of people in every city that you can count on to be afraid of nothing. They think they're invincible. They take great pride in knowing what they're not supposed to know, and they sell information cheap."

The light changed. "Who are you speaking about?"

"Children," I said, then slapped down my visor and rode on.

A few minutes later, I parked the bike on the side of the road in front of an old church. A block back, I'd seen a park packed with eager informants.

"Wait here," I told Ana, setting my helmet down on the bike.

When I got to the park I surveyed the crowd for a group of teenage males standing around, trying to look hard. Wasn't difficult. I immediately spotted a pair in black leather jackets, leaning up against a metal fence, cigarettes dangling from their lips.

I walked up to the fence, said from the other side, "Got an extra one, guys?"

They both went for their front pockets; the smaller of them was quicker on the draw. He slipped a fag through the fence, while the other pulled out an old Zippo. They lit me up. I took a deep drag and blew a thin stream of smoke up at the gray sky.

"Dziekuje," I said. "I needed that." I made a show of looking around, making sure there was no one else within earshot. "I'm looking for a couple of fellows," I told them. "Maybe you guys can help me out."

They both appeared more than happy to be part of the conspiracy.

"Who do you look for?" the smaller one said.

"A couple of Kazmer Chudzik's boys," I said.

The larger one appeared suspicious. "Are you the police?"

"Do I look like the police?" I said. "I'm not even Polish for Christ's sake."

The smaller one poked the larger one in the ribs. *"Idiota,"* the kid said. He pointed to me. "You see many police dress like this?"

The larger one looked appropriately chastened.

"There is a warehouse," the little guy said, "over on Promyka. Pan Chudzik owns it. He and his men, they do business there and take their coffee at a café across the street."

"Dziekuje," I said, handing them each a few banknotes through the fence. "We never had this conversation, okay?"

From across the street, the warehouse looked to be at least two hundred square meters. Ana translated the signs as advertisements for flooring, doors and doorframes, and outdoor furniture. Several large men were carrying boxes out of open hatches on the loading dock at the side of the building. Other large men stood in the backs of mammoth trucks, accepting the packages.

"It looks like a legitimate business," Ana said.

"Probably is. A legit business provides the perfect cover, and it's an effective way to launder large sums of money. And look at the size of those guys. On-call muscle. They could replace the Ravens' defensive line in a heartbeat."

"What does this mean, defensive line?"

"It's an American football term," I told her. "I'll explain later."

"So what is your plan, Simon?"

I looked down at my suit. "Well, clearly I'm overdressed for the occasion. The goons on these trucks probably don't have the faintest idea who Dabrowski is. For that, I'll need to get inside. But first I'll need a change of clothes."

The men were dressed in denim from the waist down. On top each wore a dark peacoat over a black turtleneck. Black wool skullcaps rested atop their heads.

We watched as two men finished loading one of the trucks, then pulled down the rear hatch. Minutes later, the truck started up, its tailpipe belching out thick black smoke. Only one man had climbed into the cab, the driver.

I turned to Ana. "Good thing you insisted on coming with me," I said. "Looks like I'm going to need your help after all."

The truck turned left out of the lot and we followed on the bike. After a few blocks we sped past. As long as the truck was heading into Warsaw, it wasn't about to leave the main drag. About two miles up the road, I pulled the bike to the curb and gave Ana her instructions. Then we stood on the deserted sidewalk and waited.

When we saw the truck rise over the hill, Ana stepped out into the middle of the road, waving her arms in the air. For a moment, I thought the driver might run her over, but then the truck slowed, rolled to a stop a good ten feet in front of her. The driver squinted, took one hard look at Ana, and didn't seem the least bit annoyed at the inconvenience.

Ana stepped around to the passenger side of the cab. She climbed up and stuck her head into the open window. Spoke to the driver in Polish.

There were other cars on the road, so I had to act quickly. I rolled under the truck and popped out on the other side. I knew that if the driver glimpsed into his side mirror, he'd take off. But he didn't. His eyes remained fixed on Ana.

I leaped onto the driver's side of the cab and raised my Glock. Held the barrel against the back of the driver's head. He turned, and the barrel was pointed right between his eyes. He looked more confused than scared.

"Czy mowi pan po angielsku?" I said. Do you speak English?

The driver shook his head.

"Ana," I called out. "Tell him to slide to the middle of the cab. We're getting in."

Chapter 26

It felt strange being out of the suit. As though I'd lost an extra layer of skin, a kind of armor. Ridiculous, because I rarely wore suits at all these days. When I was with the U.S. Marshals I had to wear them when escorting prisoners into courthouses, but now that I was on my own, I saw no need, unless dressing up would aid me in gaining access. Otherwise, a T-shirt and jeans were just fine with me. Maybe because my father had always hated them.

Ana waited down the street with the bike as I drove the truck, the driver unconscious and tied up in its belly. When I reached the warehouse, I backed up to the loading dock just as the other drivers had, then I buttoned the peacoat, adjusted my skullcap, and hopped down from the cab.

My Polish was far too limited to engage in conversation, so I brushed past the other drivers as though I didn't see or hear them, leaving them with bewildered looks on their rough faces. I entered the warehouse and moved through the maze of equipment and boxes as swiftly as possible without drawing any unnecessary attention. In the rear I spotted a door marked BIURO, which I assumed meant "private," so I headed for it.

I didn't bother to knock.

I opened the door and stepped into a spacious office, smoke so thick it looked like London fog. Through the cloud I saw a long metal desk, one heavy Pole sitting behind it. Two others sat in front of the desk, though they looked more like tough guys than clients.

"Morning, fellows," I said. "I'm looking for Pan Chudzik."

"Who the hell are you?" said the one behind the desk.

His nameplate read ALBIN JANKOWSKI.

The others turned in their chairs but seemed unsure what to do, whether to draw their guns or lay out the red carpet. They should have drawn their guns because I wasted no time reaching into my peacoat and drawing mine.

"Nobody move," I said calmly.

Ana had had no problem at all pulling up photos of Kazmer Chudzik on her smartphone's browser, so I knew after a brief review of the trio of faces staring back at me that Chudzik wasn't in the room.

"Where can I find the boss?" I said.

No one answered, no one said a word. It was as though someone stepped into this office and held a Glock to their heads every day. I admired their coolness, but I didn't have time for this. Lindsay didn't have time. Time was slipping away.

I swung my arm, pointing the gun at the nearest Pole's kneecap. He didn't flinch. His eyes simply floated behind me, just as I heard the hammer cock on a pistol, felt the cold steel of a barrel just to the rear of my left ear.

Everyone in the room laughed.

Everyone but me.

Jankowski spoke first. "Welcome to Pruszkow, Pan Fisk." He placed a lit cigarette between his lips and smiled. "I think maybe you should drop your weapon, no?"

This was an ambush. They knew my name, knew I was coming. Only way that was possible was if they had received a call from Gasowski. Wasn't the first time I discovered that a cop was dirty. Happened all the time in my line of work. Especially in Mexico. The border towns and Mexico City never failed to disappoint as far as police corruption went.

Corruption, dirty cops. It was how multibillion-dollar criminal enterprises continued to exist throughout the world. Greed feeding on greed. It was a sickness, a wound in the heart of humanity that I was sure would never be healed. At least not in my lifetime—which seemed to have just shortened considerably.

I glanced at the floor. Behind me, the door was open, light spilling in from the warehouse. A single shadow melded with mine. Meant there was only one man holding a gun to me. I could still feel the steel pressed against my skull, so he was close. Too close. Get in close like that with a man on his feet and you risked getting the weapon taken away from you.

"Set down your weapon," Jankowski said again. "*Now.* And kick it toward me."

Slowly, I bent at the knees and set my Glock on the floor. Kicked it over to the desk as instructed, then rose, placing my hands in the air. I studied the three faces in front of me. Confident grins all around. Good. These men weren't trained. They thought they'd neutralized the threat. Not a single one of them was reaching into his suit jacket for a weapon.

Jankowski removed the cigarette from his mouth and said, "Who else besides Staszak and Gasowski have you told about the lawyer Dabrowski?"

"No one," I said. "I thought it best to contain the information so that something like this wouldn't occur."

He smirked. "Ironic, no?"

"No," I said. "Unfortunate. For you."

"For us?" Jankowski stuffed the cigarette back into his mouth, took a drag, and laughed. It seemed that the laughter was contagious.

Everyone in the room laughed.

Everyone but me.

"That's right," I said as the sound faded into chuckles. "See, I came here with the intention of asking you where I could find Kazmer Chudzik and his lawyer. I had no intention of hurting anyone. Now you've forced my hand. I've got to defend myself. I've no choice but to hurt you all. Quite badly, from the looks of things." I smiled, mimicked Jankowski's voice. "That is unfortunate for you, no?"

The room erupted with another round of laughter.

This time I joined them.

Harming your fellow man is a hell of a thing. Even when it's human garbage like the men in this room. I'd hurt my fair share but I'd never get used to it, never stop regretting the very need to do what had to be done. I'd never get any pleasure out of it. Even when I finally found the man who took my daughter, Hailey. I would experience the thrill of relief, sure, like the end of a forever hangover. I imagined it'd be like pulling a stiletto out of my gut. Just knowing it was no longer in there, violating my organs, would be enough. I'd be able to push aside the thought of losing blood. Be able to die without feeling as though I'd left something unattended to.

As the laughter faded I swiftly turned my head to the left, out of the line of fire, jerked my left elbow to alter the gunman's aim, wrapped his gun arm around my own, and with my right delivered an open-palm strike to the side of the head. I followed with a punch to the jaw to snap the head back, then delivered a blow to his throat. I placed my right leg behind his and threw him hard to the ground while ripping the gun from his hand. I spun and delivered a round kick to the jaw of the Pole immediately to my right. His gun was out, and as my foot connected with his face, he fired, wide, clipping the Pole to my left in his right shoulder, causing him to drop his weapon.

Jankowski had risen from his seat behind the desk. His pistol was aimed at my chest and he was about to squeeze the trigger. It was him or me, I decided. And if it was me, it was Lindsay Sorkin, too, so I fired.

The bullet struck Jankowski square in the chest and he fell back into his leather chair. A red rose bloomed where a beating heart had been just moments earlier.

The stench of blood and burning flesh now accompanied the foul smell of cigarette smoke, reminding me of Ostermann and his justification for knocking Dietrich and Karl out cold in the alley. Our lives hadn't been at risk then, and I had thought I sensed some pleasure in Ostermann after he'd swung the butt of his gun the second time.

Rest assured, he'd said to me, *my beating two child kidnappers in a back alley of a Berlin nightclub will not cost me a single hour of sleep.*

I'd believed him. And though I'd derived no pleasure from what I'd just done, I didn't think it would cause me much anguish, either.

I looked down at the man who'd held the gun to the back of my head. I'd broken his larynx, so he'd be of no use at all. The two men who'd been seated in front of the desk had passed out, one from the pain of a bullet to the shoulder, the other from my round kick to the face.

I emptied the chamber of the gun I'd taken, wiped it down, and dropped it at its owner's side. Then I picked up my gun. I stood and surveyed the men one at a time. Each of them had been in the process of raising a firearm. This offered some relief. I'd defended myself. Done nothing wrong at all.

Still, one man lay dead and three lay unconscious, and I was no closer to finding Lindsay Sorkin. No closer at all.

Chapter 27

By the time I left the room, the warehouse had cleared out. Maybe the men on the loading docks weren't muscle after all. I concealed my Glock and moved swiftly down the street toward the motorcycle. I'd instructed Ana to remain right next to it, explained clearly that we might need to make a fast get-away. But now, although I saw the bike, she was nowhere in sight. Sirens sounded in the distance, and I now knew none of the police was on our side. We needed to get the hell out of Pruszkow, and fast.

When I reached the bike I scanned the immediate area. All industrial. Nothing around but the café directly across from the warehouse, and I thought she wouldn't dare go in there, after I'd told her what the kids at the park had said about Chudzik's men taking their coffee there. *Where the hell are you, Ana?* The sirens grew louder; the police were getting closer. We had a minute, maybe two. I peered up the street, back down. Finally, my gaze fell on my feet. Directly beneath my boots on the blacktop were tire marks I was sure hadn't been there before. A vehicle had peeled away from this spot within the past hour, since I'd parked my bike.

The realization hit me like a sack of rocks. Someone had taken Ana.

Gasowski had observed the ferocity in Ana's eyes when I forbade her to come along. He knew she wouldn't give up, that I'd be forced to bring her along to Pruszkow. Gasowski had warned them—Fisk won't be alone. The lawyer Ana Staszak will be with him. Take her. She may be used as a bargaining chip down the road.

But no. It was worse. Ana knew too much.

They wouldn't keep Ana alive for very long.

As the sirens rounded the corner, I jumped onto my bike and started the engine. Peeled away just as the first cruisers screeched into the warehouse parking lot, no doubt responding to a call of shots fired.

M arek Staszak was a member of the Sejm, the lower house of Polish parliament, not so dissimilar from the United States' House of Representatives. His party was the Lewica i Demokraci, or the Democratic Left Alliance, which was a center-left political coalition, formed because its founding members felt that the largest opposition party, the Civic Platform, was too close politically to the right-wing Law and Justice majority. Currently, the Civic Platform party, a center-right coalition, was in power.

But just now, Poland's politics didn't matter. Finding a particular member of parliament did. Specifically, Ana's brother. Marek Staszak was the only person in the country I knew I could trust, especially now that his sister's life hung in the balance.

I rode back to Warsaw as fast as the BMW would carry me and made it in under ten minutes. I'd seen the semicircular Sejm building when I first went looking for Dabrowski's law office the morning before. The complex had stood for more than eighty-five years and was unmistakable.

The trick, of course, would be to gain access.

"I am sorry," said the guard at the gate, "but a visit to the Sejm must be booked by phone at least seven days in advance."

"This isn't a visit," I said, still on my bike. "It's urgent that I speak with Marek Staszak. He's a member."

"I am sorry," the guard repeated, "but the Sejm is in session and the members cannot be disturbed."

Too bad. I intended to disturb them.

"Listen to me," I said, reaching into my peacoat. "Pan Staszak's sister is in grave danger."

The guard turned from me, looking annoyed. "Then you should call the police."

When he turned back to me, he saw the Glock leveled at his heart.

I said, "I'm afraid that calling the police isn't an option." I gestured to his phone. "Now, rip that cord from the wall and open the gate."

The guard did as I'd said, but I couldn't trust him not to sound the alarm before I reached the Assembly Room.

"Now, turn around," I said as I dismounted the bike. "Place your hands on the back of your head and walk slowly backwards until I tell you to stop."

As he stumbled backward, the poor bastard pleaded for his life.

"I'm not going to hurt you," I told him.

I turned the pistol and cracked the handle across the back of his head and he toppled.

"At least not much," I said.

I powered past the standing guard at the front door and got lucky with the layout of the building. The Assembly Room wasn't too far from the entrance and members were already filing out. I asked a young woman in a smart suit where I might find Marek Staszak and she pointed to a group of men turning to the right.

"Marek," I called out.

The statesman squinted in my direction. He had a boyish face. Had the same reddish brown hair as his sister, only it was cut short, and his eyes were a light brown. "Pan Fisk?"

I pushed through the crowd toward him.

"Yes, we spoke on the phone earlier," I said, keeping my voice low. "Listen, we need some privacy."

"My office is—"

"No, I mean outside this building. I had a bit of a bother getting past the guards."

"What's happened?" he said nervously.

I took his arm and led him to the exit.

"It's Ana," I said gently. "She's been taken."

Chapter 28

asowski!" Marek shouted, firing a water glass across his living room. It smashed against the top of his fireplace and fell to pieces. "I should have known the son of a bitch is dirty. But my *sister.* I never dreamed he would put her life in danger."

"If it's any consolation," I said, "Gasowski tried to talk her out of accompanying me to Pruszkow. Ana wouldn't hear of it."

"That's my sister," Marek said. "But no, it's no consolation. When this is over I will have the son of a bitch killed."

"First we have to find your sister," I said, trying to get him to focus. "Any idea where Chudzik's men might have taken her?"

"None," Marek said, shaking his head as he tried to calm himself. "Without the police, I would not even know where to start."

"Well, the police are out of the question, Marek. We can trust no one now except each other."

"Any ideas, Simon?"

"The meeting," I said. "Dabrowski will still be meeting with Talik. We need to determine the location. If we find Dabrowski, we'll find Ana."

"But how the hell do we do that?"

"Ana said there was a planner in Dabrowski's office. Today's date contained the initials T.Y. Maybe there's more information about the meeting place. Besides that, Chudzik was a client. If we can gain access to Dabrowski's files, we may discover some of the addresses Chudzik's used in the past. We could get lucky."

"How do we gain access to the files?" Marek said. "I am sure Dabrowski's staff has been given instructions. As soon as we enter, they will call the police."

"We'll just have to make sure no one's in the office when we enter," I said.

Marek glanced at his watch.

"We cannot afford to wait," he said. "Dabrowski's office won't close for hours. Ana might not have that long."

I shook my head. "No need to wait until they close," I said. "I have a plan."

My plan wasn't terribly original, but it had worked well in the past. Specifically in Japan. In Osaka. A wealthy businessman had kidnapped his daughter from her high school in Maui and flown her across the Pacific to sit in his office on the twenty-ninth floor of a high-rise in the Diamond District. I watched them for days. He never let the girl out of his sight. He was cool, had everything and everyone under control, just the way he liked. When that's the case, you need to create chaos.

It was March 2005 when I arrived in Japan to retrieve the girl, and the country was bracing for the ten-year anniversary of the sarin attack on the Tokyo subway. Fueled by the media, tensions were high, fewer people were riding the Tokyo Metro, and people in Osaka were already fearing a copycat crime. Creating chaos was easy. All it took was a single phone call.

The entire Diamond District evacuated at once. The businessman did just as I'd anticipated, made straight for the garage and his waiting Mercedes-Benz GL350. He shoved his daughter into the back of the SUV and rounded the rear to get to the driver's side. He never saw what was coming.

With the father unconscious, I snatched the keys and jumped into the vehicle. Told the girl I'd been sent by her mother to bring her back to Hawaii. She threw herself onto the front seat and hugged me. Kissed my cheek. That was the thing with my job. You never knew what kind of reaction you were going to get from these kids. Sometimes they loved you. Sometimes they stepped out in front of a night bus.

Here in Warsaw I didn't want to scare anyone, but Marek and I really had no choice. Time was running out on Ana, running out on Lindsay. A sarin scare wouldn't do the trick, but a small fire in a restroom on the second floor of Dabrowski's office building just might.

As before, I had no difficulty getting past security. I didn't even bother to stop at the desk, just bolted straight for the elevators and punched the button marked 2, while Marek waited for me in a nearby stairwell.

All it took was the book of souvenir matches I'd swiped from Pierogarnia and the small canister of Zippo lighter fluid Marek kept in his house. I balled up some brown paper towels from the dispenser and stuffed them into the wastebasket. I placed the wastebasket in the corner where the fire would do the least amount of damage. Then I sprayed the paper towels with lighter fluid and lit a match. Gray smoke billowed to the ceiling, finally kicking the sprinkler system on.

An alarm sounded. Tenants began spilling out and the building and it was empty in under ten minutes. I waited for the sprinklers to extinguish the small blaze, then Marek and I made for Dabrowski's office on the ninth floor.

The entrance to the law office was locked, but it was all glass. A fire extinguisher parked down the hall did the trick. I told Marek to stand back while I wielded the extinguisher like a baseball bat, shattering the glass near the padlock. A few more smacks and I was able to get my hand through to unlock the door.

"We won't have long," I said over the sound of the fire alarm. "The firefighters will be checking each floor once they know the small blaze downstairs is under control."

We went straight to Dabrowski's private office, the one I'd watched Ana enter just the day before from my seat in the conference room. I thought about the strawberries and felt a pang of hunger deep in my gut. No time for strawberries. No time for *thoughts* of strawberries.

I lifted my right leg and kicked just below the doorknob with the heel of my foot. The door swung open and Marek and I entered.

"I never liked this sleazy bastard," he said.

I moved behind Dabrowski's desk and opened his drawers. The top contained a few thin manila file folders; the second down, pens and paper clips and such. The bottom drawer held his day planner. I lifted the brown leather book out of the drawer as Marek booted Dabrowski's desktop computer. I flipped through the pages, found today's date marked with the initials T.Y., just as Ana had described. No place or time. In the front of the planner were a number of pages devoted to entering important addresses and phone numbers, but not a single entry had been scratched in.

"Password protected," Marek said in a huff, staring into Dabrowski's monitor.

"Try your sister's name."

He glared at me. "Why?"

"Just try it."

He punched it in. "Doesn't work," he said with an air of relief.

"What's the Polish word for 'password'?" I said.

"Hasło."

"Try it."

He tried it. "No good," he said.

"Try the Polish word for 'money.'"

"We will be here all *year,* Simon."

"Type it."

He typed it. *"Nothing."*

"Move," I said.

I bypassed the screen by hitting Escape, then clicked on the Internet Explorer icon. Facebook popped up. His e-mail address sat in a box at the top of the screen. In the box next to it was his Facebook password, represented by five black dots.

"Five characters," I said.

Marek ran his hands through his damp hair as I exited back to the password screen. I had a friend named Kati Sheffield who used to work in the Bureau as a computer scientist. Over drinks one night, she'd given me a crash course in hacking. She'd said at least one of five people used a weak password, and these people typically used the same password for every e-mail address, social network, and bank account. It was often the name or birth date of a partner or spouse, a child or pet. Frequently it was an anniversary, sometimes just a series of numbers like 1-2-3-4-5-6. Hometown, current city, university, the name of a favorite sports team. Often followed by a 0 or a 1 because many institutions required numbers as well as letters these days, and all your passwords had to be the same because you had hundreds of them and you'd never remember them all and you didn't want to write them down. Might as well have no passwords at all then, right?

If you didn't have your target's information—birthdays, anniversaries, names of pets and favorite sports teams and such—you tried common words. *Password* itself was one of them. *God, money, love,* things that were important to the average person. Some variation of the phrase *let me in.* In the target's native language, of course. Then in English. Hell, everyone nowadays knew English, didn't they? Dabrowski certainly did.

Five characters. M-O-N-E-Y. Dabrowski struck me as that kind of guy.

I typed it. I was in.

Thanks again, Kati.

"Unbelievable," Marek said. "When I get back to my office I'd better change my passwords."

I glanced at him. "Something patriotic, I'd bet."

He nodded. "Poland's coat of arms," he said. "In English. Plus a one at the end."

A fter locating Chudzik's physical file, we did some further exploring on Dabrowski's computer. The images on the lawyer's hard drive stunned us like a surge of electricity. They were vulgar, exhibited unspeakable crimes against children, depicted unfathomable violations of the young, pictures that would forever be trapped in my head, would haunt my mind like specters, rising at any moment to steal my breath, paint my skin as pale as paste, chill me to the bone. What bile there was in my stomach threatened to empty onto Dabrowski's desk. Marek, too, appeared faint, even as he helped steady me on my feet.

"Dear God," he said.

For the first time since arriving in Poland, I wondered whether the lawyer Dabrowski was more than just a middleman, a broker. Hundreds of images of child pornography were buried in organized fashion under innocuous file names on Dabrowski's hard drive. All of them depicted children between the ages of four and fourteen. Both boys and girls. Made to pose either alone or with one another, frequently with a faceless adult man, or men.

None of the images were of Lindsay Sorkin, of course. It didn't make sense that she'd have been caught up in this net. She'd been specifically targeted. Why her when there were any number of kids from the West who could have been snatched up just as easily, if not more so?

Still, I couldn't help but feel that time had just become even more paramount than it had been before. As sure I was that Lindsay Sorkin hadn't been taken to be sexually exploited, I was sure that these were the type of people we were dealing with. There was a network in place and Lindsay's kidnappers would have used it, regardless of their ultimate purpose for taking her. Like it or not, this was the trail of bread crumbs we'd have to follow if we hoped to find her.

Next to me, Marek shook his head in disgust. "My sister has worked in this office for ten years. How could she not know this man was a monster?"

"Monsters can be clever," I said softly. "A good deal of evil can be hidden behind a human face."

"This monster was her mentor," Marek conceded. "Her lover. To Ana, he must have been beyond reproach."

I glanced at my watch. "We'll need to be leaving," I said. "The firefighters will reach us soon."

"There were no addresses in Chudzik's files," Marek said.

"No," I agreed. "But I did see something in Dabrowski's discovery files that may lead us to him."

"What?" he said as footfalls sounded from the hallway.

There wasn't time enough for me to answer.

Chapter 29

We hid in Ana's private office, lowering the blinds and locking the door behind us. As we waited for the firemen to pass, I looked around the room at Ana's framed photographs. Many of the pictures were of her and Marek at various ages and in different cities around Europe. There they were in London as teenagers, then Dublin and Edinburgh around the same age. Here they were in Milan in their early twenties, a trip that apparently took them north to Switzerland. More recently they'd traveled to Finland and St. Petersburg, Barcelona and Madrid.

Studying the photos, I couldn't help but think of my sister, Tuesday, and what kind of relationship we might have had as adults. Hell, what kind of relationship we might have had as kids.

"People are beginning to return to the building," Marek said from his spot at the window. "The firefighters may be leaving but they will be calling in law enforcement about that glass door we smashed in, so we had better be on our way."

I nodded, tearing my eyes from a photo of Ana and Marek as children on the beach by the Mediterranean Sea.

We hurried out into the hallway, then bounded down the stairs to the first floor.

Once we were safely away from the building, I stopped him so that we could catch our breath.

"The witness list for the prosecution," I said, after a few moments. "One of the men who testified against Kazmer Chudzik is a former member of a rival syndicate, the Wołomin mob. In the file there was an English summary of his testimony that stated that he'd had dealings with Chudzik under the guise of a general contractor seeking protection in exchange for a piece of his action. Sounds to me like a guy who might be willing to talk."

"Know where to find him?" Marek said.

The witness was a convict-turned-informant named Piotr Denys and he was employed by a construction company based in Warsaw. Marek called the company and was told that Denys could be found at a renovation project in the vicinity of Lodz, a large city eighty-four miles southwest of our location. It was a hell of a long ride that would eat up at least another two hours, but we had no choice. We mounted the BMW and drove off.

When we arrived, we discovered that the address was an old Catholic church undergoing massive reconstruction. The beauty of the ancient exterior was evident even with two stories of scaffolding obscuring our view. On one side of the church stood a mammoth excavator, its bucket lifting heavy pipes from the earth. On the other side, a cemetery overgrown with grass and weeds remained untouched, undoubtedly out of respect for the long-dead who resided there.

I parked the bike across the street and Marek and I moved swiftly toward the site.

"This church is at least seven centuries old," Marek said.

Having spent most of my life in the United States, its oldest structures built no earlier than the seventeenth century, it always amazed me to see edifices built during the Middle Ages. At times it felt almost as though the Old World existed in an alternate universe.

At the edge of the site stood a fence, its gate open, a foreman standing at its maw. He adjusted his hard hat, held up a hand, and spoke directly to Marek in Polish. When Marek responded, I caught the name Piotr Denys and watched the foreman nod his head. He then barked something to another man, who appeared moments later with a pair of well-worn orange hard hats. The foreman handed the hard hats to us, and we placed them on our heads.

We walked past other workers without a word, the foreman as our personal escort.

I turned to Marek as we stepped over the threshold into the church. "Kind, isn't he?"

"He's a working man," Marek said. "These are the men I fight for, the working poor and middle class."

Inside, the church looked as though it had been rocked by an explosion. Large chunks of cement—what I assumed was the old foundation—lay haphazardly over an earthen floor. We stepped cautiously three feet above it all on shaky wooden planks, connected to one another in the shape of a tic-tac-toe board. Hoses from a compressor and cords from a generator snaked through two of the ornate stained-glass windows, the hum of the outdoor machinery flowing upward, echoing against the vaulted ceiling. As we walked, my gaze settled on a colossal out-of-place crucifix situated on the rear wall, and remained on the oversize cross until we reached a group of men, their pale skin slick with soot and sweat.

The foreman motioned one of the men aside and introduced him to Marek as Piotr Denys.

Denys was a rough-looking fellow, short and stocky, rock-hard arms colored with plenty of ink. His head rested directly on his broad shoulders, exhibiting no sign of a neck. He regarded us suspiciously as we led him away from the group.

Marek spoke a few words with him, then turned to me and said, "He doesn't speak English."

"No worries," I said. "Just ask him where Chudzik might hold an important meeting. One he'd value as particularly private."

Marek translated. As Denys spoke, the politician's face grew red.

"Pan Denys wants to know what's in it for him if he talks," Marek said. "Shall I tell him his bones will remain intact?"

"No, no," I said, staggered at how much Marek reminded me of his sister. "We don't have time for that." I reached into my pocket and plucked out a wad of euros, handed them to Marek. "Here. Negotiate instead."

Marek peeled off several bills, held them tight in his fist as he repeated the question to Denys. Denys leaned in and quietly supplied an answer.

Marek said, "Chudzik owns a lake house in eastern Pomerania near the Gulf of Gdansk. Every private meeting Denys had with him was held there."

"Ask him about security," I said.

A few moments later Marek said, "The lake house is set off from its neighbors. Lots of land surrounding it. Pan Denys suggests that if we are hoping to gain the element of surprise, we go at night. Otherwise, we'll be spotted a mile away."

"All right, then," I said. "If you're satisfied."

Marek handed him the bills and Denys quickly stalked off.

"I am confident he is telling the truth," Marek said to me.

"That's all well and good," I told him. "But what if he sells the information back to Chudzik and we step right into an ambush?"

"Doubtful," Marek said.

"Oh?"

"Denys told me that if we are successful at killing Chudzik, he will pay us five times what I just handed him."

"Is that so?"

Marek nodded. "He testified against one of the most dangerous men in Poland. Unless Chudzik is dead, Piotr Denys will be looking over his shoulder for the rest of his natural life."

Chapter 30

Marek proved he had even more in common with his sister by insisting he accompany me to Chudzik's lake house in Pomerania. I didn't put up much of a fight. I anticipated that, after what had happened in the warehouse in Pruszkow, Chudzik would be prepared with even more men, and they'd be looking for me, specifically. Undoubtedly, I would require a distraction at some point in time. The operation was dodgy to say the least. Normally, under such circumstances, you can finally rely on the police. But not now, not here in Poland. There was no way to know which cops were connected to Chief Inspector Gasowski—or to the network that had recruited him—and which were clean. And there was certainly no time to find out.

By the time we reached Gdansk, it was night, so the cover of darkness was a given. One of the few advantages we could count on. The layout of the great house, however, would present a distinct disadvantage. Though it was secluded, nestled among towering trees, the house rested high on a hill, making it impossible to gain higher ground. In addition, the roof was as flat as ancient cultures once thought the world. The perfect watching post. On the roof stood four men, one in each corner, looking out over the grounds.

There was really only a single approach, from the west. On the east side of the house lay a large deck, perched over a six-hundred-foot drop into a canyon. Directly behind the house lay a body of water. In the front of the house, two more men stood guard in front of a garage, large rifles hanging from their shoulders. These men didn't look like gangsters. Chudzik had hired professional security. This wouldn't be anything like stepping into a single room and threatening three men used to sitting on their fat asses, drinking coffee.

"I see six of them," I said to Marek, lowering the field glasses he'd been gifted by a Polish soldier, one of the original two hundred who had joined the United States, the UK, and Australia in the 2003 invasion of Iraq.

"What's the plan?"

"To eliminate them," I said. "Quietly."

Each of the men wore a walkie-talkie on his belt, so the two downstairs had to be taken out together or at least out of each other's sight. If they were able to communicate a problem to the men upstairs, it would make things decidedly more difficult.

"Do you want me to create a diversion?" Marek said.

I shook my head. "There are too many of them," I said. "Any diversion would only put the remaining men on high alert. But I think an opportunity is about to present itself."

We watched as one of the guards on the ground tapped a box of cigarettes. As he did, he began walking down the long gravel driveway away from the house. If he stayed on course, he'd be out of his partner's line of vision in less than a minute.

"Wait here," I told Marek.

Quickly and quietly, I moved through the trees to intercept the smoker. He stood only ten feet from the woods as he dug into his pocket, presumably for a lighter. From where I stood, it looked like a cheap yellow Bic, and he had trouble getting it started. He flicked the flint wheel again and again, but no flame presented itself. He turned and started back up the driveway.

I had only a few seconds to catch him before his partner would be able to see him again. Boots on gravel would give me away in a heartbeat, so I kicked them off and shot toward him quick as I could in socks.

He was about to round the corner when I caught up with him. From behind, I wrapped my right arm around his neck, making sure the crook of my elbow was positioned directly over the midline. Assisting with my free hand, I pinched my arm together, successfully compressing the carotid arteries and jugular veins on both sides of his neck. This would cut off the blood flow to his head and render him unconscious without the risk of strangling him. He struggled for mere seconds before his body went limp. I waited until I was certain he was out cold, then laid his body gently on the ground and dragged it back toward the woods and out of sight.

One down. The second should be easier.

Now I had something to lure the gunman away. I removed the walkie-talkie from the unconscious man's belt. Motioned to Marek to join me.

As Marek crept to me I slipped back into my boots. When he reached me, I handed him the walkie-talkie.

"When I'm in position," I said, "I want you to switch this on, but don't say anything into it."

Marek nodded. "Make like the guard switched it on accidentally?"

"Exactly." I pointed to the garage. "I'll be in position once you see me flush up against the garage, smoking a cigarette."

I took the Bic off the unconscious guard and shook it. There was plenty of lighter fluid left in it. The guard must have been having trouble with the wind, which was picking up and turning wicked.

Cigarette hanging from my lips I made for the garage, careful to stay out of the downstairs guard's line of sight. When I reached the garage, I leaned my back against it, cupped my hands, and tried the lighter. Lit the cigarette on the first try.

I nodded to Marek, who turned on the walkie-talkie. I heard the wind blowing through it from the other guard's handheld. He shouted something in exasperation, then I heard his footfalls on the gravel, coming toward me. I blew smoke out the side of my mouth, hoping he'd catch sight of it.

When his footsteps were just a few yards away, I took a deep breath and braced myself. I tossed the cigarette in exchange for my Glock.

The guard rounded the corner. His eyes went wide when he saw the gun aimed point-blank at his forehead. I held my finger to my lips and he complied.

"Understand English?" I said.

He offered up a barely perceptible nod.

"Good," I told him. "If you make a sound, it'll be the last thing you hear." I pointed to Marek's position. "Now, let's you and I go for a stroll over there where we can chat a bit."

Chapter 31

Who's inside the house?" I said, once I had the guard under the cover of trees.

I had to act quickly in case someone poked his head outside and saw that the two downstairs guards were missing. And I wasn't sure if either of these men was supposed to check in. I could ask, but he could lie, and there would be no way I'd know it. Not until it was too late.

"The boss," the guard said. "He is inside."

"Kazmer Chudzik?"

"Yes."

"Who else?" I said.

"His lawyer." The guard swallowed hard as he stared at his partner's body a few feet away. The guards were dressed warmly, and thus he couldn't see the rise and fall of his partner's chest. There was no way for this guard to know that the other was still breathing. In any event, he was taking no chances, and that was good for our purposes. "And two Turkish men," he said. "One is old, the other is young. I think maybe they are father and son."

Marek grabbed the guard by the lapels of his jacket. "How about a woman? Her name is Ana. Have you seen her?"

"No," the guard said, breathing heavily. "But earlier someone arrived and pulled straight into the garage. They removed something large from the trunk. It could have been a person, I don't know."

My stomach instantly sank into my pelvis. I couldn't move.

Meanwhile, Marek's eyes caught fire. "This person was *dead*?"

"I assumed so, yes. But I didn't see—"

Marek grabbed the guard by the throat and squeezed.

I nearly fell to my knees, thought I might hyperventilate.

"Easy, Marek," I finally said, my voice cracking. "I have a few more questions, then we'll head inside and find her."

Grudgingly, Marek released the guard's throat.

I gathered myself and said, "Aside from the four men on the roof and you and your friend over there on the ground, are there any more guards inside or outside the house?"

The guard shook his head.

"Are you sure?"

He nodded.

"Because if I find out you're lying, I'm going to come back here and break your neck. But only after I cut off your fingers and toes one by one by one."

"I swear it," he said. "Chudzik hired only six of us. But he has two of his own men. And they have many weapons inside. Pistols, shotguns, knives, everything you can imagine."

I carefully lowered myself onto my haunches and asked him to describe the layout of the interior of the house and where the weapons could be found. Where Chudzik and his lawyer and the two Turks and Ana might be. He answered as best he could, and I listened as best *I* could, but I could hardly concentrate.

I needed to snap out of this fog and the only way to do that was to convince myself that Ana was still alive. Alive and in danger and in need of my help.

"All right, then," I said, rising off my haunches and stepping behind the guard. My muscles were sore and tired but my mind suddenly felt as though it had just been struck with an electric charge.

"Please don't," he said. "Don't kill me. I have children."

"I'm not going to kill you," I said, placing my arm around his neck, same as I had done for his friend. "I'm just going to put you to sleep for a bit."

There was no way to deal with the men on the roof without alerting the men inside. I handed Marek the guard's rifle.

"Know how to use this thing?" I said.

Marek nodded. "I am not a big fan of guns, but our father, he was a hunter. He taught Ana and me how to shoot when we were children."

"All right," I said. "Today that knowledge comes in handy." I handed Marek one of the two walkie-talkies and pointed to the single guard visible on the roof from our vantage point. "I want you to shoot that guy in the leg on my signal."

"What about the other three?"

"If they truly are professionals, they're not going to come to their fallen comrade's aid, so you may not get a shot at them. If you do, take it. Always in the leg; try not to do any serious damage. But the more you drop, the fewer I'll have to deal with inside the house."

"When do I follow you in?" Marek said.

"You don't. You're far more valuable outside. I'll keep the walkie on me. If I need you, you'll hear from me. Otherwise, maintain your position. Keep out of sight." I pointed to the windows. "If you see a target through the glass, take it out. But make sure it's not me or Ana. And remember, even if it's one of Chudzik's men, try to simply wing them. I'm going to need someone alive at the end of all this to pump for information."

Marek placed a firm hand on my shoulder.

"Please, Simon," he said. "Find my sister, and bring her out unharmed."

I nodded.

"But if Ana is dead," he added, "please keep alive the son of a bitch who killed her. I will need some time alone with him."

Marek's words struck me like a rock between the eyes. Hearing the possibility uttered a second time gave it too much power and I immediately wanted to rewind time so that I could return the words to his throat. If Ana was dead, it was my fault. I'd known the risk of taking her with me when I first met her at the law office. I'd thought then that involving her was probably a mistake.

I took a deep breath, tried to conceal my renewed worry in front of her brother.

"All right," I said.

The men on the roof were looking out into the distance, so entering the house wouldn't be much of a bother. It was once I got inside that my problems would start.

I bolted up the drive, keeping low, my Glock already in hand. I pressed up against the garage as I'd done before. I was about to round the corner to find an appropriate window when I spotted a side door into the garage. I tried the knob. The door wasn't locked so I gave it a go.

The garage was dark and windowless, but I made out three vehicles, all fairly new and pricey. One Jag and two Mercedes. On the far end, I saw a door that would presumably lead into the house.

I hurried to it, my heart racing. I tried not to think about all that was at stake. Ana. A little girl. Their families. My head was garbled with sentiment. I knew I needed to clear it or else I would be putting myself and everyone else at risk.

I felt overwhelmed with hatred. Emotions wouldn't help me inside this house. Only clear thought. Logic. Reason. All else would serve only to hinder my efforts.

But there wasn't time to run an analysis. I tried the knob. This door was locked. I removed the walkie from my belt, put it to my mouth, held the button, and said, "Now, Marek."

I stepped back, drew in a deep breath, and lifted my right leg. Soon as I heard the shot, I aimed my foot just below the knob and kicked.

The door flew open.

I stepped inside and raised my Glock.

Chapter 32

The garage opened into a foyer. I turned left, heard movement from two rooms over. If the guard's description of the interior was correct, the commotion was coming from the living room. I kept low, darted behind an island in the kitchen. Allowed myself a peek and spotted a heavy man running toward me, his weapon raised. I planted myself and fired into his chest. The shot took him down.

A round buzzed over my head. Not from the guy I'd just taken out but from someone just around the corner. I ducked back down, maneuvered around the island to a point where I hoped I'd have a clear shot at him. I got to my feet, aimed, and fired. The bullet struck the corner of the wall. The man just behind it fired back. Once, twice.

The shots were wild. He was no marksman, so I felt better about what I was going to have to do: take him head-on. I rose from my position and moved forward, walking straight toward him. The boldness of the move froze him for a moment, enough time for me to get off a shot. He tried to duck, so the bullet caught him in the throat. I now presumed that Chudzik's two men were down.

The living room was empty and there was no way anyone could have escaped without running past me. Which meant they'd either headed to the back of the house or gone upstairs. I quickly cleared a bathroom and a guest bedroom and a small space turned into a library.

I then rounded the final corner and found a set of carpeted stairs. Footfalls were headed down the steps in my direction. I didn't wait until I saw full bodies. I cut the first man down with two shots to the knees. He tumbled the rest of the way down the steps, dropping his weapon directly in front of me. I kicked it away.

The second man turned to retreat. I chased him back up the steps. When he reached the top, he turned and fired a pistol. The shot grazed my right arm. I fired back, took him down with a gut shot, just as a third man fired a rifle over my head. I turned and shot him square in the chest.

On the third floor, I heard doors slamming. It was where Chudzik, Dabrowski, and the Turks would make their stand.

I raced up the stairs.

Just before reaching the landing, I lay on the stairs, my gun raised, glimpsing the layout. Looked as though there were four doors. Three were closed, one open. The open door led to a toilet. The three other rooms, according to the guard, were bedrooms, one of which Chudzik had made into a den, which opened onto the grand deck. That was the room in which he stored most of his weapons. Chudzik would be behind that door, the door to my far left. That door would be the most dangerous.

I paused for a moment, checked my right arm. Barely a flesh wound. I gathered my courage and picked myself up off the stairs. I went to the far right and back-kicked the door. As it flew open, I pressed myself up against the wall, expecting shots. None was forthcoming, so I chanced a careful move into the room with my Glock raised. From the corner of my eye I caught the glint of a blade. I tried to turn but I was a moment too late. The knife slashed my left forearm, a deep cut that caused me to drop my gun.

The man who had slashed me kicked my gun aside and came after me again with the knife. He was a large man, dark, with a mustache wrapped across a wide face. Talik, I presumed.

With my good right arm I snatched him by the wrist before he could drive the knife into my chest. I twisted his wrist until I heard a snap, then back-kicked him hard in the chest.

As I bent to retrieve the knife, someone leaped from the closet and jumped onto my back. It was Alim. He wrapped a phone cord around my neck and tried to strangle me. With all my strength, I threw my body back against the wall, slamming him into the Sheetrock. His grip around my throat loosened but he remained on my back.

As I tried to pry him off, I glanced up. Talik was again on his feet, coming at me with the knife. He held it awkwardly in his left hand. I blocked the blow with my right and, with the aid of my injured left, turned the knife back on him.

We struggled for what felt like forever. The big man was even stronger than he looked. Sweat dripped down my forehead, stung my eyes so badly I had to blink them closed. My face was burning up, and the purple vein in my exposed right forearm looked as though it might break free from my skin. My muscles were tiring. It was now or never. I took a deep breath and summoned every last bit of strength.

Finally, the blade plunged into Talik's chest.

Alim jumped off my back and made for the door as I moved for my Glock. By the time I picked it up and spun around, Alim was gone. As I listened to his footfalls fade down the carpeted stairs, I looked down at his uncle. Talik was either dead or dying. I didn't bother to waste a bullet on him.

As I took my first step back into the large hall, the door to the far left burst open and Kazmer Chudzik fired a shotgun at me.

In a single motion, I turned and threw myself behind the wall of the room I'd just left.

The blast just missed me and I landed on my stomach next to Talik's body. I considered lifting the corpse and using it as a shield, but surely Talik was too heavy.

I pulled myself up, crept over to the doorframe.

I chanced a quick look into the hallway. The moment I showed myself, Kazmer Chudzik fired a second time.

Big mistake.

Wasting no time, I stepped into the hall and began firing, leaving Chudzik no chance to reload. A bullet nicked his shoulder and a spray of blood shot across his large round face. He tossed the shotgun, turned, and ran into the room.

I followed.

When I reached the doorway, Chudzik was halfway through the sliding glass door to the deck. He hadn't grabbed another gun. He didn't appear to be armed.

I moved swiftly across the room, my left forearm bleeding profusely, my right still aiming the Glock at his head.

I stepped onto the deck. Yelled over the howling wind, "Nowhere to go, Chudzik."

With his back now against the wooden rail that looked over the canyon, Chudzik held his arms out at his sides.

"You do not want to kill me, American," he shouted. "If you do, you will never find the little girl. I am the only man in all of Poland who can lead you to her. No one else—not the Turk, not the lawyer—has the slightest clue where she is, or where she is going."

Chudzik's tone was defiant, his face set in a sneer. I believed him. He was too smart to have made it otherwise. I needed him. He was the man I needed to keep alive.

"All right, then," I said. "You live to lead me to the little girl. Under one condition. You tell me where Anastazja Staszak is. I know your men took her from Pruszkow."

Chudzik's eyes flickered over my shoulder. The moment they did, I dropped hard onto the deck.

The sound of an automatic weapon spilling its chamber filled the air as holes peppered Chudzik's ample chest, throwing him backward into the wooden rail. The rail splintered and his body, covered now in red, burst through and fell hundreds of feet into the canyon below.

I rolled and leveled my Glock at Dabrowski's chest. Before I could fire, I heard the click of his weapon, signifying it was empty.

"Drop it, Dabrowski," I shouted. "Drop it and don't move an inch."

The lawyer's face flushed with shock. He did as he was told, raising his hands above his head, his entire form trembling.

With the aid of my injured left arm, I rose to my feet.

"Where's Ana?" I said.

Chapter 33

Dabrowski led Marek and me into the basement of the late Kazmer Chudzik's lake house. The lawyer was still trembling, his voice little more than a rasp. Several times he stumbled on the creaky wooden stairs, as though he might faint. It was understandable: Dabrowski's life had instantly turned to shit. He'd just killed the most fearsome mob boss in Poland. If Chudzik's associates didn't ice him in revenge, Dabrowski would spend the rest of his life in prison for murder and kidnapping, not to mention possession of hundreds of images of child pornography.

Several times on the stairs I heard the lawyer mumble, "You should have killed me, Fisk."

In the cold, dark basement, I pulled down on a chain overhead. A single bare bulb threw light over the large space, exposing Ana, who lay clothed but motionless on a dirty mattress in the shadows. Ana's hands and feet were bound together; a gag was stretched across her mouth. Marek ran to her as soon as he saw her. He nudged her and pleaded for her to wake as he untied her bonds. A lump formed in my throat, another in the pit of my stomach, as Marek gently slapped his sister on her pale, round cheeks.

Finally, she came awake.

Something inside me soared. We'd just met, yet looking at her, I suddenly felt as though I'd known her a lifetime. Realized her death would have killed so large a piece of me that there would have been nothing left but bones.

Marek, crying, hugged her with all his might.

Next to me, Dabrowski breathed a sigh of relief.

"*Woda*," Ana begged as soon as Marek undid her gag.

Marek was prepared. He'd snatched a bottle of Naleczowianka from Chudzik's fridge upstairs. Now he pulled it from his pants pocket, twisted the cap, and held it to her lips. She drank hungrily, as though she hadn't ever tasted water before.

I wanted to run to her, throw my arms around her, but how could I deny her brother?

"Are you okay, Ana?" Marek said, once she finally pushed the water bottle away. I knew he was speaking English for my benefit and I was warmed by that fact.

"Yes," she said, her eyes moving from him to me, then settling on Dabrowski.

She stared fiercely at Dabrowski—her boss, her mentor, her friend, her lover, her betrayer. When she started to rise from the mattress, Marek helped her up, but wouldn't allow her to approach the lawyer.

"You bastard," she hissed at Dabrowski. "How could you?"

"I did nothing, Ana," he said softly. "You have to believe me."

The shock was clearly wearing off; Dabrowski was going into professional mode. From here on out, we'd be dealing with a defense lawyer.

A sudden rage coursed through my veins and I shoved Dabrowski to the ground.

"Didn't do anything, eh?" I said. "Upstairs you tried to spray me with an automatic."

"I *saved* you," he cried from his spot on the cold cement floor. "I killed Chudzik."

"The hell you saved me. Chudzik was unarmed. If I didn't hit the deck, I'd be full of holes right now, and you and your client would be long gone." I stepped toward him. "But we're not down here to put you on trial, Dabrowski. Frankly, I don't care what happens to you once I leave this basement."

And it was true.

"Thing is," I said, "if you want me to leave you here alive, you're going to tell me where I can find that little girl."

"You are mistaken," he cried.

I leveled my Glock at his knee. "I don't think that I am, Dabrowski."

"I only represented Kazmer Chudzik in a professional capacity. All I did was arrange his meeting with Talik Yilmaz and Alim Sari. I have no idea what you are talking about when you say 'that little girl.'"

Ana stepped toward Dabrowski with a look of pure hatred in her eyes. "If you do not tell us where Lindsay Sorkin is, Mikolaj, I promise you, I will kill you myself."

Dabrowski seemed more convinced of Ana's threats than of the threats from the guy holding the gun on him.

"I—I—I . . ." he stammered, searching his mind for an answer. "I can only tell you what I overheard, Ana."

"Make it quick," I said.

"Then you will go?" Dabrowski said, regaining control of his voice. "Then you will all leave and I will be free to go?"

Marek stepped forward. "You son of a bi—"

Ana held a hand on her brother's chest. "No, Marek. Mikolaj is not important now. Only the girl."

I had to tear my eyes from the corners of her mouth, which were irritated from the gag. Had to look away from Ana's reddened wrists or else I might have killed the lawyer on the cold cement floor on which he sat.

"Fine," I told him. "You share with us everything you know, and if we're satisfied that you're telling the truth, not holding anything back, then the three of us will leave. What happens after that will be left to you."

He considered it. But what choice did he have? At least a half-dozen men at the house were already dead, including Chudzik himself. What was one more? He had nothing to gain by keeping silent. If he talked, at least he had a chance that we'd let him live, let him go free.

"This is what I know," he said tentatively. "Two weeks ago, Chudzik was behind bars, still awaiting his trial. He could not talk to anyone in prison, except for his lawyer. All other conversations were recorded by his jailers. So, early one morning, he called me and asked me to come in, said he needed to speak with me about something urgent. Naturally, I assumed it had to do with his case. But when I arrived, he simply gave me a telephone number and instructed me to call it. The number was to a lawyer in Berlin, a man who represented Alim Sari. The lawyer's name was Ulrich Unger. I was to tell Unger that Alim's uncle needed to pick up a package in Paris and deliver it to Warsaw.

"I made the call. This Unger, the lawyer in Berlin, seemed as much in the dark as I was. But he said he would deliver the message to his client and call me back later that day. When Unger called back, he said simply, 'Send the details, and my client will tell you his price.' I returned to the prison that evening and gave Chudzik the message. Chudzik instructed me to call the lawyer back with the details. I took out a pen, ready to scratch them down. But Chudzik ripped the pen from my hand and threw it on the floor. He said, 'Nothing in writing!' He told me to memorize what he said and repeat it verbatim to the lawyer in Berlin.

"Now, mind you, I had no idea what any of this meant. I thought maybe Chudzik needed someone to retrieve stolen diamonds or laundered money or drugs. I never dreamed it was a person, let alone a child. Chudzik said only this: 'Lindsay Sorkin, six, Hotel d'Étonner,' then he gave me a date. I confess I was curious at this point. I told Chudzik that I would rather not get involved in anything so nefarious. He told me, 'You are already involved.' He seemed dead serious and I became scared, but then he smiled and told me there was nothing to worry about. I figured this Lindsay Sorkin was a courier. She was to deliver six of something. Maybe six diamonds, six million laundered euros, six kilos of heroin. Anything but a girl.

"I passed the information along, and I thought that was the end of it. But Unger called me back again, late that night at my home. I was shocked; I hadn't given him my home number. It is unlisted because of the business I am in. It frightened me that he was calling. I said, 'What do you want? Why are you calling me?' Unger said, 'My client insists on five times the usual amount. He will drop the package off at Hauptbahnhof Station.' I hung up on him. The next day, I visited Chudzik and relayed the message. I said I was done. He said, 'Fine. Just call Unger and tell him that you agree to the price.'

"After the call, I heard nothing about it until after Chudzik's acquittal at trial. Unger called me. His client wanted to know why I hadn't paid. It wasn't until then that I realized that Unger did not even know the name of my client. Unger said Alim and his uncle Talik were threatening to kill me. That I needed to come up with five million euros or I would be dead by the end of the week.

"I went to Chudzik's office in Pruszkow. I was a mess. I yelled at him and he laughed at me. I cursed at him and he said that if I was any other man, he would kill me where I stood. I asked him what I should do. Chudzik told me to call Unger and to arrange a meeting here in Poland, at his lake house. But I don't dare ever use his name. He said I would meet with Talik Yilmaz and negotiate a settlement.

"I was scared, but he said I would have protection. He'd hired private security for the meeting. Chudzik himself was not supposed to be here, but today he showed. He spoke with Talik and Alim for a long time. It was only today that I learned what the package was, that the Turks had had two Germans steal that little girl from her parents in Paris. Just before you arrived and all hell broke loose, I realized why Chudzik had arranged the meeting. He intended to kill Talik and Alim. And I became certain he was going to kill me as well."

Dabrowski was lying—at least the part about not knowing what the package was until today. Just about everyone in the civilized world knew the name Lindsay Sorkin by now. He'd heard the name on television and recognized it; he'd had to. But that didn't matter now. I wasn't here to prosecute him. I just needed a lead on the girl.

My left arm throbbing, I leaned over and grabbed Dabrowski by his jacket, pulled him to his feet. "What was said at the meeting? Where's Lindsay Sorkin now?"

Dabrowski dry heaved. "I swear," he said, "I do not know. All I gathered was that Talik was upset because his two men—the Germans who kidnapped the girl—had to be killed because an American and a Berlin investigator nearly got to him and Alim. Of course, they were speaking about you and whoever accompanied you in Germany."

"Why did Chudzik want the girl? Why specifically Lindsay Sorkin?"

"I swear I do not know. But if I had to guess, I would say that he was selling her to someone else, someone who requested her specifically. Chudzik has sold girls before. Never that young, but teenagers, even preteens, yes, I am sure."

"Who did he sell them to?"

"Who, I do not know. Only that, geographically, they usually go the other way. They are purchased from someone in Eastern Europe, someone from Moldova or Odessa. And they are sent west to the EU or the United States."

"What about children?" I said. "Who handles the child pornography?"

"*Child pornography?*" he cried. "I have no idea."

"Enough lies." I threw him back to the floor and raised my Glock.

Marek said, "We saw what was on your computer in your law office, you filthy pervert."

Ana's eyes went wide. "What?"

"Those pictures, they have nothing to do with this girl. You must believe me. I paid for the photos. I have no idea who makes them."

He was being truthful, I knew. At least about Lindsay Sorkin having nothing to do with the photos. Not only had she been specifically targeted but now we were talking millions of dollars. Could be that the same conspirators were involved, but we'd have to pick up the trail from where we had left it in Berlin, avoid getting too far ahead of ourselves. That's when you get clumsy. That's when mistakes are made.

"Who picked Lindsay Sorkin up at Hauptbahnhof Station?" I said. "Who are they and where can I find them?"

Dabrowski took a deep breath. "That I do not know. But it doesn't matter. The girl has been passed off already."

"To whom?" I said, my stomach turning at the thought that we had arrived too late once again. "To Chudzik's men?"

Dabrowski shook his head. "They are not Chudzik's men," he said. "I do not know their identities. Only that they are not Chudzik's men."

"Whose men are they, then?"

Dabrowski took several more deep breaths, then looked away from me and stared up at Marek.

"They belong to Chief Inspector Aleksander Gasowski," the lawyer said.

Chapter 34

We had Dabrowski call to set up an urgent meeting with Gasowski in Warsaw. "It has to be tonight," Dabrowski insisted, even though this night had few hours left. Gasowski bristled but ultimately acquiesced once Dabrowski told him that his meeting with Talik had gone sideways. And that Gasowski might not get paid.

"What do we do with Mikolaj?" Ana said to me while Marek tied up Dabrowski.

"What's there to do with him?" I said. "I suspect the Pruszkow mob will make your boss's future their first priority. After all, he did murder their boss."

"How will they know?"

"We'll be sure to tell Gasowski. Perhaps pass the information along to Piotr Denys as well."

"Who is Piotr Denys?"

"A former member of the Wołomin mafia. He helped Marek and me find this place. So he helped lead us to you."

"And the child pornography?"

"We'll make sure an anonymous tip gets called in before Dabrowski can make it back to his office. And we'll make sure his arrest makes the headlines. Mikolaj Dabrowski certainly won't have an easy time in prison, considering his offenses."

"I would like to cut off his testicles," Ana said.

"Yes, well. I think we've all seen enough carnage for one day. Besides, we need to reach Gasowski before daybreak. His men will have had a significant head start. But if we find out where they are headed, maybe we can still cut them off."

She looked at my left arm. "This wound is bad. You need to go to hospital."

"It can wait," I said.

"And what about this crime scene? We cannot just leave things like this. There are bodies."

"We have no choice," I said. "We call it in right now and the news will make its way to Gasowski before we reach him."

"But the authorities—"

"Once our meeting with Gasowski is over and we know everything that he knows, then it'll be safe to call it in."

Ana didn't like it, but she did understand.

Marek stepped over to us. "The bastard is all tied up," he said.

Ana and I gazed at the weakened figure on the dirty, bare mattress. His wrists and feet were bound, same as Ana's had been. The same gag stretched across his mouth.

I wondered if I'd ever get that damn image of Ana tied up on a dirty mattress in this basement out of my head, whether I'd ever forgive myself for allowing her to get taken.

I looked into her eyes, allowed myself to imagine what things might have been like if I'd met Ana in a different time and place.

"Right, then," I said finally. "Let's head back to Warsaw, shall we?"

Gasowski insisted Dabrowski meet him at the Kyriad Prestige in Warsaw. No doubt it was a place where Gasowski thought he'd have the upper hand; the hotel was not within the city center, and a quick glance at a map showed us that the location left Gasowski plenty of escape routes. Marek informed us that politicians often used the three-star hotel because of its soundproofed rooms. Such walls could come in handy if Gasowski had decided to use a gun on Dabrowski.

"Let me go alone," I said once we'd reached the hotel. "We need information, and Gasowski's the only source left in all of Poland. Things could get ugly."

"Not a chance," Marek replied. "This bastard betrayed me and delivered my sister into the hands of a monster. I want to see his face as he attempts to justify what he's done."

I turned to Ana. "We'll need you as a lookout." She started to protest but I cut her off. "For all we know, Gasowski's men may be waiting not far off. Trust me, I'd rather have you with us if Marek insists on coming. I don't want to risk having you snatched again. But we need someone to watch our backs. I don't want to step into an ambush. Lindsay Sorkin's life hangs on our survival."

"Very well," she said. "Tell me where you would like me positioned."

With Ana in place in the lobby, Marek and I headed up to the third floor.

"Stand casually three feet away with your back to the door," I said to Marek. "From behind, you can pass for Dabrowski."

Marek positioned himself and I gave the door a light rap. I leaned up against the wall, listening to Gasowski's heavy footfalls as he approached the door. Listened to him twist the lock. I watched the door handle turn. Saw the door inch open, glimpsed the chain at around eye level.

"Dabrowski?" Gasowski said.

I stepped in front of the door, and before Gasowski had time enough to slam it shut, I kicked it in, snapping the chain and knocking the overweight cop to the floor.

I shoved the door open fully and Marek and I stepped inside, Marek closing the door behind us, locking it. I held out my Glock but there was no one else in the room.

"Watch him," I told Marek. "I need to check the toilet."

All clear. There was a small pistol on the table in the far corner of the room near the window, but unless Gasowski was a hell of a lot faster than he looked, the gun wouldn't come into play. The curtains were already closed.

I helped Gasowski to his feet and sat him on one of the two double beds. I smelled vodka on his breath. A near-empty bottle of Chopin stood next to the pistol and a single bullet, along with some hotel stationery and what looked to be an expensive pen.

Gasowski's face was turning green before my eyes. I handed him the small brown plastic wastebasket, thinking he might vomit. He thanked me and set it between his feet.

Marek and I remained standing.

"I'll save you some breath, Chief Inspector," I said, "and tell you what we already know. Your friend Kazmer Chudzik contacted a Turk named Talik Yilmaz through his lawyer, Mikolaj Dabrowski, with whom you are already well acquainted. Chudzik wanted a little girl named Lindsay Sorkin stolen from her parents while they were on holiday in Paris. Talik traveled to Berlin and stayed with his nephew Alim Sari, a heroin dealer in his hometown of Kreuzberg. Alim introduced Talik to two men—Dietrich Braun and Karl Finster—who agreed to travel to Paris to kidnap the girl. Braun and Finster were to take the girl to Hauptbahnhof Station in Berlin and leave her in the third stall of a men's room that was closed for repair. They did. Then someone else retrieved Lindsay Sorkin from that stall and brought her here to Warsaw. Let's start there. Who took her from Berlin and where are they now?"

Gasowski refused to look at either of us, but rather stared intently into the wastebasket.

"If you are standing here," he said slowly, "you probably already killed them."

Marek and I exchanged glances.

"What does that mean?" I said.

"The girl was picked up in Berlin by two of Chudzik's men. They were to go with Chudzik to the meeting today, presumably to kill Dabrowski and the two Turks."

"You're sure of this?"

"Certain," he said. "It was a matter of contention between the parties. Chudzik wanted only Germans to take the girl and escort her from Paris to Berlin, from Berlin to Warsaw. He thought dark men like the Turks would draw too much suspicion and jeopardize the operation, so ultimately Chudzik sent his own men to Berlin. But he wasn't happy about it. He felt the Turks didn't fully deliver so he refused to pay them. Dabrowski, of course, got caught in the middle of it."

"Where did Chudzik's men take the girl?" I said. "Is she still in Poland?"

Gasowski slowly shook his head. "They brought her to the Polish military museum in Warsaw. From there, two of my best officers took her."

"Took her where?"

He shrugged. It was a slight movement but enough to make his entire body sway.

"I do not know precisely where," he said. "They were given their orders directly from Chudzik. We all thought it better I not know where they were going."

"Which country?"

"Ukraine," he said.

Marek spoke up. "Why? To be sold into prostitution?"

Gasowski shrugged again, still refusing to look at us. "I do not think so, Marek. The amount of money that is changing hands, it is far too much to have anything to do with prostitution. Someone who is very wealthy wants this little girl, and whoever it is, wants her very badly."

"Why?" Marek said again. "Why do you think someone wants this particular child?"

"I can only speculate from what I have seen on the television, Marek. Given the price that is being paid for this girl, I would say that it has to do with her father's business. His remote-controlled automatons that could replace soldiers in war. From Ukraine, they can take the girl through southern Russia to Iran, Iraq, Syria. Think what such a design could do for any one of their armies. Hell, with those drones, the Palestinians could retake Gaza."

I thought about it. I was still bothered by the fact that Vince Sorkin hadn't been contacted. But then, it could be that whoever was behind this was waiting until Lindsay was safely at her final destination. The true kidnappers would need complete control over her themselves. Vince would want to talk to his daughter before giving in to anything. He'd demand proof of life.

I glanced at the curtains and realized day was breaking. I'd have to get on the road. I'd have to get to Ukraine as soon as possible. It was a large country, a lot of ground to search.

Marek reached forward and gripped Gasowski's face in one hand. Squeezing his cheeks with enough pressure to break bones, he lifted Gasowski's head until the cop's eyes met his own.

"Why, Aleksander?" Marek said. "Why betray my family?"

Gasowski pulled his face away, the flesh of his cheeks a terrible crimson.

"Money," he said, holding Marek's gaze. "Being from the far left, you may never fully understand this, Marek. But Poland is now a capitalist society."

Marek shook his head, narrowed his tired eyes, and frowned deeply.

"What *you* will never understand, Aleksander, is that people like me, we are fierce supporters of capitalism. It is only greed we despise. Because it is greed that produces monsters the likes of you."

I rested my hand gently on Marek's shoulder and led him away, out of the room. As we stepped into the hallway, I closed the door to Gasowski's room.

"We're just going to leave him here?" Marek protested.

"You saw the table over by the window?" I said.

Heads down, Marek and I slowly made our way back to the elevator bank at the end of the corridor. When we reached the bank, I punched a button and silently we waited.

Some thirty seconds later, a set of elevator doors opened and we stepped inside. I turned and pressed the button for the main lobby. As the elevator doors closed, we heard a report so loud that it felt as though it had emanated from right there in the elevator.

It hadn't, of course.

It had sounded from Aleksander Gasowski's room.

Part Three

THE KILLERS OF KIEV

Chapter 35

Our Air Baltic flight landed at Odessa International Airport just over five hours after taking off from Warsaw. We'd had to leave the motorcycle behind. It would have been a nine-hour drive; over a day by train. We needed to save as much time as we could. And we desperately needed the sleep.

Ana, of course, had insisted on coming with me. Her brother Marek hadn't been able to talk her out of it. I hadn't even tried. By now I was well aware that there was no saying no to the lawyer Anastazja Staszak. I imagined the police and prosecutors of Warsaw trembling on the courthouse steps when in her presence. Were I in their shoes, I knew I certainly would have. She was undoubtedly a formidable opponent in the courtroom, a zealous advocate too familiar with swaying judges and juries in her favor. If I were ever charged with a crime in Poland—a better than-average possibility in my line of work—I wouldn't think twice about from whom to seek counsel. I'd trust my freedom in Ana's capable hands any day of the week. Indeed, I'd trust her with my very life.

Together, Ana and I rushed through the gate as though we were late for a connecting flight. In all of Ukraine, Odessa was the logical place to start. Situated in the south, on the northwest shore of the Black Sea, the city had long been considered a hedonists' playground, a haven for sex tourists and wife hunters, a sanctuary where con artists, drug dealers, and prostitutes could safely ply their respective trades. Moreover, since the collapse of the Soviet Union, Odessa had become a hub for the international sex industry.

The city was a major seaport, a bustling gateway linking the most poverty-stricken parts of Ukraine, Moldova, and Romania to the wealthiest sections of western Europe and the Middle East. Thanks largely to the corruptibility of Odessa's destitute police force, organized crime continued to thrive, particularly among those gangsters engaged in the ever-growing business of sex trafficking. A generation of girls born behind the Iron Curtain—and thus, impoverished and ignorant of the outside world—had become easy prey for entrepreneurial mobsters.

In general, victims no longer had to be abducted or even manipulated, but merely recruited. Indigent teenage girls dreaming of riches were now more than happy to be given free passage to Abu Dhabi or Dubai in order to turn tricks. There was no longer a need for lies or false promises of jobs as waitresses or dancers or fashion models in Paris, London, or Milan; it was enough to say, "Have sex with men for money for a few years and you will return here affluent, covered in gold, diamonds, and furs."

Of course, I was under no illusion: this wasn't what had happened to Lindsay Sorkin. The amount of money involved, the specificity with which she'd been chosen—none of it fit with the usual goings-on in Odessa. But if Lindsay had indeed been taken to Ukraine, as Gasowski had assured us, chances were she was moving through the network that was already in place here.

Outside the airport, we hopped into a taxi, which took us straight to the Mozart Hotel. After what had transpired at the guesthouse in Krakow, Ana had generously permitted me to select the accommodations. The Mozart was a luxury establishment with forty rooms, all individually decorated with elegant European furnishings. As our taxi pulled up to the hotel, I watched Ana gaze longingly at the Opera and Ballet Theatre just across the street.

I checked us in. This time, one room with two beds. Given every-thing that had occurred in Poland, we weren't taking any more chances with respect to security. In Ukraine we'd be sticking to-gether whenever we could.

"So, what is the plan, Simon?" Ana said when we were finally alone in the room.

"Once night falls we'll head to the city center and explore some of the clubs. I suppose I'll pose as a john, see if I can find someone will-ing to introduce me to some girls. Maybe I can get one of the girls to talk."

Ana folded her arms and frowned. "Really?" she said. "You are going to start at the very bottom? Talking to a teenage girl who has no doubt been heavily dosed with heroin and who is unquestionably afraid for her life?"

"Do you have a better idea?"

"Of course," she said. "And I am sure you have already consid-ered it but your chivalry will not permit you to share it."

I sat on one of the beds and folded my hands in my lap. I indeed knew what she was going to suggest, and I agreed that it was the smartest course of action. Still, it would be terribly dangerous. I couldn't allow Ana to put herself in harm's way like that; not again. This was my job. Any way you looked at it, I'd chosen this life fol-lowing Hailey's disappearance. If not for my recovering the boy in Bordeaux, neither of us would have been sitting here in a hotel room in Odessa, contemplating how best to infiltrate an organiza-tion devoted to human trafficking. Ana was a volunteer, helping me purely out of her generosity. If anyone had to take the serious risks, it was I.

"Well?" she prodded.

"Impossible," I said. "For the very reasons you yourself just pointed out. They drug the girls, or at the very least expect them to drug themselves. And the girls are scared for their lives for good reason, Ana. These are ruthless men we're going to be dealing with."

She glared at me. "And Chudzik's men were not?"

I rose off the bed. "*You* insisted on coming with me to Pruszkow. I never meant to put you in danger of being kidnapped."

Taking a step toward me, she said softly, "I know that, Simon. We were not prepared for that. We had not properly planned. For this, we will be ready. We will make sure you know where I am at all times." She wrapped her arms around my neck and gazed into my eyes. "If things get too hot, you can save me. And you will not have to run around an entire country looking for me to do so."

Looking into her eyes was like gazing into the calm Caribbean Sea. All the tension flowed out of me.

"It's too dangerous," I said softly.

"I cannot think of a better reason to put my life in danger than to save the life of an innocent little girl, Simon."

She was right, of course. People risked their lives for all sorts of senseless reasons. For sport, for instance. To get home under one's own volition following a night of serious drinking. The wealthier among us often put themselves under the knife for things as silly as a smaller nose, larger breasts, or, worst of all, a tighter tummy, while people all over the globe were starving to death. I flashed on my father ascending mountains, attempting to convince me of how noble it all was.

I thought, *What's more noble than trying to rescue an imperiled child?*

"All right, then," I said. "We'll—"

Suddenly, Ana's lips were on mine, her tongue probing my mouth with a hunger I hadn't known since my first months with Tasha in college. This time, the mere thought of turning her away was physically painful, and I quickly rid my head of it, allowed myself to savor her flesh without that unfounded sense of guilt that creeps into too many of us. I wanted her and I'd be damned if I was going to deny myself again.

In a tangle, we dropped onto the bed, our hands clawing at each other's clothes as though our very existence depended on our being undressed, on our melding our bodies together as one.

Over the next thirty minutes all the fear I knew would melt away, and the past would cave in on itself. For a time it would be as though all the troubles of this world had never truly existed, that they'd been figments of our imagination. For one half hour, there would be no danger to consider, no horror. There would be no war. No violence.

For the next half hour, I would be perfectly at peace.

It wouldn't last, of course; I knew that.

Neither sex nor peace ever did.

Chapter 36

Ana dressed herself in peasant clothes from a local thrift shop and worked for nearly an hour on her background story, talking it out with me in our hotel room. She would pose as an unemployed seamstress from Bialystok, the capital city of one of the poorest regions of Poland. Bialystok, which was located in the eastern part of the country, not far from the Belarusian border, was currently cursed with an unemployment rate of nearly 40 percent, and those unskilled laborers fortunate enough to have jobs took home roughly $180 per month. Ana subtracted ten years from her true age, then turned to me and asked if she'd pass, and without a second's hesitation I said, "Yes, of course," and it was true.

"One problem," I said, when she stepped out of the bathroom in her peasant clothes. "Dressed like that, you won't get into the clubs we'll need to go to in order to find our way to a pimp."

She looked down at her thin cotton beige blouse with matching skirt, then tore off a large piece of fabric that hung over her midriff and another that covered her legs to the knees. She spun, showing off her exposed belly and back, her perfect bare thighs.

"You do not think so?" she said.

"I stand corrected."

As for me, I finally traded the bloodstained turtleneck, peacoat, and jeans for one of the suits Davignon had procured for me in

Paris. The suit had just been pressed, courtesy of the Mozart Hotel. While my own exposed stomach might get me into Shede, one of Ukraine's most popular openly gay nightclubs, it wouldn't gain me entry to Palladium, which was where we would need to start at this time of year. Had it been summer, the action would have been at Arkadia Beach, where two colossal Ibiza-style nightclubs were packed to overflowing seven nights a week. But with Ukraine's current biting temperatures, the crowds moved inland, closer to Odessa's city center.

We waited until nightfall, then took separate taxis downtown. It was imperative that no one in or near the nightclub noticed Ana and me together. One minor slip could easily get both of us killed. I was especially concerned for Ana; in fact, I could hardly stop thinking of her.

I entered the club first. It was just after 11:00 P.M. and there was a show being performed on the stage. A half-dozen half-naked women and a single half-naked man moved to pulse-pounding house music in front of an immense screen displaying quick cuts of Ukrainian words and psychedelic images. Palladium was brimming with sexual energy, with both the chemical and mind state of Ecstasy, with all levels and constructs of debauchery.

It wasn't my scene, of course. Having aspired to become a federal agent from a young age, I hadn't dared experiment with illegal substances as a teenager. And I'd married Tasha straight out of college, so I'd never really experienced the singles scene. Thanks to work, I'd been in my share of bars and clubs around the world, but searching for kidnappers or deadly armed fugitives was one sure way to put a damper on an evening.

As the whole of my body tingled with adrenaline, I surreptitiously watched the entrance for Ana's arrival. I'd already spotted several men who fit the successful eastern-European mobster mold—flashy cashmere suit; silk shirt with no tie, the top few buttons undone, revealing multiple necklaces nearly lost in a jungle of chest hair; a gold Rolex, rings on at least three fingers; shoes so shiny they'd blind you in sunlight; and the clincher, prison tattoos covering almost every inch of the hands and neck.

When Ana sauntered in, she turned heads, just as I'd expected. For the briefest of moments our eyes locked on each other's from across the club, then she turned and vanished into the sea of sweating bodies on the dance floor.

I moved down the length of the bar, pausing once to order a glass of Glenlivet on the rocks. If you didn't drink in social settings in Ukraine, Ana had told me, you were regarded with suspicion, as someone who couldn't be trusted. So, scotch in hand, I continued along the bar until I spotted Ana gyrating on the dance floor. Just watching her move was a complete aphrodisiac, and as much I hated to admit it, a pang of jealousy struck me deep in the gut every time I saw another man place his hands on her.

I did what I could to remain inconspicuous, talked to a few women, flirted, bought each a drink or two. My background story was much less elaborate than Ana's. I was a bar owner from Brooklyn, here in Ukraine on holiday; exploring Odessa's nightlife would allow me to enumerate the costs as a tax write-off. "That damn Uncle Sam," I joked more than once.

After a solid hour and a half, I saw Ana move toward the bar with a man in tow. He was dressed well, but not flashy, and for a moment I wondered what the hell Ana was doing. But as per our plan, she picked a spot at the bar immediately next to where I was standing. I turned the other way, put my rocks glass to my lips, and prepared myself to eavesdrop.

I heard Ana call the man Pavlo, and made a mental note. I listened to her deliver her background and was particularly amused when she improvised, adding an absent father, a sick mother, and a paraplegic brother with two kids. She often had to have sex with her terribly overweight landlord in lieu of rent, she told him.

And there, I realized, was her segue.

"Well," Pavlo said loudly in broken English, "you enjoy certain physical attributes that should make money not so much of an issue, I would think."

"Really?" she said, as though relishing the compliment.

"I am being dead honest," he told her. "Your landlord is not the only man who would forgive your debts just for a taste of you."

"Unfortunately," Ana said coyly, "the grocer does not accept blow jobs in exchange for fresh fruits and vegetables, and the baker no longer welcomes hand jobs for bread."

"How about the plumber?" Pavlo said, laughing raucously. "Surely, he enjoys laying pipe."

Ana joined in with a forced chuckle. "You are too funny, Pavlo."

"But in all seriousness," he said, "if you are willing to trade your services for money, I can introduce you to the right people. Just say the word."

Ana jumped at the opportunity. "Consider it said. As long as I can send money home to my family. I cannot simply abandon them. Especially my disabled brother and his two kids."

"Of course you can send money back to Bialystok. Sending money home is what most of the girls do." Pavlo motioned to the bartender. "Two Nemiroff martinis, *proshu.*" Turning back to Ana, he said, "Let's enjoy a drink and then I will take you to meet my friend Marko."

"That's sounds perfect," Ana said over the music. "Really, I do not how to thank you."

"I know a way," Pavlo said with an unmistakable snigger. "Later tonight, my dear, you can allow me to sample the goods."

I closed my eyes and took a swallow of scotch and reminded myself that deep down I was really a man of nonviolence.

Chapter 37

Follow that black ZAZ," I said from the rear of a taxi. "The vehicle that man and woman just stepped into."

I sighed deeply and leaned back in my seat, wishing I still had the motorcycle. I didn't want to lose sight of Pavlo's car even for a second. The plan was for Ana to text me once they reached Marko's location, or before, if there was any trouble. But any number of things could go wrong. Pavlo could stop the car and take Ana's phone away before she had a chance to use it. She could lose her signal. Her battery could die.

I removed my mobile from my pocket, checked the battery and the signal; both were fine. So I took the opportunity to call Ostermann's number in Berlin, but there was no answer. Next I called Lieutenant Davignon in Paris.

"Simon," he said the moment he answered. "What in the hell is happening in Poland? The lawyer Mikolaj Dabrowski is all over the news. He is apparently being questioned in connection with a shootout at his client's house in Pomerania. The client, they are saying, is some notorious gangster named Chudzik who was recently acquitted in a racketeering trial. Is this the man behind Lindsay Sorkin's kidnapping?"

"I'm sorry, Lieutenant, but I don't have time to fully explain. Suffice it to say that I had a chat with Dabrowski, who led me to a corrupt chief inspector in Warsaw named Aleksander Gasowski."

"Why does that name sound so familiar?"

"If you've been tuned in to the Polish news, you no doubt heard it mentioned during the broadcasts. Gasowski blew his brains out at the Kyriad Prestige in Warsaw. But not before he admitted to his role in Lindsay Sorkin's abduction. Two of Gasowski's officers picked the girl up from the Polish military museum after two of Chudzik's men delivered her there."

"Chudzik the gangster?"

"Precisely," I said. "Chudzik's men had retrieved her from the men's room at Hauptbahnhof Station in Berlin, where Dietrich Braun and Karl Finster had dropped her off after taking her from Paris."

"Wait a minute, Simon." Davignon lowered his voice, presumably so that Vince and Lori Sorkin wouldn't hear. "So, you are telling me that the girl is now with the police in Poland?"

"Not exactly," I said. "Before Gasowski committed suicide he said that Chudzik had ordered his men to deliver her somewhere in Ukraine. That's where I am now."

"You are in *Ukraine*?"

"Odessa, to be exact. Gasowski didn't know which city in Ukraine, or even which region. He was kept in the dark just in case someone like me got to him."

In the background I heard a woman's voice repeating a statement in French; it sounded as though it was coming from a loudspeaker.

"What is that?" I said. "Where are you?"

Davignon sighed. "We are in hospital, I am afraid. Lori Sorkin collapsed in the elevator of the hotel. No word yet from her doctors. My fear right now is that she suffered a miscarriage."

Life is like dominoes, I thought. *Once one tile falls . . .*

Once Hailey went missing, I lost Tasha, then slowly Tasha's parents and brother as well, who'd become a surrogate family to me over the years. I couldn't fault them for distancing themselves from me, of course. Seeing me was too painful. I was a glaring reminder of all they'd lost. A daughter. A granddaughter. A sister, a niece.

Trying to forget was a defense mechanism I understood too well. Hell, even years after the incident I couldn't drive past the parks Hailey had played in, couldn't shop in the grocery stores Tasha had favored. I certainly couldn't live in our house.

"Which reminds me," Davignon said. "We haven't been able to get in touch with Keith Richter."

"Keith Richter?"

"Lindsay's pediatrician back in the States. We get only an answering service, and no one returns our calls. Apparently the doctor is on vacation this week. But we were able to track down a hospital that drew Lindsay's blood. Santa Clara Valley Medical Center. Where Lindsay received her stitches as a toddler. The medical-records department is faxing over her lab report, which will contain her blood type and anything else you may require."

I hoped I wouldn't require anything more than the photo I had of Lindsay Sorkin smiling.

Through the windshield of the taxi I saw Pavlo's ZAZ make a sharp right turn.

"I need to leave you for now, Lieutenant. I'll call you with an update as soon as I can."

I ended the call and shouted, "Make that right!" to the driver.

Our tires squealed as we turned nearly ninety degrees onto a narrow roadway. I could almost sense Pavlo staring into the rearview. Did he know he was being followed? Had Ana somehow tipped her hand? Was she already in grave danger and unable to contact me?

Sure enough, seconds later, the ZAZ accelerated. The car shot into the wrong lane and passed several slower-moving vehicles before kicking back into the right just in time to avoid an oncoming SUV. Horns blared all around.

Within sixty seconds, the black ZAZ was entirely out of sight.

Chapter 38

We crawled the streets of Odessa for a solid hour, the taxi's meter running up like the National Debt Clock on Manhattan's Sixth Avenue. I despised myself for having made such an egregious error with so much at stake. I'd never thought of myself as reckless, but that's exactly what I was. In attempting to locate Lindsay, I'd gotten Ostermann arrested and Ana kidnapped, now possibly killed.

I glanced at my watch. I saw no choice but to start from the beginning, to enter a club and spark up some conversations, to find someone who knew Pavlo, to learn where he might have taken Ana.

Just as I was about to instruct the driver to return me to Palladium, my mobile finally chirped in my lap. It was a text message from Ana: CHILLAX HOSTEL NEAR BLACK SEA.

I immediately leaned forward and gave the location to the driver.

"No good," he said in battered English. "That place, it close down two years in the past."

"But you know where it is," I said.

"Yes. I am taxi driver eighteen years."

"Good," I said, passing forward a couple five-hundred-hryvnia banknotes to keep him interested. "Then take me to it."

At the next intersection, the driver made a precarious U-turn and headed toward the Black Sea at an acceptable rate of speed.

Learning that the hostel had closed was unsettling, made me even more uneasy. Ana was alone in an abandoned building with Pavlo and Marko and whoever the hell else might be there. I continued to loathe myself for moving forward with this plan when I'd had so many reservations. I was more than willing to trade my life for the chance of finding Lindsay alive, but I had no business at all risking Ana's. She was a lawyer. This wasn't her fight; it was mine.

We arrived only minutes later. I'd instructed the driver to announce when we were near, and when he did, I asked him to extinguish the headlights. A block away, I ordered him to pull over and let me out. I paid the remainder of the enormous fare and exited the taxi, softly shutting the door behind me.

I'd considered asking the driver to stay in case we needed to get out of the area quickly, but I didn't want to risk someone's hearing an idling engine or seeing a taxi driver sitting alone in the dark. Nothing that might tip these guys off, send them on the run.

Chillax was a two-story structure shaped like a box, surrounded by buildings most likely condemned. The entire block was as silent as the dead, the hostel sitting like a sentinel on the corner. No lights were visible from where I stood.

Hostels are the poor man's motels, places where backpackers can grab an empty cot on the cheap. They are most frequented by the young, including spoiled American kids traveling on their parents' dime but choosing to spend their spending money not on four-star hotels but on liquor and drugs. For some, backpacking through Europe is an initiation into adulthood; for others, it's one last hurrah before settling into serious study at an Ivy League college.

At seventeen, I begged my father for the opportunity to backpack through Europe. He promptly and vehemently said he'd have none of it. From the day we arrived in Providence, my father had done everything he could to keep from flying across the Atlantic. That, I had always thought, was the real reason I had requested a transfer to international investigations when I was with the U.S.

Marshals. Not to run away from my wife and child, as Alden Fisk had.

The closer I got to the abandoned hostel, the darker it seemed to get. The Eli Roth film I'd caught on pay-per-view in a Stockholm hotel room a few years earlier crept into my mind. I was pretty sure *Hostel* had been set in Slovakia but right now that provided little comfort. Who knew what hell was waiting for me inside this building. But then, who knew what hell Ana would suffer if I hesitated even another minute.

At the back of the building I climbed a six-foot fence, the metal pulling at the delicate threads of my jacket and pants as I leaped over the top. I hoped Davignon wasn't expecting the suits back once I finally returned to Paris.

The rear entrance appeared to be locked up tight, a padlock and chains crisscrossing the doorway like a birthday present with an unpleasant bow. I didn't carry a set of bolt cutters on my person, so entering through this door without making a racket would make for one hell of a trick. I was sure it wasn't possible.

Which left me only the windows and an imagination operating on little sleep.

There were no windows on the bottom floor so I looked up. The windows on the second floor were boarded up. If there was no glass behind them, that would work wholly to my advantage as far as noise went. Unfortunately, it also meant that I wouldn't be able to see in. So, while I was prying off the boards, someone on the other side could be waiting for me with a machete.

All right, I thought. *Definitely time to remove all horror-movie memories from my mind.*

Scaling the wall didn't look like it would present too much of a problem. The building was made of brick and there were unintentional handholds and footholds just about everywhere I looked. I chose the path of least resistance, drew a breath, and started up.

Of course, everything is much more difficult to do in a suit and dress shoes. And climbing the brick wall of a hostel proved no exception. The soles of my shoes slipped on nearly every brick and my fingers were almost immediately covered in nasty cuts. My lungs burned like hell and my left forearm ached, but I continued up, trying futilely to extinguish the height-induced panic gripping my gut.

Once I reached the second floor, I balanced myself on a ledge and surveyed the boards. Plywood, I guessed. Attached to the window frames with thick nine-inch nails. The wood looked weather-beaten and would probably collapse under the strength of a good, solid kick. Gaining leverage to make such a kick, however, was an entirely different story. My best shot would be to rip the plywood from the frame in a single move, then hurl myself through the window, land with a shoulder tumble, and come up raising my Glock.

Only this wasn't an action movie, either. And I sure as hell wasn't Jason Statham. But I'd seen enough of his films to give it a go.

Chapter 39

I t wasn't the most graceful entrance ever made, but it certainly served its purpose: I was inside. I'd hit a bit of luck as well. Not only was there no one in the room I'd hurled myself into, but the door was closed, and it seemed unlikely that anyone had heard me enter. The room was empty except for two sets of bunk beds with bare, badly stained mattresses. Briefly I thought of Ana, bound and gagged on that filthy mattress in Chudzik's basement, and I began to seethe. Finally, I made for the door, opened it slightly, and peered out into the dark hall. I didn't see anyone, but I did hear some mumbled conversation, which seemed to be coming from the first floor.

Quietly, I hurried to a stairwell at the end of the hall. I pushed open the door, winced at the slight squeak, and squeezed through as small an opening as I could. I had switched off the ringer on my BlackBerry, clicked off the safety on my Glock. I was as ready as I'd ever be to head down the steps.

The closer I came to the first floor, the better I heard the conversation. By the time I reached the bottom, it was as if they were speaking right to me. A sliver of light peeked through. I looked down and noticed that the door was wedged open a crack with an old aluminum beer can.

I risked a quick peek. The door opened onto a large sitting room, possibly the hostel's main lobby. Two large sofas—the kind you'd find in the common room of a college dormitory—faced each other in the center of the space and were surrounded by several beat-up chairs. From my vantage point I could see Ana and Pavlo seated next to each other, she leaning into him, he with his arm around her shoulders, his lips dangerously close to her left ear.

Holding my Glock at the ready, I pressed up against the door and listened intently. I heard Pavlo's voice first.

"Come on, Ana. Listen to Marko. He has been in this business a long time. He knows what he is talking about."

Ana said, "But Marko cannot even assure me which country I will be sent to. What if I end up somewhere I do not wish to be?"

"Ana, Ana," said the man I assumed was Marko, "what did I tell you before? The most beautiful girls are taken to the most beautiful cities. And you are one of the most beautiful girls to walk through these doors. I have a customer driving in later tonight to pick up two girls for three months in Antalya; it is a wonderful city on the Mediterranean coast of southwestern Turkey. You will love it there. Three hundred days of each year are sunny. *Three hundred.* I guarantee, if we get you down to the pickup spot in time tonight, you will be one of the two selected."

"Antalya," Pavlo said with the same obnoxious laugh I'd heard at the club, "it even goes well with your name."

"And what about the police?" Ana said. "I do not want to get into any trouble."

Marko and Pavlo laughed simultaneously.

Marko said, "The Ukrainian police? Are you kidding me? You will see a police cruiser drive up to the beach tonight. The police will be there for one reason and one reason only. To collect their money."

"It is feeding time for the police," Pavlo added. "Like pigs at the trough."

More dirty cops. No surprise there, or anywhere else in the former Soviet Union for that matter. Organized crime and law enforcement enjoyed a parasitic relationship in the former communist states, with organized crime constantly growing into a bigger, tastier host.

"And once you arrive at your destination," Marko said, "you will have no worries at all. You will work in the lobbies and at the poolsides of some of the world's most luxurious resorts. And these resorts, not only will they not shoo you away like flies, but they will lure you with honey like bees. These resorts, they *need* you there. *You* are why businessmen make reservations and continue to return year after year after year."

"So you are saying, I will not be walking the streets like some common call girl?"

"Who knows what the future holds?" Marko said. "Who cares? After three months in Antalya, you may become homesick or feel like you have enough money to live off of for the next ten years, and decide to return to Bialystok covered in priceless jewels. Or you may get deported and then return here, ask to be shipped out again. You may find yourself on the streets of Paris or Madrid or Dublin. Is that so bad? Wherever you go, I promise your presence will be more than welcome, and you will make more money than you ever dreamed of."

"Marko speaks the truth," Pavlo said.

"Now come, Ana," Marko said. "We have to get to the beach before my customer arrives. There will be at least two dozen girls there for the competition. But don't be intimidated; you will be the prettiest girl there."

"All right," Ana said. "Let me just use the restroom before—"

"There is no time right now," Marko said. "Let's go. You can pee when we arrive at the beach." He paused. "Pavlo, thank you for the recruit. I have called Yuri and he is sending two girls here as your commission. Spend as much time as you would like with them. Just return them in the same condition in which you received them, or you will have Yuri to answer to."

"I can use one of the rooms downstairs?" Pavlo said.

"No," Marko replied. "Use only the rooms upstairs. The rooms on this floor are where Yuri likes to break in new girls, and if he discovers that you put your dirty ass on his sheets, you will end up in hell with his cousin Osip."

I heard two sets of feet walking away—no doubt Marko's and Ana's—and one set of feet coming toward me. I had a decision to make. Pull the gun on Marko now, before he could leave, or wait and follow him and Ana to the beach. To the other girls. To the customer. And quite possibly to Yuri.

I heard the front door open and close, then I felt pressure against the door I was leaning up against. I let the door give a bit, let Pavlo take a step or two in, then used my shoulder to crush him between the door and the doorframe.

Pavlo let out a scream and I promptly covered his mouth, hoping that Marko hadn't heard the commotion. My worries were quelled when I heard an engine start up and a vehicle quickly peel away.

I slapped Pavlo's face so that he wouldn't pass out from the pain. From the way he was breathing, I guessed he had a few broken ribs. I hoped none had punctured his lungs.

Not because I gave a damn what happened to him, really.

But because I needed to know precisely where Marko was taking Ana.

This time, I had no intention of waiting on a text.

Chapter 40

Pavlo was kind enough to lend me the keys to his vehicle. He was fading into unconsciousness at the time, but I was sure I detected a bob of the head when I queried. Fortunately, Pavlo's ZAZ was equipped with a GPS. Unfortunately, the female voice spoke to me in Ukrainian. I didn't have time to tinker with the device to determine whether I could switch the setting to English, so instead, I ripped the GPS off the dash and tossed it onto the backseat so that it wouldn't distract me. From studying maps of Odessa back at the Mozart Hotel, I had a general idea of where I was heading: to a port off an unnamed beach on the Black Sea.

The spot was less than a ten-minute drive from the hostel, and when I saw it I realized Pavlo had been right in that the scene was unmistakable. Thirty or so stick-thin women, none older than her midtwenties, stood in a crowd on a pier next to a sizable boat. Despite the frigid air, none of the girls wore more than a thin dress. All their midriffs and legs were exposed. Each of the girls rocked gently in absurdly high heels and carried a smoke. I searched the crowd for Ana but couldn't find her at first. Finally, after a few minutes, I spotted her off to the side, speaking with two other women, both of whom appeared to be teenagers.

I didn't see any men at all and assumed Marko was on the boat.

From the looks of things, it became pretty clear that was where I needed to be. These girls would be able to tell Ana only so much. I needed to speak to Marko. And, I hoped, to Yuri himself.

I parked Pavlo's ZAZ well out of sight. I double-checked my Glock, then exited the vehicle and started toward the pier. I stopped when a pair of headlights came into view.

I ducked behind another car and peeked through its side windows. The headlights were coming from a police cruiser, with two cops sitting in the front seat. They shone a large spotlight directly into the crowd of girls, but the girls didn't seem the least bit perturbed. In fact, many of them appeared to be posing in the glare of the spotlight.

A lone woman who'd been standing at the edge of the crowd sauntered to the cruiser. She looked slightly older than the others. When she reached the vehicle, the driver's-side window glided down. She leaned in, spoke to one of the officers, then clearly passed something off to him. I couldn't quite make out what it was, but I had little doubt that it was an envelope filled with cash. Just as Marko and Pavlo had suggested back at the hostel.

It's feeding time for the police, Pavlo had said. *Like pigs at the trough.*

Apparently satisfied, the officers extinguished their spotlight, rolled up their window, and slowly moved on.

I edged forward behind the row of cars. Less than two minutes passed before another set of headlights appeared. A new black Lincoln Town Car rolled to a stop before the crowd of girls. Unlike the police cruiser, this car garnered a significant reaction. The girls swarmed into the beams of light and exhibited their bodies with all the intensity of the dancers onstage at Palladium.

The windows of the Town Car were tinted, but that didn't prevent a few of the girls from flocking to the sides of the vehicle, some lowering their tops, some raising their skirts, no doubt in the hopes of being chosen by whomever was seated in the backseat, leering out.

Finally, the woman who had presented the envelope to the police pushed her way through the throng. When she reached the rear window on the driver's side, the glass glided down, and I saw a dark man in a gray suit and sunglasses greet her.

Negotiations were about to commence.

With everyone distracted, this was my chance to get aboard the boat. There was little cover except for darkness but that darkness was nearly complete. A sliver of moon sat high in the sky, throwing off little illumination on the starless night. Between that and my black suit, grass and sand to muffle my footfalls, I was pretty damn certain I'd make it just fine. If I was spotted, I'd duck behind the nearby retaining wall and ready myself for a firefight.

The boat was approximately sixty feet in length, with no one on the deck providing security. There had been no one watching the hostel, either, as far as I could tell. These men were either brazen or stupid or legitimately had little to fear. If I'd been a betting man, I'd have put my money on the latter.

Once I was aboard the boat, I glanced out at the crowd of girls. They continued to flaunt themselves in front of the Town Car, so I assumed the customer hadn't yet made his selection as to who would accompany him to Antalya. Ana remained on the fringes, clearly not putting forward her best effort to be chosen.

I headed down the stairs to the cabin, my weapon drawn. There were lights on inside the cabin, the voices of carefree men carrying through the door. I pressed up against the door and listened. Surprisingly, I heard only two voices. I tried, but couldn't make out what they were saying.

I gave it a minute, then twisted the knob and it turned. For a moment I feared that the boat didn't have anything at all to do with the sex-trafficking operation—that I was about to walk in and point a Glock at a pair of retirees from Bulgaria exploring the Black Sea.

But when I pushed the door open, I found two well-dressed men in their midthirties, staring back at me. They barely reacted at all.

I said, "Marko and Yuri, I presume."

"I am Yuri Bobrovnyk," said the blond man seated to the left. He pointed to the dark-haired man seated to the right. "This is Marko Dyachenko." He lifted a brandy snifter and took a sip. "And you are?"

"I'm the man looking for Lindsay Sorkin," I said. "The six-year-old girl abducted from her parents' hotel room in Paris six days ago and dragged across the European continent by thieves and lawyers and gangsters and police."

Marko chuckled. "That sounds a bit redundant. I do not see much difference between those four groups, do you, Yuri?"

Yuri smiled, shrugged. "I could not pick one or the other out of a lineup." He looked up at me. "Would you mind not pointing that gun on me? I assure you it is not necessary. I am unarmed." He turned to Marko. "Are you armed?"

Marko shook his head. "I am not armed."

"He is not armed either," Yuri said in his thick Ukrainian accent. "See? Neither of us is armed. We present no threat."

I lowered the Glock a few inches, pointed it at the floor between them, ready to raise it if I glimpsed any sudden movement. I stood at an angle so that I could see if anyone was about to descend the stairs to the cabin.

"Thank you," Yuri said. He had a smooth, clean-shaven face with a dimpled chin. "Now, how can we help you, Mr. Guy with the Gun?"

"Where's the little girl?"

"Why do you think we would know this?"

"You're a sex trafficker," I said. "You peddle women."

"Exactly," Yuri said. "Women, not children. Tell me, Mr. Guy with the Gun, who wants little girls? Sickos, perverts. Why would I risk my business, destroy my reputation to deal with such deviants? The customers who pay me hundreds of thousands of euros to ship my women abroad would shop elsewhere. The police I pay off would stop protecting me. Some crazy man with a gun, someone like you, looking for his daughter or niece, would come onto my boat and blow my fucking head off. Why would I want that, tell me."

"So," I said, "you expect me to believe that if I went out there right now and talked to those young girls, I would hear nothing but good things about you and your operation. Is that right?"

"No," Yuri said, setting his snifter down on a coffee table. "The girls who were not selected this evening will be very disappointed that they are not going to Antalya. Many of them stood out there in the freezing cold for several hours dressed in practically nothing, hoping to impress my customer. If you survey those girls tonight, most will probably express very little job satisfaction. But that goes for most businesses, no?"

"Most businesses don't drug their employees," I said, "or use violence when they don't do as they're told."

"Drugs?" Yuri said with a laugh. Marko joined him. They looked like two partners who'd recently started a successful dot-com and were now basking in all its glory. "You think I provide these women with drugs? Heroin, cocaine, oxy, it is all expensive. Let them buy their own fucking drugs. I offer no health plan. As for violence, if I was prone to violence, right now I would cut out your tongue. My mother did not raise me to strike women. Never in my life would I harm one of these girls."

"How about men, then?" I said. "How about your cousin Osip?"

"Osip?" Yuri said, puzzled. "You know my cousin?"

"Holy shit," Marko said to me. "You were listening in on our conversation at the hostel."

"My cousin Osip," Yuri continued, "is in Moldova recruiting women."

"Not according to your buddy Marko here," I said. "According to Marko, Osip's rotting in hell."

Marko smiled broadly. "What do you think Moldova is? Heaven?"

Yuri said, "My cousin Osip is a fuck-up. He screwed around with too many girls, passed around the crabs. So I sent him to Moldova. According to a study I read in a magazine, it is the unhappiest place on earth."

"Actually, it was in a book," Marko corrected him.

Yuri nodded. "Oh, yes. A book. What was it called?"

"*The Geography of Bliss.*" Marko turned to me. "Amazon. Currently under ten dollars U.S."

Yuri didn't bother with any threats, just asked that if I had any further questions about his business I contact him beforehand to set up an appointment. I had half a mind to pistol-whip the two of them and drop them overboard just to see how well they could swim.

Once I stepped off the boat, I turned the ringer to my Black-Berry back on. A few moments later, I spotted Ana. The crowd had thinned, but there were still a few girls left, smoking and engaging in conversation, perhaps waiting for another Town Car to arrive. Ana stood with two other girls, both thin as rails and scantily dressed. When she noticed me, Ana motioned me over.

"This is Mariya, and this is Lavra," Ana said by way of introduction. "Girls, this is my friend Simon."

"Pleased to meet you," I told them, then turned to Ana. "I'm sorry, but we have to get going."

"I understand." Ana reached into my front pants pocket and removed a small wad of hryvni. She divided them equally and handed one half to Mariya and one half to Lavra. To me, she said, "I promise to pay you back."

"No worries," I told her.

The girls thanked us and kissed both of us on both cheeks before stumbling away.

"I know those girls will spend that money on drugs but I couldn't help myself," Ana said as we walked through what was left of the pack.

As we passed them, I glimpsed each girl's pale, skeletal face, and I felt as though I were looking at the walking dead. Some of them appeared no older than sixteen.

Sixteen, I thought. *Sweet sixteen. Hailey's sixteen. Would be sixteen.*

I looked into the eyes of a brunette who appeared to be from the West, and I was rocked by a sudden certainty that I was looking into the face of my only child. The resemblance was too striking for it not to be her.

"Hailey?" I whispered.

The girl looked at me oddly, then muttered something in Russian and turned away.

Ana must have heard me. She placed a cool palm on my cheek and guided my face down to hers.

"Simon," she said softly.

For a moment the images in my head froze in place. If asked where I was or what I was doing there, I wouldn't have been able to answer. I'd have drawn a complete blank.

Finally, Ana nudged me forward. "These girls, they are all volunteers," she said sadly. "Simon, I am afraid we have hit a dead end."

My head turned back to the brunette, almost of its own accord, and my eyes followed her as she made her way up the beach's incline to the street.

I continued watching her as she staggered to a waiting car. I was mesmerized, in a complete trance, my thoughts floating back a decade to Georgetown, Washington, D.C., to holding Hailey in my arms while she unwrapped presents on Christmas Eve.

Then a chirping noise smacked me like cold water in the face and returned me to the present. I looked at Ana, lost myself in her eyes again.

"Answer it," she said, obviously still concerned about me. "It is your phone."

Chapter 41

An hour later, Ana and I were on an overnight train heading north to Kiev, the country's capital. The call I'd received was from Ana's brother, Marek Staszak, back in Warsaw. He said he wasn't about to leave Lindsay Sorkin's fate in the hands of the Polish police. So, after Ana and I had left for Ukraine, he had returned to Mikolaj Dabrowski's office with a private investigator and seized the lawyer's desktop computer. He and the investigator then took the hard drive to a private company that handled the extraction of encrypted data and personally waited in their office for the final results.

The experts determined from where the images on Dabrowski's computer originated, and Marek thought it more than a mere coincidence that most of the obscene material came from a so-called children's modeling agency based in Kiev. Known as Ukrainian Darlings Studios, the alleged agency posted photos and sold images using several domains on the Internet, including UD Models, UD Dreams, UD Holidays, UD Magazine, and UD Island, among others.

Once he gathered this information, Marek contacted a close friend in the Senate, the upper house of Polish parliament. His friend had widespread connections that included the deputy head of the Criminal Investigation Department of the Ministry of the Interior in Ukraine. The deputy head quietly confirmed that there was an ongoing investigation involving both the Ukrainian authorities and Interpol. The modeling agency was indeed a front for a hard-core child-pornography ring that had been in operation roughly seven years. More than eighteen hundred girls and boys between the ages of eight and sixteen had allegedly visited the agency voluntarily, though it was clear that the images sold on some of the UD sites depicted children as young as four.

No raids had yet been conducted and none was expected for several months, so authorities had ample time to use surveillance and other techniques to acquire evidence that would result in an airtight case. There was also the issue of rounding up as many users of the sites as possible. The users ranged in age from twenty-two to seventy-eight and spanned at least forty-two countries.

"Who is the leader of this agency?" I had asked Marek after he provided me a location. "I need a name."

"I can give you two names, Simon. They are brothers. Dmitry and Viktor Podrova of Lviv. At least one of them is thought to be running the day-to-day operations in Kiev."

Now, as the train rumbled along the flat Ukrainian countryside, Ana dozed with her head on my shoulder. We had a first-class sleeper compartment for two, yet we hadn't moved to the bed. Wired on espresso, I stared absently out the window at pitch-black fields and thought of the girl at the beach who had resembled Hailey.

You're out of your mind, Simon. How the hell would you even know what Hailey looked like today? You can barely picture her as a child anymore. You constantly need to pull the photo of her and Tasha from your wallet, or else you'll risk losing the faces of both forever.

I turned my head for just a second, and when I did, I could have sworn I saw someone's face, a man staring into our compartment.

Just a trick of the imagination, Fisk. You're tired, possibly hallucinating. You should go to bed, get some sleep.

But I knew I wouldn't get any sleep tonight. My adrenaline was pumping, my blood running too hot. I felt as though Odessa had been a big waste of precious time—Lindsay's precious time.

The kidnappers consistently remained one step ahead of me, and I knew that if this game of cat and mouse continued this way, I'd leave an ugly number of bodies in my wake without ever locating Lindsay Sorkin. As things stood, it would be a hell of a risk to return to Germany. And surely I was now wanted in Poland for questioning. If charges were ultimately brought against me in either country, I'd be red-flagged by Interpol and confined to a nation averse to extradition treaties. Even then I wouldn't be entirely safe. I'd forever be looking over my shoulder.

But this wasn't about me, I had to remind myself; it was about Vince and Lori Sorkin and reuniting them with their daughter.

In my years as a U.S. Marshal, then (for lack of a better term) as a private investigator, I'd always known that anticipating my target's next move was key. Usually you found your subjects because of the research you did before the chase. You learned where your targets had family and friends, what type of jobs they were qualified for, the kind of climate they preferred or at least could endure. But in this case, that essential preparation was impossible.

Again I stared out the window into the night and tried to picture the person or persons capable of pulling off this elaborate kidnapping of Lindsay Sorkin. For a moment, I locked on a reflection coming from the window into our compartment. That face again. I swung my head around but the visage was gone.

Must have been the provodnik.

Each carriage had one: an attendant who collected tickets, distributed sheets and pillows, made morning wake-up calls, served cups of tea. Or maybe it was someone in a second- or third-class sleeper, or even a fourth-class traveler with nothing but a hard bench seat, looking for an empty compartment with a bed so that he could stretch out and catch some z's before arriving in Kiev.

I thought of lowering the curtain, but I wanted to be able to see out. I hadn't been having the safest week of my life, after all.

The motion of the train threatened to lull me to sleep, but I knew it wouldn't keep, that I'd just wake up feeling miserable after eight or ten minutes, so I kept myself awake with a Ukrainian travel guide some previous passenger had left behind.

I opened to the section on Kiev, the birthplace of Eastern Slavic civilization. Somehow, the city had persevered despite having been conquered by the Vikings, captured by the Nazis, and controlled by the Soviet Union. While under the control of the Soviet Union, Ukraine had suffered the world's worst nuclear disaster at Chernobyl.

After a few minutes, my sore eyes wandered above the guidebook and there in the window I saw that face again. Staring directly into our compartment.

He's checking to see if I've fallen asleep.

I gently moved Ana's head off my shoulder and she stirred. I propped her up in the corner and covered her with my suit jacket. Then I made for the door, unlocked it, and slid it open.

I stepped out of the compartment, spun my head around, and scanned the aisle in either direction. To my right, in the distance, I saw the back of a man in a denim jacket walking swiftly toward the front of the train.

I followed.

As I got nearer I noticed he had a small pack swung over his right shoulder. I picked up my pace in order to catch up to him.

I'm being paranoid. I've had too little sleep. He's just a kid backpacking through eastern Europe. Probably heading to a hostel in Kiev for six bucks a night. All he can afford. That's why he was peeking into our compartment. He's staying in fourth class. He was simply looking for a place to crash.

I wasn't convinced. My feet were carrying me almost in a jog, my pulse racing. I saw my arm reaching out to grab the kid. As I put my hand on his shoulder he spun around. He couldn't have been more than twenty years old.

"What do you want?" he shouted in awful English.

His lips were trembling, his eyes darting back and forth. He was terrified of me.

Or at least of someone.

Or *something*.

"Why were you looking into my sleeping compartment?" I said.

"Why do you accuse me of this, you stupid American?" he roared, earning dirty looks from the other passengers.

It was *what* he said, not how he said it, that bothered me. How did he know I was American? Everyone who met me assumed I was British. I looked British. I sounded British. Hell, I *was* British, truth be told.

"What's in your pack?" I said.

He turned his head and glanced at the carriage door. The train was rounding a bend, so we weren't moving all that fast. The bastard was thinking of making a run for it.

"You want it?" he shouted at me as he removed the pack from his shoulder. "Here, you take it!"

He shoved the pack into my chest, turned, and went straight for the door. As he did, I noticed him reach into his denim jacket and pull out a mobile phone.

I tried to piece it all together. Here was a kid who'd been peeking into our compartment, who'd thrown a fit when I asked him a simple question, who'd somehow known where I was from. I looked down at the bag he'd pushed on me, then glanced at his right hand as his thumb worked the button on the old mobile phone.

Christ. The phone's a detonator. The kid just handed me a goddamn bomb.

I immediately darted after him through the aisle, the contents of my stomach rising in my throat. I finally caught up with him just as he jumped the four short steps to the door. He pushed the door open and I watched tall brown grass and rail blowing by us. He hesitated for just a second, but a second was all I needed. I tossed the strap of the pack over his head and around his neck.

The kid spun around, trying to remove the pack to toss it back to me.

Meanwhile, I saw green digital numbers decreasing on the phone he now held in his left hand.

Six.

I used the banister as leverage and raised my left leg, throwing a back kick straight into his chest. The kid flew out the door, his back striking the ground with great force.

Five.

Gripping the banister, I jumped down the stairs and watched him tumble away from the train as I counted down in my head.

Four.

I closed the door, bounded back up the four steps, and saw every passenger in the car staring at me.

Three.

I started up the aisle, staring out the side window, looking for the kid.

Two.

At the very last second I spotted him.

One.

The explosion was so powerful that it blew the kid to bits, and very nearly knocked our night train off the bloody rails.

Chapter 42

We arrived at Kiev's Central Station two hours later than scheduled. Police had come to investigate the scene of the explosion, and explained that no one would be permitted off the train in Kiev until everyone had been questioned.

"That means we will be trapped aboard this train for another three or fours hours," Ana said in exasperation once we pulled into the station.

"Not necessarily," I said. "I suspect we'll be among the first to be questioned. Once they have their information, they will either arrest me or let us both go."

"Arrest you? Why would they possibly arrest you?"

"Because most of the passengers who witnessed the incident were half asleep, and chances are, most of them don't speak English. So they're going to explain to the police not what occurred but how they perceived it. Some of them probably just caught the tail end. Which means the police will have accounts of a larger man wrapping a pack around a skinny kid's neck before physically kicking him off the train. Followed, of course, by an explosion that rocked the train and blew the kid to kingdom come."

"And you are certain we were the intended target?" she said.

I nodded without looking at her. "No doubt about it."

There was a quick rap on our compartment door, then it slid

open, revealing a short, completely bald Ukrainian man and a pale, gangly woman.

The man said, "Simon Fisk? Anastazja Staszak?"

We both nodded.

"My name is Martyn Rudnyk," he said. "I am the deputy head of the Criminal Investigation Department of the Ministry of the Interior here in Ukraine. This is Agent Jess Kidman of Interpol. She is from South Africa, currently based in Harare, Zimbabwe." He looked from me to Ana. "I spoke to your brother, Marek. After putting up a fight and learning of the bomb on the train, he explained the situation and the reason the two of you are presently in Ukraine."

"Word travels fast," I said.

Rudnyk ignored me. "It is important that the four of us speak privately. If you wouldn't mind coming with us, the ministry's headquarters are here in Kiev."

"Do we have a choice?" Ana said.

Kidman stepped forward. Her suit was too large for her frame. She'd purchased it off the rack and was either too tall or had recently lost a lot of weight. "We are not the enemy, Ms. Staszak."

After what we had learned about Chief Inspector Aleksander Gasowski back in Warsaw, it was difficult to trust anyone in authority, especially here in eastern Europe. Just the night before, we'd witnessed firsthand a perfectly fine example of the corruption within Ukraine's police force down at the pier in Odessa. We had no reason whatsoever to trust these two.

"Given a choice," I said, "we'd both prefer to provide a statement, then be left alone."

Kidman appeared unperturbed. "As I am sure you are aware by now, Mr. Fisk, both of your lives are in grave danger. And you cannot possibly complete your objective of finding the American child if both of you are dead."

ne way or the other," Kidman said in a cramped room at ministry headquarters, "the attempted bombing on the overnight train from Odessa suggests that you have run afoul of Ukrainian organized crime. In such cases, we have no choice but to extract you from the situation."

"With all due respect, Agent Kidman," I said, "we don't require extraction. As you can see, we can take care of ourselves."

"Perhaps," Rudnyk piped in. "But our first concern must be for the public at large, and if that bomb had exploded on the train, it would have killed dozens of innocent people. Such risks—such *close calls*—you must understand, are unacceptable."

Ana's face glowed red. "In case you have not noticed, Simon and I did not attempt to bomb anyone. We are victims. Maybe if your police force spent more time investigating and attempting to prevent such crimes—as opposed to, say, taking bribes—this incident would not have occurred."

Rudnyk nodded affably. Behind the veneer of an agreeable cop, however, I detected a man burning with rage. The lines on his forehead and the hooded eyes reminded me of idealistic cops who'd been bludgeoned by the job. Cops sickened by what they'd seen and heard over too many years on the force, too many rounds of the same fight. Cops who'd taken on too much friendly fire, who'd been blocked by bureaucrats and colleagues who played on both sides of the line. Bitter cops who nevertheless continued to slip into their wrinkled suits each day, cops who'd never bend or break, never surrender their convictions, right up to the moment they slept their last sleep.

"Your point is well taken," Rudnyk said. "I, of all people, am not blind to the corruption that plagues my country. It is not my intention to make excuses for it. However, it is a plague that presently afflicts all post-Soviet states. I could sit here and list the various academic causes for the corruption, but that will not aid you in finding the young girl you seek. So for now, let us just say that my nation is experiencing, for want of a better term, 'growing pains.'"

Kidman nodded. She seemed more of a pragmatist. It was a consequence of worldliness, of experiencing enough of humanity to know that change came, if it came at all, in barely perceptible increments, and of accepting the fact that it wouldn't be you but maybe your great-grandchildren who would reap the benefits of the good you did today.

They made a good match, Kidman and Rudnyk. The world needed both types of cops.

"Back to the matter at hand," Kidman said. "As I said back on the train, we are not the enemy. We are certainly not here to thwart your attempt at locating the missing American girl. We wish to provide assistance. But there are conditions."

"Conditions?" Ana said.

"Consideration must be given with respect to our ongoing investigations. Our work over the past several years cannot be jeopardized."

I said, "We've no interest in interfering with your investigations. We just want to find Lindsay Sorkin."

"Very well," Kidman said. "Then we understand each other. And our objectives do not conflict." She turned to Rudnyk. "Let's proceed."

We waited as Rudnyk left the room to retrieve a file. I was surprised by all the formality, the mechanical way in which our presence was being received. It was unlike any law enforcement collaboration I had ever seen. There was no yelling, no threats or ultimatums. Just cool heads and an almost frightening air of patience.

When Rudnyk returned with the file, he sat across from us and said, "Last night, shortly before the incident on the train, we intercepted a communication that we believe was commenced by Yuri Bobrovnyk in Odessa."

"You *believe* it was him?" I said.

"Yes, it was not his line that was being tapped."

"Whose was it?"

Chapter 43

Ana and I stood in the blistering cold, surveying Kiev's eclectic cityscape, which was far more beautiful than I'd ever imagined. It was a few minutes before we were finally able to hail a cab. Travel sites advised foreigners against taking taxis in the former USSR, but right now getting ripped off was the least of our worries. We needed to get somewhere fast, and we didn't want to put any more lives at risk by hopping on a bus or a tram. One incredibly close call with a bomb was enough to convince us that we needed to be more vigilant, and avoiding public transportation for the remainder of our time in Ukraine was probably a wise precaution.

I hoped we wouldn't be here all that long. We were desperate to recover Lindsay Sorkin and return her to her parents in Paris. I was terribly concerned about Lori. I'd spoken to Lieutenant Davignon again immediately after leaving Rudnyk and Kidman, and though Lori hadn't suffered a miscarriage, doctors were concerned about the effects the excessive stress might have on her pregnancy.

Even if Lori hadn't been pregnant, I knew from experience that there was more than one ticking clock in any missing-child case. A parent can endure only so much. I'd witnessed Tasha's breaking point, and I'd have been remiss not to consider Lori's.

I stepped into the taxi after Ana and provided the driver with our destination: the Ukrainian Darlings Modeling Agency.

"We will get to that. In any event, you, Simon Fisk, were mentioned by name. A description that fits yours was given, along with a summary of events that apparently transpired on a boat docked in the Black Sea."

I didn't say anything.

"The conversation between Yuri Bobrovnyk and one of our suspects was heated. From everything we know about them, these men do not get along, but they have formed some unholy alliance to further their own respective interests."

"You're speaking about the Podrova brothers," I said. "Dmitry and Viktor."

"Yes," Rudnyk said without any discernible reaction. "Yuri Bobrovnyk, as he may have told you, considers himself a legitimate businessman. And in our current political and economic climate here in post-Soviet Ukraine, an argument can be made that he is not being entirely inaccurate."

"The Podrova brothers, on the other hand," Kidman said, "are purveyors of materials that depict unspeakable crimes against children."

"Therein lies the conflict," Rudnyk added. "Yuri Bobrovnyk knows that despite the undeniable disparity in their offenses, he and the Podrova brothers are inextricably linked under the designation 'organized crime' in general, and 'sex trade' in particular. It is an inescapable fact that, if not the Ukrainian government, the world community will ultimately step in to put an end to these atrocities against children."

"Bobrovnyk fears that the Podrova brothers are bringing far too much attention to Ukraine," Kidman said, "and that at some point, the outrage over crimes against children will expand into outrage over crimes against women."

"Unlikely," Ana noted.

Kidman bowed her head in acknowledgment. "Agreed."

"But there are other reasons behind Yuri Bobrovnyk's fury with the Podrova brothers," Rudnyk said. "Under the delusion that he is a legitimate businessman, Yuri is indignant over the fact that many of the teenage girls who come to him are already 'worn out,' as he puts it. There are fewer and fewer virgins, which, for Yuri, demand the highest price. And the girls are often so strung out on drugs that they either steal from him or accept an assignment abroad only never to return. Some overdose and die. Those who survive have inevitably added years to their faces, so they are difficult to sell, or at least demand a much lower price."

"Why doesn't Yuri take the Podrova brothers out?" I said.

Rudnyk displayed his first hint of a smile. "Because I have never been so lucky. But also because, believe it or disbelieve it, Yuri Bobrovnyk and his associates are not violent men, or at least do not consider themselves to be so. However, even if they have considered violence as an option to deal with the Podrova brothers, surely they came to their senses. Yuri would never win a war against the Podrovas. The brothers are ruthless, and—as much as I hate to admit it—smart. It is why we have not yet been able to take them down despite the abominable nature of their crimes."

"So now that we have all this background information," I said, "where does that leave us in terms of rescuing Lindsay from the Podrova brothers?"

Kidman spoke up. "First, let me say that we have no confirmation whatsoever that Lindsay Sorkin is in the possession of the Podrova brothers. As Martyn pointed out, the Podrovas are very clever and they successfully evade most attempts at surveillance. Gathering intelligence has proven both extremely dangerous and sadly unrewarding. But from what Marek Staszak told us—particularly that the girl was being taken to Ukraine—we think that there is a more than fair chance she is with the Podrovas. And that a cautious look into it would be worthwhile."

"Cautious?" I said. "What exactly do you mean by cautious?"

"What Agent Kidman means," Rudnyk said, "is that this opera-

tion to retrieve the missing American girl must be like a surgery. A surgery requires a tool of precision, like a scalpel as opposed to a butcher knife. We want you to succeed, but not to make a mess of things."

"We understand," I said.

Rudnyk nodded, finally wore a genuine smile. "Good. No offense, Mr. Fisk, but your coming from America, we thought that particular concept might require a bit more explanation."

"We will get to that. In any event, you, Simon Fisk, were mentioned by name. A description that fits yours was given, along with a summary of events that apparently transpired on a boat docked in the Black Sea."

I didn't say anything.

"The conversation between Yuri Bobrovnyk and one of our suspects was heated. From everything we know about them, these men do not get along, but they have formed some unholy alliance to further their own respective interests."

"You're speaking about the Podrova brothers," I said. "Dmitry and Viktor."

"Yes," Rudnyk said without any discernible reaction. "Yuri Bobrovnyk, as he may have told you, considers himself a legitimate businessman. And in our current political and economic climate here in post-Soviet Ukraine, an argument can be made that he is not being entirely inaccurate."

"The Podrova brothers, on the other hand," Kidman said, "are purveyors of materials that depict unspeakable crimes against children."

"Therein lies the conflict," Rudnyk added. "Yuri Bobrovnyk knows that despite the undeniable disparity in their offenses, he and the Podrova brothers are inextricably linked under the designation 'organized crime' in general, and 'sex trade' in particular. It is an inescapable fact that, if not the Ukrainian government, the world community will ultimately step in to put an end to these atrocities against children."

"Bobrovnyk fears that the Podrova brothers are bringing far too much attention to Ukraine," Kidman said, "and that at some point, the outrage over crimes against children will expand into outrage over crimes against women."

"Unlikely," Ana noted.

Kidman bowed her head in acknowledgment. "Agreed."

"But there are other reasons behind Yuri Bobrovnyk's fury with the Podrova brothers," Rudnyk said. "Under the delusion that he is a legitimate businessman, Yuri is indignant over the fact that many of the teenage girls who come to him are already 'worn out,' as he puts it. There are fewer and fewer virgins, which, for Yuri, demand the highest price. And the girls are often so strung out on drugs that they either steal from him or accept an assignment abroad only never to return. Some overdose and die. Those who survive have inevitably added years to their faces, so they are difficult to sell, or at least demand a much lower price."

"Why doesn't Yuri take the Podrova brothers out?" I said.

Rudnyk displayed his first hint of a smile. "Because I have never been so lucky. But also because, believe it or disbelieve it, Yuri Bobrovnyk and his associates are not violent men, or at least do not consider themselves to be so. However, even if they have considered violence as an option to deal with the Podrova brothers, surely they came to their senses. Yuri would never win a war against the Podrovas. The brothers are ruthless, and—as much as I hate to admit it—smart. It is why we have not yet been able to take them down despite the abominable nature of their crimes."

"So now that we have all this background information," I said, "where does that leave us in terms of rescuing Lindsay from the Podrova brothers?"

Kidman spoke up. "First, let me say that we have no confirmation whatsoever that Lindsay Sorkin is in the possession of the Podrova brothers. As Martyn pointed out, the Podrovas are very clever and they successfully evade most attempts at surveillance. Gathering intelligence has proven both extremely dangerous and sadly unrewarding. But from what Marek Staszak told us—particularly that the girl was being taken to Ukraine—we think that there is a more than fair chance she is with the Podrovas. And that a cautious look into it would be worthwhile."

"Cautious?" I said. "What exactly do you mean by cautious?"

"What Agent Kidman means," Rudnyk said, "is that this operation to retrieve the missing American girl must be like a surgery. A surgery requires a tool of precision, like a scalpel as opposed to a butcher knife. We want you to succeed, but not to make a mess of things."

"We understand," I said.

Rudnyk nodded, finally wore a genuine smile. "Good. No offense, Mr. Fisk, but your coming from America, we thought that particular concept might require a bit more explanation."

Chapter 43

A na and I stood in the blistering cold, surveying Kiev's eclectic cityscape, which was far more beautiful than I'd ever imagined. It was a few minutes before we were finally able to hail a cab. Travel sites advised foreigners against taking taxis in the former USSR, but right now getting ripped off was the least of our worries. We needed to get somewhere fast, and we didn't want to put any more lives at risk by hopping on a bus or a tram. One incredibly close call with a bomb was enough to convince us that we needed to be more vigilant, and avoiding public transportation for the remainder of our time in Ukraine was probably a wise precaution.

I hoped we wouldn't be here all that long. We were desperate to recover Lindsay Sorkin and return her to her parents in Paris. I was terribly concerned about Lori. I'd spoken to Lieutenant Davignon again immediately after leaving Rudnyk and Kidman, and though Lori hadn't suffered a miscarriage, doctors were concerned about the effects the excessive stress might have on her pregnancy.

Even if Lori hadn't been pregnant, I knew from experience that there was more than one ticking clock in any missing-child case. A parent can endure only so much. I'd witnessed Tasha's breaking point, and I'd have been remiss not to consider Lori's.

I stepped into the taxi after Ana and provided the driver with our destination: the Ukrainian Darlings Modeling Agency.

It was Ana who'd come up with the plan. Rudnyk and Kidman had run into several dead ends in their investigation of the Podrova brothers' so-called modeling agency. They had tapped phones, run stationary surveillance, even broken in, rummaged through their files, and installed hidden cameras. All to no avail. Nothing damning was kept on-site, nothing of any import discussed over the phones. As far as things looked to the naked eye, nothing nefarious was being conducted on the premises at all. The front was exceptional as far as fronts go.

No one who worked for the Podrova brothers would talk to the authorities. Everyone was too scared. Unlike Yuri Bobrovnyk, the Podrovas were cold, calculating killers who pulled the trigger immediately upon discovery of the slightest transgression. But then, Ana and I already knew that firsthand from last night's nearly tragic train ride.

"The *children*," Ana had said back at the ministry's headquarters. She turned to me. "You said it yourself, Simon. Back in Pruszkow when we were searching for Kazmer Chudzik. They are the one group of people in every city that you can count on to be afraid of nothing."

Kidman had held up her hand. "I don't think you understand. These children have been severely traumatized. They are living in nightmares."

"We have approached many of the children we suspect are being victimized," Rudnyk said. "They are terrified and they are convinced no one in the world can help them."

The thing was, Rudnyk had gone on to explain, these children weren't snatched off the streets, nor were they volunteers in the true sense of the word because they were far too young to provide their consent. Thus, it wasn't the Podrova brothers whom they had to fear—it was their parents. Their guardians or loved ones. Uncles, aunts, stepparents. In some cases, their older siblings. There was an absurd amount of money to be made exploiting children, and some monsters were intent on cashing in. With so much at stake, it had proven impossible to penetrate what Kidman called the "Child Wall of Silence." None of the children would speak of their abuse.

"I am not suggesting we inquire about their abuse," Ana had said. "Only that we show them a picture of Lindsay Sorkin. With the proper background story, I think it could work. These children do not care about their own lives—they have had those stolen from them. But it is far more difficult for criminals to steal empathy. Children have a natural inclination to protect other children. I have witnessed this consistently during my decade as a criminal lawyer."

Rudnyk and Kidman disagreed that this was the precision instrument that was called for. For the record, they refused to sanction our operation and insisted that it would be entirely unethical for them to provide us with a list of names, ages, and addresses for some of the Podrova brothers' suspected victims.

Ana and I didn't waste much time arguing. After all, Rudnyk and Kidman had obtained the list of alleged victims from the modeling agency itself. There was no reason we couldn't do the same.

The agency was located on the second floor of a small, inconspicuous building near the edge of the city. When we arrived in front of the building, Ana and I stepped out of the taxi and surveyed the hand-drawn layout that Rudnyk and Kidman had been kind enough to provide us—off the record. Although they couldn't aid us in any official capacity, Rudnyk and Kidman knew what was at stake and they weren't going to attempt to stop us. In fact, even if they didn't agree with our plan, they assured us they wanted it to succeed.

"Do what needs doing," Rudnyk had quietly said to me after our meeting. "The Podrova brothers, they are not human beings. They are monsters who have done to children things of which most of us cannot even speak. There is no such thing as justice for their crimes. The best anyone can do is rid the world of these creatures, if not all at once then one at a time."

I folded the diagram and stuffed it back into my pocket as Ana and I crossed the quiet street. Inside the agency itself, there would be a reception area with a single desk. Behind that desk were several unlocked filing cabinets that contained information for each client.

Rudnyk and Kidman had insisted that Ukrainian Darlings acted like a legitimate business—at least on its own premises—so there wouldn't be any added security. On-site, the agency's so-called clients posed for clothed photos in a large room set up with hot lights, several backdrops, and multiple cameras. These same so-called clients were then allegedly taken off the premises for their more lurid work.

We entered the building and I followed Ana up the creaky stairs. The halls had been freshly painted white with murals of unicorns and rainbows. Head shots of beautiful children were posted everywhere. To the average eye, this would have looked very much like a happy place straight out of a children's picture book. But Ana and I knew better, and as we traipsed up the stairs, the atmosphere chilled me to the bone.

I stopped just short of the second landing and nodded to Ana. She reached into her handbag, plucked out her phone, and pulled up my number.

"Soon as the receptionist moves to the back," I said, "hit Send."

Ana rapped on the door, then stepped inside.

I held my phone in my hand, waiting for the signal. Ana was posing as a destitute parent hoping to make some fast money off her beautiful daughter. Before she'd bring in her child or fill out any forms, however, she wanted to see the studio for herself, to make certain everything was on the up-and-up.

According to Rudnyk and Kidman, unless there was a photo shoot scheduled, the receptionist sat in the agency alone, waiting for intakes. Therefore, if she was going to give Ana the tour, she'd have to leave her post. Which would allow me to drop in to grab some files.

After only a few minutes I began to get antsy, started second-guessing our strategy. Maybe Ana and I were being too clever for our own good. If there truly was only one woman standing between us and the files, trickery wasn't particularly necessary. Of course, I'd never hit or pull a gun on a woman unless she was a deadly threat. But I wasn't above demanding that she stand in the corner for ninety seconds.

As I debated whether to make a move, my BlackBerry buzzed in my hand. I slipped the phone back into my pocket and rushed to the door. I saw the green filing cabinets as soon as I stepped inside. This was going to prove easier than I'd thought. I heard Ana engaged in cordial conversation with the receptionist in the rear.

The cabinets were indeed unlocked. The files were organized by year. I grabbed a few of the most recent, along with a handful from last year. I turned to make my exit as planned.

As I opened the door, I thought of something Marek had told me over the phone. The Ukranian Darlings Modeling Agency had been in operation for roughly seven years. Seven years ago, Hailey would've been only nine. And what if the agency had really been operating for ten? What if it had simply been operating under a different name?

I turned and walked back to the cabinets. I set my stolen folders on top of the first cabinet and began flipping through the files, one at a time. These older files weren't as organized as the newer ones, but they did contain photos. There was a single photo—a head shot—stapled to the inside front cover of each file folder.

Of course, it would be a waste of time to search for Hailey's name. If she was in one of these cabinets, it would surely be under an alias. So instead I started looking at each photo. Each child. Each victim. I flew past the boys but each time I reached a girl's photo I stopped and studied it. I had to be absolutely sure it wasn't Hailey before I moved on. So many had Hailey's dark hair, her tiny nose. So many had Hailey's eyes.

Over the past decade I'd been all over the world. I'd followed every lead in some form or fashion, no matter how outlandish. I'd made thousands of calls, knocked on thousands of doors. With the help of volunteers from communities large and small, I'd posted and handed out tens of thousands of flyers, combed hundreds of miles of forests. I'd watched dozens of landfills being searched, dozens of lakes being dredged. I'd been in every police station, hospital, and morgue in North America. I'd searched graveyards, dug up private land and public property with abandon. Hailey had to be *somewhere,* why not here?

Halfway through the first cabinet, I was all but certain I would find her.

"*Excuse* me?"

The woman's voice startled me. I glanced up and saw the receptionist, with Ana standing directly behind her. I snatched the files I'd taken originally off the top of the cabinet and made for the door.

"*Hey,*" the woman shouted as my feet hit the stairs.

I bounded down the creaky steps and bolted once I was through the front door. I rounded the corner and ran up the block to the rendezvous spot I'd arranged with Ana.

When she finally reached me, I tried to explain.

But I didn't have to.

Somehow she already knew. Somehow she understood.

Chapter 44

A few blocks away, we hailed another taxi. We'd looked through each of the files I'd filched and found that a number of the children were clustered together in the Podil district, also known as Lower City, one of Kiev's oldest and poorest neighborhoods. That seemed like the obvious place to start.

The taxi dropped us off in front of a run-down apartment building, the address at which three of the alleged victims were listed as living. The newer files had contained no photographs to go with the children's names. All we knew was that two of the victims living in this building were girls, ages seven and nine. The other was a boy, age five. It was noted that both girls spoke English; the boy did not.

Outside the cab, I glanced about.

"There looks to be some kind of a playground round back," I said. "Let's check that first. I'm sure we'll fare better in a place with no parents around."

It wasn't much of a playground. A pair of swings with worn chains, a set of monkey bars that probably wouldn't withstand forty pounds, a big red plastic slide cracked down the middle. The only thing that looked remotely fun for a kid was the dirt. But even that was rock hard now in the dead of winter.

"No one here," I said, not terribly surprised.

I looked over at Ana, whose gaze seemed locked on the small enclosed perch at the top of the slide.

"Yes. There is," she said quietly.

I followed her eyes to the top of the slide and squinted, trying to see inside the uncovered window. There was a flash of color—a kid's winter jacket, probably—and I knew that Ana was right.

"Shall we?" I whispered, but Ana was already moving toward the center of the playground. I considered remaining behind; a woman might relate better to a child. But then I remembered I had Lindsay Sorkin's photo in my jacket.

"Dobry den," Ana was saying to the little girl when I arrived. I assumed she was speaking Ukrainian, though I knew nothing of the language. *"Me ne zvaty Anastazja. Yak vas zvaty?"*

The little girl didn't respond.

"Do you speak English?" Ana said.

The girl made the slightest incline with her head.

"What a relief," Ana said to her. "Because my Ukrainian is terrible."

"It is not so bad," the girl said without inflection.

Ana's face lit up. It appeared as though she was genuinely pleased with the girl's appraisal of her Ukrainian.

"Really?" Ana said. "Because I am from Poland and I studied only Russian in school. Ukrainian, I had to learn all on my own."

The girl said, "My mother came from Poland."

I felt an instant wave of hope. The seven-year-old on our list was Dorota Wojcik—a Polish name, Ana had assured me.

Ana said, "That is terrific, to make a friend from Poland all the way here in Ukraine. Tell me, what is your name?"

The girl glanced at me and said, "I am not supposed to talk to strange people."

Ana tried to make a joke out of it. "Oh, that is my husband, Simon," she said. "He is not strange; he just *looks* strange."

The girl's lips slowly turned up.

"My name is Dorota," she said.

"That is a beautiful name," Ana remarked. "If Simon and I ever have a little girl, we are going to name her Dorota. Right, Simon?"

"Of course," I said. "You've been saying it for years."

"So," Ana said to Dorota. "Simon and I are in Kiev searching for his niece. She became lost more than a week ago, and her parents are very sad. I was wondering if you would take a look at a picture of her and tell us whether you have seen her. Would that be okay?"

The smile disappeared from Dorota's face.

"Please," Ana said. "It will only take a moment, then we will leave you to your playing."

The girl searched Ana's eyes for any sign of treachery. Then she searched mine.

Finally, the girl nodded.

"Thank you," Ana said, turning to me for the photo. When I handed it to her, she carefully unfolded it and set it on Dorota's lap. "Her name is Lindsay. Lindsay Sorkin. She is about your age, maybe a year younger. She comes from a state called California, far away in America. It is where Hollywood is located, where they make all the best movies."

Dorota stared hard at the picture, tracing Lindsay's face with her thumb.

"Have you seen her?" Ana said. "Have you seen this little girl?"

Slowly, almost imperceptibly, the little girl nodded her head.

My heart began to pump so hard and fast it felt as though it were going to break through my rib cage.

"You *have* seen her," Ana said with delight. "Where did you see her? When?"

"Yesterday," Dorota said. "In the afternoon."

I looked down and saw that my fists were clenched. I bit the inside of my mouth until it was raw.

"Where?" Ana nudged her. "Where did you see Lindsay, Dorota?"

Dorota took a deep breath, glanced over at me again.

"On the television," she said.

Dizziness swept over me; I thought I might fall. Sweat began to pour from my temples despite the brutal cold. I'd felt as though we were close, so close. It now felt as though Lindsay had been taken all over again. I suddenly realized I was really no closer to finding her than I had been in Paris the morning I met Davignon and Vince and Lori Sorkin. Lindsay, I was convinced, would never be found. Like my daughter, Hailey. Mankind, in its most abhorrent form, had eaten up these girls, swallowed them whole. These children had succumbed to the worst the world had to offer.

Ana was asking the girl more questions but I could pay no more attention. I needed to get to a hotel and drop onto a bed, sleep for as long as was possible. My ears ringing, I began to walk away, just as it started to rain. A cold drizzle quickly became a freezing torrent by the time I reached the fence.

I heard Ana's footsteps behind me, heard her calling my name, but I couldn't stop, couldn't so much as turn around. For the first time in forever, I actually felt tears running from my eyes.

Ana caught up with me and matched me stride for stride, saying nothing as we made for the street. Then I heard the unmistakable patter of tiny footfalls and I felt sorry for turning away from little Dorota Wojcik. She was seven years old, possibly a victim herself. It wasn't her fault.

"Ana!" the girl cried from behind us. *"Proshu!"*

Ana and I turned at the same time.

"Go home, Dorota," Ana said, not unkindly. "It is raining; you will catch cold."

The girl froze. She wiped her eye, then turned around, only to spin back again.

"The girl you showed me," Dorota said desperately. "I saw her not only yesterday, but the day before."

Ana sat on her haunches to face the little girl.

Sadly Ana said, "On television, yes?"

"No," Dorota said, shaking her tiny head in the cold rain, and I saw that tears were streaming from her eyes as well. "I saw her here. In Kiev."

Chapter 45

Night draped itself over northern Ukraine, and with it came temperatures well below freezing, and a heavy snow blown almost horizontally by a violent wind. Ana and I had the taxi drop us off several blocks from the address Dorota had given us.

The girl *had* seen Lindsay Sorkin. Alive and in the flesh. Dorota had been at a two-story duplex in the Svyatoshinsky district of Kiev for a "session," which she reluctantly described as a clothes-off photo shoot with Dmitry Podrova and two of his Russian associates. As Dorota was being escorted out by Dmitry, one of the Russians opened a bedroom door, and Dorota glimpsed a young girl tied up and gagged on a cot in the corner of the room. Dmitry quickly slammed the door shut and hollered at the Russian for being so careless. Dmitry then turned to Dorota and asked what she had seen. Nothing, she'd assured him. If she had seen something, Dmitry told her, and she spoke about it to anyone, he would kill her in her home while she slept. Then he would kill her baby brother.

"Do you think Lindsay is still in there?" Ana said as we watched the duplex from across the street.

I couldn't speak. Dorota's story continuously played out in my head and I thought I would be sick. Both Ana and I were a bit stunned that the young girl remembered the address—not only the street name but the number outside the door—and before we left, I'd asked the girl how.

"I always remember the bad things," she'd said. "The bad things are easy to remember. The bad things you even remember in your sleep."

"Do you think Lindsay is still in there?" Ana said again.

Again I didn't answer. Truth was, I had no idea. The Podrova brothers knew we were in Ukraine, searching for the girl, knew by now that their attempt on our lives on the train from Odessa had failed. They would have moved her. But then, these men had been able to act with impunity for so long. Most of the police were on their payroll. Those who weren't didn't have the resources or manpower to conduct a proper investigation. Their egos could have driven them to leave the girl right where she was. There was only one way to find out.

I glanced at my watch. It was just after midnight.

"Time to go in," I said. "I need you to remain here as a lookout."

Ana didn't raise a fuss. She knew too well that if someone snuck in behind me I was a dead man.

I moved down to the end of the block and crossed the street against the driving snow. I then moved behind the row of houses as silently as possible so that I could approach the duplex from the rear. With the wind biting my face, I wasn't sure if Ana was safer outside or whether she should have come with me after all. The Podrova brothers would probably have guns, lots of them. But at least she wouldn't freeze to death.

When I finally reached the rear of the duplex, I let fly a sigh of relief. The duplex was nothing like the fortress into which Kazmer Chudzik had turned his Pomerania lake house. I stared at the window leading to the right side of the basement and thought entering should be no bother at all.

Only there was a good chance—if the basement was used for nefarious purposes—that the door leading up to the rest of the house would be locked, even dead-bolted. I'd have to find another way in without making much of a racket.

I stepped around to the side of the house and spotted a window that opened onto the first floor. Not perfect by any means, but it was the best entrance available outside of ringing the doorbell.

The first thing I did was quietly remove the screen and set it down in the snow. Breaking into a home wasn't all that difficult. Go on the Internet and you'd find all manner of forums discussing the fine art of burglary—but all of it was for shit. Criminals weren't especially adept at breaking into houses. They were often far too concerned with making an escape. Law enforcement, on the other hand, didn't have to worry about getting away; we just needed in. And if we were fast enough, making noise didn't matter so much. You just needed to be able to get the drop on your targets. Problem here was, there was probably more than one of them and I was alone. And I wasn't here to make an arrest. Later, with or without Lindsay, I'd need out every bit as much as I now needed in.

There were no lights on downstairs, just one dim lamp on the second floor. So I took out my Glock, turned it around, and used the handle to break a hole in the upper right corner of the window. I was satisfied that the noise level was low enough, especially with the wicked wind blowing against the house. I reached in and unlocked the window. Slid it open and quickly climbed in.

I was in a downstairs bedroom that held only a cot. Could well have been the room Dorota described. Only Lindsay wasn't here. There was a small amount of what looked like dried blood on the sheets and I instantly felt as though I might drop to my knees. But a set of footsteps pounding down the stairs gave me the adrenaline rush I needed. I ran to the closed door, pressed up against the wall next to it, and waited.

Three seconds later, the door swung open and a man swept in. I grabbed the guy from behind, put him in a choke hold, but didn't squeeze, as I didn't want him passing out. If no one else was in the house, I needed him conscious. He could be my only source of information as to Lindsay's current whereabouts.

He struggled. I pressed the barrel of my gun to his temple and suddenly he wasn't struggling so much.

"Don't gamble your life away by lying," I said quietly. "How many people in the house?"

"Just me," he said gruffly, struggling for breath.

"You're sure?"

"I'm sure."

His cologne flamed its way up my nostrils and threatened to make me sick.

"What's your name?" I said.

"Dmitry."

"Where's Viktor?"

"Out," he growled. "At a party."

In the full-length mirrors that made up the closet doors I saw his eyes darting around the dark room, searching for a weapon. Finally, he threw his arm forward and swung his elbow back into the right side of my ribs. I'd been expecting it and the blow had little effect, except to loosen my grip. He pulled away from me, but as he turned to swing at me, I struck him across the face with my Glock.

Dmitry fell backward onto the cot.

I grabbed him by the shirt, lifted him, threw his body hard up against the wall, then I used the Glock to break his nose. Slammed it again against the lower half of his face. Blood spewed from between his lips. He spit, and several crimson teeth shot out of his mouth.

"Another move like that," I warned him, "and losing a few teeth is going to be the least of your worries."

He didn't say anything.

I pressed the barrel of the Glock into the flesh next to his left shoulder and told him I'd squeeze the trigger if he failed to provide a single accurate answer. He knew I wouldn't kill him until I had the information I needed; that would have been counterproductive. But it was clear that he believed that I'd cause him a whole hell of a lot more pain.

"Where's the American girl?" I said.

"Not here," he said, his head trembling from the blows he'd taken. "Not in Ukraine. Not anymore."

"Who has her?"

Dmitry tried a smile but it was difficult to pull off with a broken face.

"Two of my best men," he rasped. "Russians. Former KGB."

I rapped the Glock against his ear to keep him from trying to smile again. He shouted in pain as I dug the Glock into the flesh next to his shoulder again.

"The Russians," I said. "What are their names?"

"Jov. Sacha."

With my left I smacked him across the face.

"*Last* names," I said.

"Jov Sergeyev. Sacha Orlov." He took pains to force a grin. "Go. Marshal Fisk. Find them. They will enjoy killing you. Reuniting you with your wife and daughter."

A furious rage flowed through me, but I had to think of Lindsay now. I took several deep breaths in an attempt to maintain control.

"Where are they taking her?" I said.

"North. To Belarus."

"Why? Who's there? Who's waiting for her?"

"The man who hired us."

"Give me a goddamn *name*," I shouted.

"I do not *have* a name. You *know* that I wouldn't. And you *know* I wouldn't know exactly where they were taking her. They will receive instructions along the way."

"Why the stopover here?" I said. "What did you do to her? Why didn't your men take her straight from Warsaw to Belarus?"

"Because," he said, breathing heavily. "Because of what was on the news. Viktor and I, we decided to renegotiate the contract."

"The father," I said.

"Of course, the father. When we discovered who he was, what he could supply, we realized the girl was worth ten times what we were being paid."

"This man who hired you agreed to pay more?"

"Not at first. He said he didn't give a fuck who her father was. Her father wasn't what he was after. But we told him it didn't matter. You buy a platinum diamond ring, you pay for the diamond. Regardless of whether all you want is the platinum."

I didn't say anything as I thought about what he'd just told me, just moved the barrel of the gun a few inches downward and to the right. The question was, could the buyer be believed? Was the buyer really not after the father? Or was that just a negotiating tactic? Had to be, right? The amount of money that was changing hands, no way this could be about anything but Vince Sorkin's trade secrets. The buyer not only had an idea of the girl he wanted, he had a name. Lindsay Sorkin. He knew what city she'd be in, what hotel she'd be staying at. No, I was convinced. To use Dmitry's hideous analogy, the buyer wanted the platinum diamond ring for the *diamond*, not the platinum.

I pressed the barrel deeper into his chest, said, "Go on."

Let him think talking would extend his life. Even if only for a few minutes.

"We had to bring in another buyer," he said. "A Syrian we had worked with in the past. Smuggling arms through Turkey."

"I want a name."

"Bilal ibn Hashim," he said. "But the Syrian ultimately lost the bidding war. He said if we didn't sell her to him, he would simply take her. So, Jov and Sacha left for Belarus immediately."

From the front of the house I heard the click of a lock, followed by the squeak of the door.

"Quiet," I cautioned Dmitry.

I twisted his body so that I could use it for cover if need be, and slowly aimed my Glock at the door.

The door was open just a crack.

My heart pounding, I listened to footfalls moving in our direction. It sounded as though there were two pairs, one heavy, the other shuffling.

Then I watched the door swing slowly inward.

I saw the gun first, then the heavily inked arm holding it.

Finally, I saw where the gun was leveled—directly under Ana's jaw.

Chapter 46

With Ana positioned directly in front of him, Viktor Podrova moved cautiously into the room. With the light from the foyer spilling in behind him I clearly made out Viktor's face. His jaw was jumpy, his eyes narrowed as he took in the scene. Dmitry was bleeding badly from every orifice in his head.

"Drop the gun and step away from my brother, or the Polack girl dies."

"I am so sorry, Simon," Ana said. "He snuck up on me across the street while I was watching the house."

She had tears in her eyes. Snow caked all over her hair and clothes. A bruise was forming below her left eye. The bastard had hit her and I wanted to rip his face off for it. But I'd settle for getting her out of this room alive.

"It's all right, Ana," I told her. "We already have what we need. If Viktor is truly as intelligent as Interpol says he is, then he'll step back and allow us both to leave."

Viktor tightened his grip and Ana let out a scream. His finger trembled over the trigger of his Makarov pistol.

"You may think you know all about me and my brother," Viktor said, "but if you think you are leaving this house alive, Marshal Fisk, you know nothing."

As I looked behind Ana into Viktor's eyes, there was no doubt in my mind as to how this standoff would end. Two of us would live. Two of us would die. The only question was, which pair was which.

The smart money would have been on the Podrova brothers. Or at least on Viktor. I didn't need to read a sixty-page psychological profile on him to know he was ruthless. I could almost smell the cruelty coming off him. I was certain that if it came down to it, Viktor would sacrifice his brother to save himself. On the other hand, there was no way I would sacrifice Ana, and he knew it. Behind those menacing eyes was a knowing smile. He possessed a human shield; I held nothing but a bag of bones. To Viktor, Dmitry was already dead.

"Drop your gun *now*," Viktor shouted, "or the lawyer dies."

Calmly, I said, "You kill her. I kill your brother. What then? We fire at one another to see who can take the most bullets before he drops dead?" I shrugged. "Sounds rather unpleasant."

Viktor was through hiding it; now he did turn his lips up in a smile.

"Not quite, Marshal Fisk. You see, there is one thing that separates men like me from men like—"

Before he could finish the sentiment I turned, aimed at the mirror, and fired. The move caught Viktor off guard, but not Ana. As Viktor moved to fire on me, she sank her teeth deep into his forearm. He released her with a scream and she dived onto the carpet.

Viktor lifted his Makarov and squeezed the trigger in my direction. Once, twice.

Both shots hit his brother.

Ana lifted a piece of broken glass from the floor and swung it, burying it as far as she could in Viktor's calf.

Viktor shrieked in pain.

It was all the time I needed.

I fired.

The bullet caught Viktor square in the chest and knocked him backward into the wall. His body slid down, leaving a bright red vertical streak down the Sheetrock.

I dropped Dmitry to the floor just as he released his death rattle.

I helped Ana to her feet. Her body was shivering and I was desperate to warm it, to comfort her in any way she needed comforting. The room, I knew, reeked of cordite and spent blood and sizzling flesh, but all I smelled were fresh strawberries. I buried my face in her hair as she clung to the back of my neck. We pressed our bodies together.

"Are you okay?" I said.

"Yes," she said, breathing heavily. "I think I am getting used to this."

Carefully, I led her around the broken glass and fallen bodies.

"What did he mean?" Ana said as we passed Viktor and stepped out into the foyer. "What was he going to say about what separates men like you from men like him?"

I shrugged. "I don't know, Ana."

"Well, it is a very bad habit to interrupt people when they are in the middle of a sentence."

If she was joking, she didn't let on.

We moved swiftly through the living room to the front door, intent on not taking a single moment for granted.

Together Ana and I stepped out of the duplex and into the ferocious cold, knowing two things for certain.

The Podrova brothers were dead. And, far more important, little Lindsay Sorkin continued to live.

Part Four

THE CHILDREN OF BELARUS

Chapter 47

Ana and I were just a few kilometers outside of Gomel, the second largest city in Belarus, when our rented Suzuki Grand Vitara struck a large fallen branch, immediately overheated, and seconds later broke down. I'd been dozing off in the passenger seat of the navy SUV when Ana released a scream so loud it made me reach for my Glock. I thought our tires had been shot out. In the pitch black, the SUV rumbled to the side of the deserted road and let out a great sigh of steam from the hood. We sat in complete silence for several moments as we contemplated the repercussions of becoming stranded on a dark, rural road in southeastern Belarus in the dead of winter in the freezing cold.

A light snow dotted our windshield. I lowered my window and gazed out into the woods. More than one-third of the country was forest. Pine, spruce, oak, birch, aspen, alder—all were represented. Here, the trees stood so tall they choked off any light from the moon.

"We are imprisoned in a Grimm fairy tale," Ana said softly.

Strange how, with everything that had transpired over the past few days—the shootout at Chudzik's lake house, the standoff with the Podrova brothers—*this* could feel like our low, our rock bottom. But it did. Maybe because it seemed so completely senseless. This wasn't an obstacle raised by the Germans or Turks, the Pruszkow mob or corrupt cops, wasn't a land mine laid by Yuri Bobrovnyk or the Podrova brothers, or even the Russians we were trying to track down. This was just dumb, stupid luck—nothing but shitty fate.

And wasn't that the worst of all our fears? Something we couldn't at all control. A tumor in the colon, a drunk driver barreling down the wrong side of the road, striking us head-on because we'd decided to forgo the two-dollar delivery fee and order Chinese takeout instead. It was the ultimate mind-fuck. Those who just happened to be riding the subway in Tokyo on a Monday morning in March 1995, or flying from Boston to Los Angeles on September 11, 2001.

For me, it was Hailey. Over and over, for years, I'd thought, *Why her?* I'd blamed my career, my being in Bucharest when she was taken. I'd blamed Tasha's parents for buying us that huge house in Georgetown when all we'd needed was a two-bedroom apartment downtown. Hell, I'd even faulted Tasha herself for being at home with Hailey and not out shopping or at a Nationals game with Tasha's older brother, Benny, and his wife, Lara. But it was none of their faults. Only the man who took her, and however he came to find her, which was pure rotten luck.

Ana and I both jumped at a loud rap on her window.

Even though I'd been watching for tails fairly steadily since we'd left Kiev, I placed my hand around my Glock before telling her she could lower her window.

The man standing outside our SUV in the scudding snow was large and had a round, red face and a full, gray beard.

"Preevyet," he grunted, which I knew to be a greeting. He then followed with a few sentences I couldn't begin to understand.

Ana, not for the first time, surprised me.

"Knee puneemaiyoo," she said carefully. *"Ya plokha guvareyoo pa rooski. Vy guvareetyeh pa angleeski?"*

Grimly, the man shook his head.

"What did you say?" I asked her.

"I told him I do not speak Russian. I asked if he spoke English. He doesn't."

"Hauno," I muttered. Russian for "shit." One of the four or five words I remembered. The others would be useful only in a bar.

Fortunately, the steam billowing from beneath our hood clued the man in as to our troubles. He motioned for Ana to pop the hood and she did. I knew little about engines but felt bad about leaving him out there alone in the cold, so I opened my door and hopped out to join him. By the time I got to him he was already shaking his head and frowning.

"Nyet," he said.

It was clear that he couldn't fix it, at least not out here, in the dark, in the blizzard, with no tools and no parts. He stepped around the hood to Ana's window and pointed behind our SUV to his pickup truck, which must have been twenty years old. We then engaged him in a game of charades. After a few tries, we realized he was mimicking the act of taking us to his home, where we could spend the night.

"What do you think?" Ana said as the man returned to his truck.

"What choice do we have?" I replied. "We'll be fine. He's an older man, and besides, I'm carrying my gun."

We piled into his pickup and, after a few attempts, his engine coughed to life. He waited for the truck to warm up, then we rolled off.

As we drove deeper into the forest I saw that Ana, seated in front between me and the Belarusian, was growing more on edge. As was I. The only lights were those of the truck we rode in; it was clear that no one else was around for miles. We'd already accomplished enough twists and turns that we'd never find our way back to the Grand Vitara if need be. Not that getting back to the broken-down SUV would do us much good anyway.

More than twenty minutes later we arrived at our apparent destination, a single-story home that somewhat resembled an old barn. The Belarusian parked the pickup haphazardly on what I suspected was the front lawn. I couldn't know for sure as it was buried under a thick layer of snow. He extinguished the headlights and opened his door, providing no hint that we should follow.

"Maybe he is just going in to get his tools," Ana said quietly.

As she said it, the large man looked back and motioned for us to exit the truck.

Heads down against the blowing snow, we followed the man to the entrance of the home.

He stepped inside, while we were stopped at the threshold by a young woman, presumably the man's daughter. We waited in the cold as he explained our presence to her in his language. The young woman appeared more skeptical the more he talked, and for a minute I was certain we were going to be turned away, left to freeze to death in the forest.

Finally, the man brushed past her into the house, while the young woman remained in front of us, arms folded over an ample chest.

"I am Darja Kovalev," she said with no warmth whatsoever. An older woman materialized at her side. "And this is my mother, Olga."

"Pleased to meet you," I said, offering my hand to the mother.

From their reaction I thought I'd accidentally pulled out my Glock. The old woman took several steps backward while her daughter swatted my hand away.

"Never offer your hand over the threshold of someone's home," Darja scolded me. "It is very bad luck. You should not even say hello."

As if to avoid an utter calamity, Darja quickly ushered us inside.

The home was humble, to say the least. Small, the furniture no doubt dating back to the Soviet era, maybe even back to Stalin.

It was late; indeed, both women appeared ready to turn in. Yet, before we could stop them, they were in the process of setting a table and starting the burners. Salami suddenly appeared, and what

I was told were pickled mushrooms. Ana and I sat at the table as Olga reheated some beetroot soup—what I knew as *barszcz*—the fantasy food Ana had introduced me to back in Krakow. Not until the food began hitting the table did I realize I was famished.

I reached for a pickled mushroom and Ana immediately slapped my wrist. I looked up. The man had disappeared into the rear of the house and the women were busy with their backs turned to us.

"Not the mushrooms," Ana whispered.

For a moment I had no idea what she was talking about. Then it hit me: contamination from Chernobyl. During the ill-fated train ride from Odessa to Kiev, I'd read in the guidebook that more than 80 percent of human radioactive contamination was caused by eating contaminated food. The primary hazard was in the soil rather than the air. Radiation was transferred from the soil to the plants, and the Gomel region suffered the worst contamination of all.

We were only 120 kilometers from the Ukrainian city of Pripyat, where the Chernobyl nuclear plant was located. Levels of radiation in this region continued to be alarming and would remain so well into the twenty-second century. The guidebook I'd read made it sound as though eating berries or mushrooms cultivated in the Gomel region were tantamount to swallowing a liter of drain cleaner while playing a heated game of Russian roulette.

I quietly thanked Ana and helped myself to a slice of salami instead.

The large man returned and set a fifth of vodka down hard on the table between us. He motioned to Darja, who promptly produced two tall shot glasses.

"My father, Vladislav, wishes you to drink with him," Darja said directly to me.

I was about to demur when Ana poked me in the ribs and whispered, "It would be very bad manners to refuse. Drinking with someone is an act of friendship."

"Of course," I said, recalling a long-ago trip to Moscow to track down a fugitive from Brighton Beach. It took sharing a bottle of vodka with his cousin for me to capture him and return him to the Eastern District of New York, where he would later be convicted of twelve counts, including murder and racketeering. Before I left for Moscow, I'd read everything there was to read about Russian culture and customs, drinking being an important part of both.

So now, as Vladislav filled the shot glasses, I searched my mind for the unwritten rules. When he was through with the pour, I raised my glass and clinked it against his as he said, *"Za vstretchu!"*

"To our get-together," Ana explained, holding a glass of ice water to her lips.

I maintained eye contact with him and downed most of the shot in a single gulp. It was important not to allow your glass to touch the table again until it was empty. I finished off the last bit, then finally set it down. Before I could remove my hand from around the glass, Vladislav was already refilling it. Once a bottle was opened, I suddenly recalled, the bottle had to be drained dry. No exceptions.

"Za milyh dam!" he said, clinking his glass against mine just as Darja took a seat at the table.

"To lovely ladies," Ana explained.

I swallowed the vodka, fought the burn in the back of my throat.

As I chased the vodka with a few more slices of salami I listened to Ana make small talk with Darja.

"Your country is so beautiful," Ana told her.

For the first time, Darja smiled. "Thank you. It is a difficult time in Belarus, but then, I think it is a difficult time everywhere."

Vladislav shot his daughter a look.

Darja said, "He cannot speak English, my father. But he heard me say 'Belarus' and he feared I was talking politics."

Talk of politics was generally avoided in the former Soviet Union, especially around strangers.

"Vashe zdorovie!" Vladislav said, lifting his glass again.

"To your health," Ana translated.

That's ironic, I thought as I fired another direct shot at my liver.

"Your home is beautiful," Ana told Darja. "You live here with your parents?"

Affordable housing in the former Soviet Union was in short supply, forcing many young people to live with their parents well into their thirties. Even if they were married. Even if the couple had children. Which, as it turned out, was the case with Darja. Her husband was sleeping one off in their bedroom, their two children asleep in the small room opposite.

"Vipiem za lubov!" Vladislav said with a roll of his eyes as Darja told Ana about her husband.

Ana turned to me as I downed another shot. "He said, 'Let's drink to love.' But I think he was being sarcastic."

"Yes, I caught the sarcasm," I said. "Any way you can help us out with this bottle, Ana?"

"Sorry," she said. "I do not like straight vodka."

"Yeah," I mumbled. "Well, that makes two of us."

Dizzy, I scanned the room for something to talk about, anything that would forestall the next toast. Through the walkway into the living room, I saw a square piece of black velvet hanging from the wall.

"Is there a Monet hiding behind that curtain?" I said.

Darja and Ana turned to look at it.

"It is a mirror behind that wall hanging," Darja said.

"Is it broken?"

Darja shook her head. "We have suffered a death in the family," she said calmly. "When a family member dies, it is necessary to cover all the mirrors in the house. The dead, their spirits linger for forty days. They cannot be seen by the naked eye, of course. But they may be sighted in any reflective surface. When it occurs, it can be very unsettling."

"I can imagine," I said.

"I am so sorry you lost someone," Ana said, glancing at Olga, who was still at the burners, cooking something. "Was it someone very close to you?"

Darja nodded her head slowly, dropping her eyes to the table.

"It was my daughter," she said.

The air immediately seemed to be sucked through the windows, leaving us without oxygen. I inhaled deeply, suddenly on the verge of inexplicable panic.

Chapter 48

Elena was nine years old when she died at the end of the preceding month. She'd succumbed to complications from thyroid cancer, an unbelievably common disease in Belarus, particularly in the Gomel region, which had suffered the worst fallout from the Chernobyl disaster in the entire country. Levels of contamination continued to be dangerously high, even right here, in the air circulating in the room in which we sat. Thinking about it gave me the shivers, and I hoped we wouldn't be here long enough to suffer any ill effects.

"I have had four children," Darja said stoically. "Elena was my first. She was born healthy, which is very rare in our region. Only one out of ten infants born here are so lucky."

"Because of Chernobyl," Ana said.

Darja's expression didn't change. "Of course, Chernobyl."

The world's worst nuclear disaster occurred on a night in late April 1986, when reactor number 4 at the nuclear power plant was scheduled to be shut down for regular maintenance. Workers decided to use the opportunity to conduct an entirely unnecessary safety test. There were purportedly a number of contributing factors to the accident—design flaws, operator errors, flouted safety procedures—but whatever the cause, the result was unthinkable: nearly nine tons of radioactive material (the equivalent of more than ninety Hiroshimas) burst into the sky in a massive ball of fire, ultimately blowing north over all of Belarus and Ukraine. The fallout likely culminated in tens of thousands of deaths in the years and decades to follow, and caused an area the size of the state of New York to become unsafe for human habitation for the next five hundred years.

Because of Soviet silence, the fifty-three thousand residents of the nearby city of Pripyat were not evacuated for two full days following the disaster. Located within the deadly thirty-kilometer Exclusion Zone, Pripyat remains a ghost town even today.

But the most horrifying effects of the Chernobyl catastrophe were undoubtedly absorbed by the children of Belarus and northern Ukraine. Currently, only 15 to 20 percent of infants in the affected regions were born healthy, and even those children generally developed weaker immune systems and later contracted radiation-related diseases such as thyroid cancer.

The infant-mortality rate in Belarus was 300 percent higher than it was in all of Europe. Infants who survived birth were frequently afflicted with Down syndrome, chromosomal aberrations, and neural-tube defects. Indeed, congenital birth defects were incredibly common; in fact, such defects had increased 250 percent following Chernobyl. Congenital defects often affected the kidneys, lungs, and heart, and frequently required surgery, even organ transplants.

Presently, there were more than seven thousand children on the list for cardiac surgery. Doctors in Minsk had the know-how to treat most conditions, but not the money. Often not the organs.

"Since Elena was born healthy, my mother said we were blessed and we needed to have more children. The population of our country has steadily declined since the disaster. Soon, my mother warned, there would be no Belarusians left. We were obligated, she told us. So we got pregnant again. The second baby was a boy. He was stillborn, like so many other infants in Belarus."

Ana held a hand to her chest. "I am so sorry," she said.

"We had two more children, as you know. Polina and Margerita, both who are asleep in back."

"And they're healthy," Ana said hopefully.

Darja shook her head. "No. The older girl, Margerita, was born with Down syndrome and a cleft palate. She, too, has recently been diagnosed with thyroid cancer. The other, Polina, she was born with a hole in her heart. So many children here are born with the condition that the doctors, they have a name for it—Chernobyl Heart."

All of us fell silent.

Olga, who stood leaning against the kitchen counter, appeared to be crying, though other than her grandchildren's names, I was certain she hadn't understood a word her daughter said.

Vladislav stared motionlessly at the bottle of vodka, until he finally lifted it and poured himself a shot. He downed the shot without ceremony. And without inviting me, a slight for which I would be eternally grateful.

"My parents are angry with me," Darja said. "Such things should not be spoken about in the presence of strangers." She swallowed hard. "But I am tired of being so quiet."

"And your husband?" Ana said. "What is his name?"

"Kirill."

The moment she said the name, Vladislav spit on the floor.

Olga witnessed it and gave him hell for it.

He yelled back, pounding the table with his fist, knocking his shot glass to the floor, where it shattered.

I silently wished it were my shot glass that had fallen.

Darja continued as though nothing had happened.

"My father, he does not like my husband. Kirill is an alcoholic, like most husbands in Belarus—including my father. Both are depressed, neither have ever helped around the house. The only difference is that my husband fools around on me. Sometimes Kirill is so drunk, he brings the women to the house. This truly enrages my father."

"I can imagine," I said.

When Darja looked up at me, I wished I'd kept my mouth shut. The shots of vodka had kicked in and I was already incapable of censoring myself.

"It is very common here," Darja said defensively. "Men cheat on their wives."

"They do so in Poland, too," Ana threw in.

"In the States, too," I said, not wanting to alienate myself at the table. "But they try to be more discreet about it."

"How noble of them," Darja said.

I wanted so badly to peel myself away from this conversation that I felt ready to do another shot with her father. But Vladislav was still busy yelling at Olga, now pounding both fists on the table so hard that he knocked over the bowl of beetroot soup. It, too, shattered on the floor and made one hell of an ugly mess.

Suddenly another voice entered the fray. A male mouthpiece shouting in Russian at the top of his lungs.

"Kirill?" Ana said quietly to Darja.

"Of course, Kirill."

Darja said his name with the same acidity she'd used when saying the name Chernobyl.

The battle, meanwhile, continued as Vladislav leaped from his chair, knocking it over in the process.

Kirill, a thin, bearded man dressed in loose jeans and no shirt, had lurched into the room. He pointed a finger at Vladislav with one hand and intentionally knocked over a small vase with the other.

Vladislav bent over to pick up his chair, and I was sure the argument was over. But instead of setting it back down at the table, he lifted the chair over his head as though to swing it at his son-in-law.

Olga immediately intervened, gripping the chair legs from behind her husband.

Kirill took advantage of the opportunity and punched the old man in the stomach. The blow was so powerful, it knocked both of Darja's parents down.

I'd already jumped up. So had Ana and Darja.

When Darja witnessed her parents fall in a heap, she moved to attack her husband. Calmly, Kirill turned, gripped her by the hair with his left, and nailed her in the face with his right.

By the time Darja hit the ground, I was already halfway across the top of the table. I leaped just as I reached the end and swung my right fist, using gravity to throw more force behind it. The punch landed somewhere near the center of Kirill's face, and he hit the floor like a meteor striking a planet.

Breathing heavily, I stared down at his unmoving form, as Ana helped Darja and then her parents to their feet. I watched Kirill's chest rise and fall and was relieved that I hadn't killed him. He'd been looking straight up when I struck him, and for a moment I thought I'd driven his nose up into his brain.

Once everyone but Kirill was standing, I received hugs and kisses from Olga and Darja, and finally Ana.

From Vladislav, I received a shot glass full of vodka.

"Do Dna!" he shouted.

I took the shot in a single go as Vladislav drank straight from the bottle.

"What did he say?" I asked Ana after setting down my shot glass, waiting for him to pour me another.

Ana smiled. "He toasted you," she said. *"Do Dna.* It means, 'Until the end, the heroic.'"

Chapter 49

When I woke late the next morning, my head was on fire and the contents of my stomach had already started the return trek up my esophagus. Quick as I could I scurried to the toilet and vomited. A moment later, Ana stepped in, smiling.

"Good morning," she said.

Olga immediately swept past her into the bedroom, carrying a plate of something that resembled cucumbers. Despite my protest, she picked up one of the smaller ones and stuffed the tail end in my mouth, making me gag.

"Eat it," Ana said.

I allowed myself a bite and it was all I could do to keep it down.

"They are pickled gherkins," Ana said. "They will help with your hangover."

I grimaced. "They will?"

Ana shrugged. "Olga seems to think so."

Olga patted me on the arm, turned, and left the room, leaving me with the plate of gherkins in my hand. I turned and gazed out the window. The snow on the ground gleamed so brightly it set my retinas ablaze.

I closed my eyes, rubbed them with my free hand, and opened them again. For a moment I was sure I was hallucinating.

"Is that our . . . ?"

"It is," Ana said. "It's our SUV. It's fixed and ready to go, thanks to Vladislav."

A half hour later, Ana and I were back on the road heading north to Minsk, the capital and largest city in Belarus. From what we had elicited in Poland and Ukraine, one thing was clear: a terribly large sum of money was being paid for Lindsay Sorkin.

That had long ago ruled out any conventional ransom, long ago ruled out any fear that she'd been taken to be sexually exploited. It made no business sense: the buyer would never recoup his losses.

That left her father, Vince Sorkin, as the motive. The weapons designer. Creator of this remote-controlled automaton that could potentially replace soldiers on the battlefield. Dmitry Podrova had said that the buyer in Belarus denied that Vince Sorkin was the reason behind the kidnapping, but I remained convinced that the denial had been a negotiating tactic. After all, if not for the media, the Podrova brothers would have never known about the father's worth to other potential bidders, like the Syrian, Bilal ibn Hashim.

This was about Vince Sorkin and Nepturn Technology—what I had feared from the very beginning. This was why, all those days ago, I'd stood from the marble table and tried to leave the cottage, why I'd told Lori Sorkin that she'd be in better hands with the French National Police.

If this was indeed about Vince Sorkin, now that we were here, Minsk was the logical place to start. First, despite the fall of communism, it was believed that roughly 80 percent of Belarus's economy remained state controlled. Which meant that the Belarusian government—and by extension its secret national intelligence agency, the only intelligence agency that retained the Russian name "KGB" following the dissolution of the Soviet Union—was one of the few holders of enough wealth to make such an offer for Lindsay's capture. And it made sense. Belarus's colossal neighbor Russia continued to exert power over the former Soviet states in any way it could. The Russian president was known to have cut off Belarus's supply of natural gas on several occasions, the sole apparent reason being to remind the former Soviet state of its powerlessness in the region.

Of course, logic also dictated that there was another possibility. That the man who had hired the Podrova brothers was yet another broker, and that Lindsay Sorkin's ultimate destination was, in fact, Belarus's big brother, Russia. This was now my greatest fear. If we didn't find Lindsay quickly in Minsk, there was a good chance she'd be taken to Moscow. Once she was there, perhaps in the control of the Russian Foreign Intelligence Service or SVR, all bets would be off. Ana and I would have no chance whatsoever of recovering her from such a goliath.

"I have never been on such a lonely freeway," Ana said, peering out the passenger-side window.

We were doing just over eighty miles per hour, so we'd passed a few vehicles, but not many. And only one or two cars seemed to be keeping pace. I checked the rearview now but it was empty.

"Speaking of lonely," I said, "did I hear Darja right this morning? Did she tell you her husband had packed his bags and left her when he regained consciousness last night?"

Ana nodded. "It is a good thing, Simon. He contributed nothing and he hit her all the time. She is very happy he left."

"Still," I said. "I feel like it's my fault."

"Probably. But think no more about it. Darja told me that almost seventy percent of marriages in Belarus end in divorce."

I checked my rearview again and saw a silver sports car I'd seen earlier. A man in sunglasses was driving. He seemed not to have any passengers, which afforded me some measure of relief. Then again, *we* were searching for the Russians. Why in the world would the Russians be following us?

"I have to call Davignon," I said, pulling my mobile phone out of my pocket. "Would you hit Speaker, then dial?"

A moment later, the sound of a muffled ring coasted through a flow of static.

"Simon?" Davignon said.

"Yes," I replied. "I have Ana with me and you're on speakerphone."

"Where are you, Simon?"

"Belarus. We're in an SUV on the way to Minsk."

I hadn't spoken to Davignon since I was in a taxi on my way to the hostel in Odessa, so I briefed him on everything that had happened since then: Yuri Bobrovnyk and the boat, the explosion meant for us on the train, the Podrova brothers, and our night in Gomel. I skipped over the vodka, the fistfight, and the hangover.

Davignon took it all in, then said, "So if what this Dmitry Podrova told you is true, Lindsay is still alive."

"Alive and heading north, Lieutenant. If so, we're on her trail."

"This is terrific news, Simon. And you, how are you holding up?"

"I'm fine, Lieutenant. Question is, how is Lori doing?"

"Better, I think. Her breakdown appears to be more mental than physical. She is still in hospital under observation. I visit every few hours. I am the only person she will see."

I frowned. "What about her husband?"

"They had a terrible fight. I don't know all the details but it seems she is now blaming Vince for everything."

I wondered if Lori had come to the same conclusion I had—that Vince was most likely the motive behind Lindsay's kidnapping.

"I need to speak with Vince as soon as possible," I said. "I have some further questions for him about his role at Nepturn Technology. Is he with you now, Lieutenant?"

Davignon hesitated. "I am afraid not, Simon."

"All right," I said. "Where is he, then? At the hotel?"

Davignon cleared his throat. "Unfortunately, at present, we have no idea where he is."

I stared down at the mobile phone resting in the center console, my mouth agape.

"What the hell do you mean, Lieutenant?"

"Of course, I had Vince under constant protection," he said defensively, "but he somehow slipped away from my men."

"Slipped away?"

I feared Vince might be on his way to Ukraine. Which would be terrible. Because if Moscow was indeed involved, Vince Sorkin might well be our only bargaining chip. If something were to happen to him, it could be to his daughter's peril.

"You need to get him back, Lieutenant."

"We are *trying,* Simon."

I sighed. I could tell by his voice that Davignon was every bit as frustrated as I was.

"All right," I said, trying to calm myself. "If Vince contacts you to find out where I am, don't tell him that I'm in Belarus. If he's left the country, do everything you can to get him to return to Paris. If he follows me, he may be playing right into the kidnappers' hands. Make certain he understands that at the end of the day, he may be his daughter's last hope."

I ended the call, exasperated. If Vince were in sight, I could have strangled him for being so stupid. But then, what did I do in the days after Hailey was taken? I'd done what I thought was right. I'd listened to the Federal Bureau of Investigation. I'd remained at home, waited by the phone, allowed them to conduct their search without my interference.

Only no one ever called.

No one ever found Hailey.

Over the past ten years I'd convinced myself that it wouldn't have mattered if I'd done things differently in the days immediately following Hailey's disappearance. Hailey would still be missing, she'd still be dead. But I wasn't sure I believed that anymore. What if I had put in the effort that I'd been affording Lindsay Sorkin right from the start? If I hadn't waited for the Bureau to give up. Could I have found Hailey? Could I have tracked down the monster who stole her from her mother's arms?

"Are you okay, Simon?" Ana said.

I rubbed away the tear that was forming in my right eye.

"I'm fine," I said, staring at myself in the rearview to make sure my face no longer betrayed the lie.

I looked well enough, I thought.

But in the rearview I'd caught something more than just my reflection.

That same silver sports car was behind us again.

Chapter 50

By the time we arrived in Minsk it was snowing again. The beauty of the capital caught me completely by surprise. The buildings didn't scrape the sky but rather ceded to it, allowing for spectacular panoramic views that instilled a sense of calm not found in other major cities. There was so little noise that had I been blindfolded, I would've feared I'd gone deaf. No traffic, no horns, no screeching brakes, not even a policeman's whistle. The city was as silent as the grave. And as clean as any I'd ever seen, even Honolulu or Helsinki.

The excitement of arriving was soon replaced by the realization that we had no clue where to go now that we were here. We knew the Russians' names—Jov Sergeyev and Sacha Orlov—but that did us little good if they were originally from Moscow and spent most of their time in Ukraine.

Of course, I would have liked to obtain more information from Dmitry Podrova, but Viktor had gone and spoiled my plan. Once we'd left the Podrova brothers, I'd called Rudnyk and told him what went down at their place. But not before asking him whether he'd ever heard the names Jov Sergeyev and Sacha Orlov. He hadn't, and the names weren't in Ukraine's system. I then tried Jess Kidman. She'd never heard the names and they weren't in Interpol's system either. Kidman was, however, able to pull up and send to my phone a grainy photograph of the Syrian, Bilal ibn Hashim. Unfortunately, given the quality of the photo, I wouldn't have been able to pick the Syrian out of a lineup.

There was no one else to call because there was no else we could trust.

After driving aimlessly for a few minutes, I pulled the Grand Vitara into a garage for an underground shopping mall beneath Independence Square.

"As much as I love shopping," Ana said, "I am not sure this is a good time, Simon."

I glanced in my rearview, hoping the silver sports car had followed us, but I saw nothing but empty blacktop in the mirror. I pulled into one of the parking stalls and told Ana to follow me.

The mall was named Stolitsa and it was as impressive in style as any in the West. But it was also rather empty, not only of customers but of stores. Muzak replaced the silence of the surface, but other than that the underground shopping center was fairly quiet. I scanned the stores that still existed. Unlike most malls throughout Europe, I didn't recognize the brand names advertised in the shops' windows.

Ana looked perplexed. "What are we doing here, Simon?"

"Maybe wasting precious time," I said. "But I hope not."

I pulled her into a clothing store with a cluttered window. We rounded a number of racks of women's clothes.

I moved up front to the window and peeked out between two well-dressed mannequins, both of which were well prepared for a winter in Siberia.

Meanwhile, a stern-looking saleswoman began her approach from the rear of the store.

I turned to Ana. "Do you know enough Belarusian to get her to leave us alone?"

"I think so," she said.

Before I could say another word, the saleswoman was upon us.

"Preevyet," Ana said, holding up a dress she'd just snatched off the rack. *"Skorlka ehya styeet?"*

The saleswoman appeared annoyed. She tore the dress from Ana's hands, fished out the sales tag, and displayed it inches from Ana's face.

"Spaseeba," Ana said.

As she said it, I turned my head back to the window that looked out onto the mall. A dark man with black hair and an elongated nose was passing by. He was dressed in a long black leather jacket and wearing sunglasses.

As my eyes followed him he reached into his jacket but continued staring straight ahead.

Suddenly, in one fluid motion, he turned and extended his right arm, aiming a 9 mm handgun directly at me.

"Down," I shouted.

As I went to the floor, the storefront window exploded and a bullet buzzed my left ear.

Ana and the saleswoman screamed.

I reached for my Glock and got to my knees, scanning past the mannequins for my target. One mannequin had fallen, another had been cut in half at the waist.

I couldn't see the shooter.

A ringing sound was piercing my left ear. I tried to shake it away, to no avail.

Behind me, the women were crying but I couldn't risk a look back. Not yet.

Finally, I heard shouts and shrieks down at the other end of the mall, and I got to my feet and leaped through the empty window and onto the marble floor. My feet slipped, but once I gained purchase I was running with every bit of strength I had, my right arm extended, still holding the Glock.

"Get down," I shouted to everyone I saw.

As salespeople poked their heads out, I yelled for them to get back inside.

It took me a moment to realize why no one was doing what they were told—no one had understood a goddamn word I'd said.

Finally, I spotted the shooter, taking aim at me again.

As he fired I dived behind a directory, stayed down as it flew into pieces just above my head.

I immediately jumped to my feet, got a clean shot off but missed him by a few inches.

He began to run again.

I chased after him.

After a few dozen yards, he made a ruinous mistake—he ducked into a store.

I came to a full halt just before I reached the entrance. I pressed my back up against the wall and readied my weapon. I wiped sweat from my brow, drew a deep breath, and moved in.

It was a candy store, full of busy bright colors that would've easily distracted someone who wasn't trained. But all I saw was the long black leather jacket in the rear. Then a face.

It was the face from the silver sports car that had been tailing us. The man was no longer wearing sunglasses. I stared into his dark eyes and saw no fear. No fear whatsoever. At that moment I had no doubt in my mind that I was staring into the eyes of a professional killer. And although I couldn't tell definitively from the grainy photograph Kidman had sent me, I thought, who else could this man be but Bilal ibn Hashim, the Syrian whom the two Russians were running from.

Somehow, the Syrian had tracked us down. No doubt the rental company had a LoJack or some similar vehicle-recovery devise installed on the Grand Vitara. However he'd done it, Bilal ibn Hashim now meant to eliminate us from the equation.

If he had tracked us, surely Bilal would have tracked the Russians, too. Which meant that I needed to figure out a way to

neutralize Bilal without killing him. No easy feat under the circumstances. Still, it seemed clear to me that Lindsay's life might well
depend on both of us surviving this standoff.

In front of him, Bilal held tightly to a young woman with light
brown hair. A human shield. She was sobbing and saying something I couldn't understand.

Bilal was pressing his gun hard against her right temple.

I scanned the back of the store and saw no door. He was trapped
but he had a hostage.

"Drop the gun, Bilal," I said calmly, sweat dripping down my
neck, dampening the collar of my shirt.

His eyes narrowed at the mention of his name. He bared a set of
coffee-stained teeth.

"Tell me where I can find the Russians," he shouted. "Tell me, or
this woman is dead."

And that mistake, his second in minutes, would prove fatal. Up
until that moment, I thought that I needed him alive. But if he was
asking me where the Russians were, then he was useless. I raised my
Glock just slightly and peered through the sight, centered it directly
between his eyes.

"Last chance, Bilal," I said.

"No," he cried. "It is *her* last chan—"

I fired.

Chapter 51

Forty minutes later, I was gripping Ana's hand in an ambulance. Bilal ibn Hashim was dead, but his first shot through the storefront window had struck the left side of Ana's chest, just above the heart.

I turned to the Minsk police officer sitting at my side.

"How far to the hospital?"

"We are not to go to hospital," he responded in a thick accent. "We are to go to clinic. It will be safer."

I was devastated. Felt as though I had put the bullet in her myself. My hands were shaking and my gut had risen into my chest. Listening to the chirping of the machinery, my mind wanted to shut itself down, take a forever rest. My very core was collapsing.

Lying on her back, Ana stared up at me with watery eyes.

"When we get to the clinic," she said, "please, call my brother."

I tried to hide the worry in my voice. "I will, Ana. First thing."

"And last," she said. "You need to promise—as soon as you call Marek you will leave."

"I'm *not* leaving you, Ana," I said.

"You *must*, Simon. Or else all of this will have been for nothing. We are so close. You must go find Lindsay."

I swallowed hard, tried to keep my eyes from welling up. Truth was, I had no idea where to go from here. My plan to allow the man following us to find us had backfired. It nearly got both of us—and a number of innocent bystanders—killed. Even the Syrian didn't know where the Russians were, where they'd taken Lindsay Sorkin. How was I ever going to find her?

Face it, Simon. She's gone.

"Find her and bring her back to Paris," Ana said, staring up at the ceiling of the ambulance. "Then, go to London. Find your sister, Tuesday. Find your mother. Everyone should have a family."

Families only break your heart, I wanted to say in my exhausted state.

They abandon you.

Steal you.

Kill themselves.

Vanish into thin air.

Ana's eyes fluttered and the monitors she was connected to began to beep in ominous tones.

No. Can't be.

"*How far?*" I shouted to the officer.

He glanced out the window and said, "We are here."

The clinic was an old, one-story building that looked more like an asylum than a hospital. I drew a deep breath as the paramedics lifted Ana's stretcher out of the ambulance and hurried her to the front door. There seemed to be no place to receive an ambulance.

I followed them inside on legs that felt like lead weights.

The interior of the clinic was no more appealing than the exterior. The lobby reeked so badly of bleach that my eyes began to water. I covered my nose with my hand and chased after Ana's stretcher. The corridor seemed endless, its floor scuffed badly enough that I couldn't tell what color it had originally been. The walls were a drab, dirty blue. The fluorescent lights above our heads flickered as though the clinic might lose power at any second. Loops of copper electrical wires hung out from the ceiling, only a few feet overhead.

Ana could die in here from an otherwise treatable wound, I thought with a sickening terror.

They burst through a set of double doors into an operating room.

"I am sorry, sir," said a large woman in nurse's garb. "You will have to wait outside."

The nurse went into the operating room, and through the double doors I caught one last glimpse of Ana, unconscious as they scissored off her clothes.

Standing there, every last bit of energy seemed to drain from my body. I couldn't recall how many days it had been since I'd left Bordeaux for Charles de Gaulle Airport in Paris. Eight? Nine, maybe?

Did it matter? My world had altered unimaginably since then. I'd taken the lives of at least a half-dozen men. All of them in self-defense yet troubling nonetheless. I'd made a promise to a mother that I wouldn't be able to keep, and for that, I knew, Lori Sorkin would never forgive me. And I couldn't blame her.

As unlikely as it was given the amount of time we'd spent together, I'd fallen for a woman for the first time since I'd met Tasha in college. And now that woman was on an operating-room table, fighting for her life. Because of me.

I bent at the waist and placed my hands on my knees.

Worst of all, I'd let down little Lindsay.

If Vince Sorkin wasn't found, the six-year-old girl was doomed to become a statistic. Even if Davignon somehow retrieved him, no government in the West would allow Vince to deal himself for his daughter. In fact, if my suspicions were correct, Vince Sorkin hadn't run anywhere; he'd been taken. By the CIA or MI6, maybe even French intelligence. The United States and Great Britain certainly wouldn't risk the possibility, however remote, of his knowledge falling into the hands of terrorists, or a terrorist state.

Chances are, I thought grimly, *Vince Sorkin is already dead.*

Which left little to no hope for his six-year-old daughter.

I straightened myself up. A few moments earlier I'd admitted to myself that I'd fallen for Ana. I knew as well as anyone how dangerous that was—how easy it is to lose someone, how painful it is, and how *permanent* that pain is.

For all I know, Ana could be breathing her final breath right now.

No, she couldn't be dying. I'd promised to take her to Hollywood, California.

I'd made other promises to her, too, I realized. In the ambulance. I'd promised to call her brother Marek, first thing. So I took out my phone and dialed the number he'd called me from the night Ana and I were at the beach on the Black Sea in Odessa. After six rings the call went to voice mail and I left him a message, asking him to call me back as soon as he could. I left out the details so as not to alarm him.

Ana had also wanted me to go to London, to locate my sister and mother.

Strange that after all these years I was even considering it. Sure, I'd always been curious. But what do you say to an estranged mother who, as far as you know, never wanted anything to do with you? What kind of bond can you form with a new sister when you're both nearing forty? Yet here I was, sorting through how I could make a meeting happen. It had been about a week since I'd met Ana. Had she had that much of an effect on me already? And what did it say about us if she had?

I swallowed hard. I *would* go to London to look for them, I realized.

But not yet. First, Ana wanted me to find Lindsay Sorkin. She'd said we were close. So close, she'd said.

How close can I possibly be, I thought, *if I don't even know where to start?*

I glanced down the hall to my right. It was nothing but a dead end.

That made things easier.

There was nowhere to go but left.

Chapter 52

I walked past the clinic's lobby and continued down a corridor as drab and endless as the last. I kept my eyes focused on the floor in front of me but in my periphery I couldn't help but notice that the rooms on either side were occupied by children. I permitted myself a glance into one of the rooms and saw a child who must have been around four, yet his body was that of an infant. His large head lolled from side to side, each arm as thin as yarn and seemingly moving of its own accord.

I kept walking, tried to ignore the sudden crying coming from rooms all around me. But I couldn't ignore it. Once it invaded my mind, it conquered all other thoughts, and colonized. I had to see what hell I'd stepped into, what awful suffering surrounded me.

I stopped at the entrance to the next room and poked my head inside. There were two children in this room. One appeared to suffer from spina bifada, the other from something along the lines of cerebral palsy.

"The poor, dear things," I whispered to myself.

A soft voice came from behind me.

"Birth defects," she said. "And not nearly the worst of the lot."

I looked over my shoulder and found a small, redheaded nurse standing there in the hallway, her hands behind her back.

I found myself unable to speak.

"Most of the children here were born abnormal, then abandoned," she said with an Irish brogue. "Some suffer genetic damage: anencephaly, open spine, polydactylya, muscular atrophy in their limbs."

"Chernobyl?" I said.

She nodded. "Even the children who aren't born sick, most of them find their way here sooner or later, with thyroid cancer or other diseases. We see a lot of cases of leukemia."

"Even after a quarter century," I said.

The small nurse shrugged. "A quarter century, it's nothing. Belarus will be lucky if it's free of contamination in another half millennium."

"I had no idea," I admitted.

"Don't be ashamed," she said. "Very few of us Westerners do. When the disaster first occurred twenty-five years ago, the Kremlin did everything they could to downplay it. The seriousness of the accident was withheld from the people for weeks. Parents watched their sons and daughters run around on outdoor playgrounds completely ignorant of the fact that their children were being exposed to deadly levels of radiation."

"How cruel," I said quietly.

"Even much later, after more than ten thousand cases of thyroid cancer, scientists paid by state governments insisted that there was no link to the fallout from Chernobyl. The Russian government blamed the people themselves for unduly panicking. Moscow said changed living conditions and restricted eating caused all the cancer. Their stress caused it. Citizens didn't go for enough walks, they said, or eat enough vegetables. That's why everyone in Belarus was dying."

"But surely the Western governments took some action," I said.

"Just as they're doing in war-torn Africa? In Darfur?"

I had no answer to that.

"Some Westerners did stand up," she said. "Some Americans, some western Europeans. The doctor who runs this clinic, for instance, is an American, and he's done so much good he should be awarded the Nobel Peace Prize."

"What does he do exactly?"

"The medical professionals here for the most part have the knowledge but not the money. The doctor helps in that regard—his charities have raised enough funds to set up clinics all over Minsk. Many of the children here in Belarus are born with a condition we call Chernobyl Heart."

"They're born with holes in their hearts," I said.

"That's right. In most cases, correcting it is a fairly simple procedure. But it's costly as well. We use Gor-Tex to patch the holes. Each patch costs over three hundred dollars U.S. That's more than most doctors earn here in Minsk in a month."

I turned my head to look back up the endless corridor, hoping to see activity outside Ana's operating room, but there was none. Not yet.

"I'd like to help," I said. "Is the doctor around for a quick chat?"

The nurse shook her head. "Not today I'm afraid. He's at another clinic, near the National Library." She sighed. "A strange twist of fate, really."

"What is?"

"Several years ago the doctor fell in love with one of the nurses on staff at one of his clinics. They eventually got married. He knew the risks, of course; they both did. But Tatsiana wanted a child so badly. The doctor finally gave in. We had seen some healthy babies born here in Minsk, far more than in the Gomel region. So they were hopeful. About seven years ago they had a girl, named her Mila. Adorable girl."

"She was born with birth defects?" I said.

The nurse slowly bowed her head. "A rare condition called hypoplastic left-heart syndrome. Mila's undergone multiple open-heart surgeries, most recently a failed heart-valve procedure. Following that she was immediately put on a list to receive a heart transplant, but there are thousands of children in Belarus on that list. And Mila has a rare blood type, which in her case actually worked in her favor."

"Really?" I said. "How so?"

Tears instantly sprang to the nurse's eyes even as her lips turned up in a smile.

"A heart came in this morning," she said. "That's where the doctor is now. Replacing his own daughter's heart at his own clinic. Amazing, isn't it?"

"More than amazing," I said, genuinely moved by the story. "It's wonderful."

"I hope you get the chance to meet him. How long will you be in Minsk?"

I thought about it. "I don't know," I said.

"Well, today, of course, he's going to be busy, but if all goes well with his daughter's transplant, I suspect he will be back to work by the end of the week."

"Terrific," I said.

The nurse smiled, then turned and started back down the corridor.

"By the way, who should I ask for?" I said. "What's the doctor's name?"

She stopped, smacked herself lightly on the forehead for forgetting to mention it.

"His name is Stephen," she said. "Dr. Stephen Richter."

Richter.

The name hit me like a brick to the head.

"*Richter,*" Vince Sorkin had said the day I met him. "*Keith Richter in San Jose.*"

As tired as I was, I couldn't get my mind around who Keith Richter was or why he was important.

Wait, I thought.

Davignon had repeated the name just recently. Back when I was in Odessa.

"We haven't been able to get in touch with Keith Richter," he'd said.

"Keith Richter?"

I hadn't been able to recall who he was then, either.

But then Davignon had reminded me.

"Lindsay's pediatrician back in the States."

Chapter 53

I had no choice but to take a taxi. I gave the driver the location and told him to drive as fast as possible. I didn't think he understood my words, but he sure as hell understood my body language. He recognized that this ride was urgent.

As the driver peeled away from one clinic and headed for another, I pulled out my BlackBerry and called Davignon. He didn't answer after four rings and I was certain the call was going straight to voice mail. Then I heard his voice.

Davignon spoke in a whisper.

"I am in Lori's hospital room, Simon, and she's sleeping, so I cannot talk right—"

"Wake her up," I shouted, trying futilely to control the pitch of my voice.

"Why, Simon? Is something—"

"Just do it," I said.

As Davignon nudged Lori out of her sleep, I watched the eerily still city of Minsk blow by me.

"Ask her about Lindsay's pediatrician," I said. "Does Lori have the doctor's phone number in the room with her?"

I waited for a moment as he inquired.

"It is in her phone," he said. "Hold on, Simon, I will get it for her."

"Ask Lori what she knows about him," I shouted, hoping he

hadn't set his own phone down. "Ask her if he has a son or a brother or a cousin or an uncle, anyone in his family named Stephen."

"I am putting her on with you, Simon. Hold on."

When Lori finally spoke I could barely hear her.

"Why are you asking about Dr. Richter?" she asked, frantic. "Has something happened? Is Lindsay injured?"

"No, Lori," I said. "Nothing like that. I'm simply trying to get a bead on her, and her pediatrician may be the key."

"Keith Richter?" she said. "How could *he* be the key?"

Gently I said, "Answer my question first, Lori. Do you know anyone in his family named Stephen?"

"Stephen," she said, clearly considering it. "Keith's wife's name is Jenny—Vince and I spotted them at a restaurant a few months ago, and they asked us to join them."

"How old is Keith?"

"In his early to midforties, I'd say."

"Think, Lori. This may be important. Did he ever mention a brother? Or maybe a cousin who is also a doctor."

"Yes, yes," she said suddenly. "A brother, I think. But I don't remember his name. I just remember him saying his brother doesn't live in California."

"Did he say *where* his brother lives? Which country or continent?"

She hesitated. "I don't know, Simon. But I think he mentioned some organization he's affiliated with—maybe Doctors Without Borders, or something?"

"But the brother definitely lives overseas?" I said.

"I think so. It was date night and I'd been drinking white wine, and—"

"It's okay," I assured her. "You've given me enough to go on. Please put Lieutenant Davignon back on the phone."

While I waited I saw a sign for the National Library—we were close.

"What's going on, Simon?" Davignon said, confused.

"Have you found Vince, Lieutenant?"

"My men are still looking. Evidently, he withdrew a large sum of cash. I thought perhaps he received a ransom demand, but I do not see how. His phones here and back home, his e-mail addresses, they are all being closely monitored."

"All right," I said. "If you locate him, get him to Lori's hospital as soon as you can. It's vital that I speak to him."

"Yes, of course, Simon. But please, give me an idea—what is going on? Do you know where Lindsay is?"

"Are you out of Lori's earshot?"

"I am, yes."

I tore off my tie and stuffed it in my pocket.

"I think I know where Lindsay is, Lieutenant. I'm almost there now."

Chapter 54

I had the taxi drive past the clinic so that I could quickly scan the exterior, then I had the driver drop me a block away. The building appeared windowless, and, just as I'd feared, it was guarded by a large man stationed at the front door.

I surveyed the structure for another entrance but found none. Like the clinic they'd taken Ana to, there was no opening to receive ambulances. No fire exits. Clearly, Minsk didn't enforce the strict building codes of a U.S. city such as New York or D.C. If I was going to get in, it would have to be by powering past the big guy at the front door.

I watched him from behind a wide tree roughly ten yards away, as my eyes burned from the heavy winds. He was heavily inked. Had to be six foot four if he were an inch. He wasn't dressed in a uniform, but he was clearly in place to ensure that the wrong persons didn't enter the clinic. He smoked a cigarette as he paced, and I realized there was a good chance I was staring at Jov Sergeyev or Sacha Orlov. Dmitry Podrova had described the Russians as his best men—both former KGB.

I had to assume this man knew what I looked like and that he'd be waiting for either me or the Syrian. As far as tools went, all I had was my Glock, and I couldn't risk making such a commotion. I needed to be clever but I didn't have time to be clever. I'd have to rely on my instincts and improvise as I went along.

I began to move out in front of the tree, then I stopped and gazed up into its branches. My eyes followed the branches from the trunk all the way to the roof of the clinic.

There was my answer.

Damn, do I hate heights, I thought.

Still, I began the climb. It felt a lot like climbing the outer wall of the hostel in Odessa. My hands took the brunt of the cuts and scrapes, and my shoes didn't want to cooperate. My left forearm was introduced to a whole new level of pain. But my adrenaline kept me moving skyward.

Finally, I reached a branch strong enough to hold my weight. The leaves shook and I worried that the sound would carry over the hard wind. I stopped and watched the man's face; his eyes remained level, so I continued.

I found a branch that reached all the way to the roof of the clinic and tested it. The branch seemed sturdy enough. It thinned a bit just before the roof but it would be only a foot or two for me to leap. After Ostermann's building in Berlin, I felt confident I could handle that.

As I navigated the branch I felt a lump form in my throat. I glanced down; it wouldn't be a terrible fall, but if I dropped awkwardly I could do some serious damage. And if Lindsay was still alive in that clinic, I'd have failed her.

It wasn't until I was just a few feet from the roof that I realized a jump of any kind would prove impossible; there was no way to gain the necessary leverage.

I looked down and saw that the large man was roughly twenty feet below me. If I could—

The branch snapped under my weight.

The sound was like the cock of a hammer in my ear.

I saw the large man look up.

Neither of us had much time to react. All I could do was attempt to control my fall and hope that his seeing me was enough of a shock to freeze him where he stood for a few moments.

With my right leg I pushed off just enough to reach him.

At the last moment he turned his body, but with my arms extended I was able to bring him down, his back cushioning my fall.

He grunted as his face hit the concrete. When he rolled over, I saw blood dripping from his forehead, and his eyes were wide with hell.

I remained on top of him, pinning his left arm. With his right he came up with a knife.

I moved to block the blow just in time and the blade drove deep into my left forearm, deeper than in Poland. The pain instantly seared all the way up to my shoulders.

With my right I punched the man flush in the face. Blood spewed from both sides of his nose. I pushed up hard under his chin so that the blood would stream into his eyes, blinding him.

He shouted something in Russian as he blindly reached for the knife still lodged in my left forearm.

I howled in pain as the blade began to come loose.

With my right I gripped his left ear and jammed my thumb into his eye as deep as it would go. His right hand released the knife and both hands went straight for his eye socket.

I dislodged the knife from my arm and made sure I had a secure grip.

I drew a deep breath, prepared to plunge the blade into his chest.

Only there had been enough killing.

Instead, I tossed the knife into the grass. With my right hand I grabbed the Russian's right lapel, positioning my bare knuckles against the carotid artery on the right side of his neck. With my left, I reached under my right and grabbed the Russian's left lapel, forming an X with my wrists. Then, with every bit of strength I had left in me, I applied pressure on the carotid. Took about twelve seconds, but by the time I finally released him, the Russian was out cold.

Breathing heavily, I glanced at the doorway. Apparently, no one had witnessed the fight.

I stood, looked down at the Russian.

His one good eye was half open, filled with blood yet staring absently at the sky.

I reached for his neck and felt for a pulse.

He was alive.

I grabbed his knife from where I'd thrown it in the grass, then quickly made my way to the entrance.

Chapter 55

I stood in front of the automatic doors and waited for them to open, but they didn't. My left forearm was useless. I gripped one side of the doors and tugged with all my might but it didn't budge.

The place was locked down.

I pulled out my Glock and stood back.

So much for not making a racket.

The shot shattered the city's disquieting silence, but also the glass on the right side of the door.

I stepped through, trying to ignore the throbbing pain in my left arm. I'd used the tie in my pocket as a temporary tourniquet. But the wound was deep and I continued to lose blood.

In the distance, a gruff voice bellowed something in Russian, the sound echoing off the corridor walls. The only word I understood was *Sacha,* which meant that the Russian running to the entrance was most likely Jov.

I pressed against the wall, then turned my body into the hallway, ready to fire.

No one appeared.

Then a gun materialized from the doorway and immediately fired in my direction.

I dodged back behind the wall just in time.

The shot ripped into the wooden reception desk just across from me.

My mind was growing cloudy from blood loss. I willed myself to remain on my feet. I couldn't faint. Not now, after I'd come so far.

I heard his footfalls in the hallway as he attempted to advance. I turned and fired just after he'd reached new cover.

I ducked back behind the wall and drew a deep breath.

There's no time for this. Lindsay may be under the knife as I stand here waiting for an opening.

If the Russian cut me down, this was all over. But if his bullets struck me anywhere but the heart or head, I knew I'd still make it into the operating room to find Lindsay. It was a chance I had to take.

One last breath, then I stepped into the hallway, Glock raised, searching for my target.

The moment I saw movement I fired, struck the left knee. The leg went out from under him, but he remained able to aim his weapon.

I fired another shot, into his right shoulder, and his hand opened.

His gun hit the linoleum and I immediately kicked it hard down the hall.

Jov continued to struggle to get to his feet, so I removed Sacha's knife from my belt.

He watched me as I maneuvered around his body. He opened his mouth to scream just I knelt behind him, lifted his right pant leg, and sliced through his Achilles tendon.

He howled in pain as his body dropped flat onto the dirty hallway floor, blood pooling all around his feet.

I strode down the hallway, leaving the fallen Jov behind with his screams. The floor was scuffed, the walls painted the same drab blue as in the sister clinic. The fluorescent lights flickered; exposed electrical wires hung loosely from the ceiling.

The operating room was positioned in the same location as at the other clinic, too—the room they'd wheeled Ana into.

Covered in blood—mine and others—I swallowed hard, steeled myself, and pushed open the operating-room doors.

Two surgical tables lay side by side. A young girl unconscious on each.

Two women and one man, all in green surgical gear, stepped away from the tables, unarmed, their hands slightly raised in the air in surrender.

Until that moment I hadn't even realized I was holding the gun on them.

One man stood between the two tables, arms down at his sides. He pressed his glasses higher up his nose, lowered his surgical mask, and removed the green cap from his head, revealing a mess of curly salt-and-pepper hair.

"Hello, Simon," he said in perfect English.

I stared down at the steel table holding Lindsay Sorkin. My eyes moved down her tiny body and settled on her chest.

"It's over, Doctor," I said.

"I don't suppose we can negotiate," he said sadly.

"Over a six-year-old's life?" I said. "No, Dr. Richter, I'm afraid that's out of the question."

I felt dizzy from the blood loss, my arms growing weaker every moment. The gun bobbed. I cleared my head and held it straight, aimed at Richter's center.

"The thing is, Simon, there are two six-year-old girls in this operating room. Lindsay Sorkin. And Mila Richter."

"I've heard about your daughter, Doctor. And I'm sorry. But you've no right—"

"And I've heard about yours, Simon," he said calmly. "You know what it's like to lose a child."

"Thanks to you," I said, "so do Vince and Lori Sorkin."

Richter smiled mirthlessly. "You have no idea, do you? Vince Sorkin is a criminal, Simon. A fucking traitor to his country. *Your* country. *Our* country."

I licked my lips. My mouth was going dry.

"Vince Sorkin is selling weapons technology to Iran," Richter said. "And his wife, Lori, knows all about it. She's known all along. Paris was just the beginning for them, Simon. They were about to cash in, change their names, and vanish."

I swallowed hard, tried to subdue my sudden thirst.

"First of all, Doctor, I don't believe a word you're saying. And even if it's true, it has nothing at all to do with the innocent girl lying on your slab."

"*Two* innocent girls," he shouted. "Don't pretend that Mila isn't here. Don't pretend she doesn't *exist*." He reached out to his daughter and ran his gloved hand gently over her forehead. "And it *is* the truth, Simon. Every word I've told you is true. You'll know it soon enough."

My left arm felt terribly weak. I didn't know how much longer I could hold the gun.

"It doesn't matter," I said. "This isn't about the parents."

Richter's eyes narrowed. "*Isn't* it, though?" He took a small step to the left and started to round the table holding his daughter.

"Stand *still*," I hollered.

The doctor stopped but otherwise ignored the interruption.

"Your wife *killed* herself when you lost Hailey, Simon. How can you stand there holding a gun on me and say this has nothing to do with the parents?"

"Tasha would have *never* traded another child's life for Hailey's," I said.

"Wouldn't she have, though? Wouldn't *you*?"

"You're mad, Doc—"

"If instead of *my* daughter," he said, "it was *your* daughter on this slab, and I told you I could bring her back right now, wouldn't you ask me to do it? Wouldn't you *beg* me to?"

I looked down and for a moment I *saw* Hailey on that slab where Mila lay.

Richter said, "Aren't you more deserving than Vince and Lori Sorkin, Simon?"

"This isn't *about* them," I shouted.

"It *is*," he fired back. "Mila has no less potential than Lindsay does, Simon. Mila is no less deserving of *life*."

"Neither is Mila more deserving than Lindsay," I said.

"What life does Lindsay have to look forward to, Simon? A life on the run from the CIA? Or more likely, orphaned at the age of six? Mila has two parents who love her more deeply than anything on this earth, two parents who have devoted their *own lives* to the sick and dying children of Belarus. If all else is equal between these two girls, Simon, then *shouldn't* the Sorkins and my wife, Tatsiana, and I be taken into account? Shouldn't the way we've lived our lives *matter*?"

"You have no right to play—"

"*God?*" Richter laughed angrily. "Don't be so fucking obtuse, Simon."

Beneath me I felt my legs turning to rubber. The image of the operating room was suddenly surrounded by a bright white glow. I needed to end this before I passed out.

"It's over, Doctor," I said again. "Wake the girl. Lindsay Sorkin is leaving with me."

Richter stood silent for a few moments. Only now there appeared to be two of him.

"The hell she is," he said finally. "You're going to have to kill me, Simon."

He moved to the table of surgical tools and picked up a scalpel.

"Don't make me do this, Doctor," I begged.

He moved over the insensate form of Lindsay Sorkin.

My finger tensed over the trigger of my Glock.

Richter lifted the scalpel.

"*Please*," I shouted.

Just as I was about to squeeze the trigger, the doctor looked me dead in the eyes.

Then pressed the blade of the scalpel deep into the flesh of his own throat and cut.

Chapter 56

The next morning, Ana and Lindsay and I were flown back to Paris on a private jet courtesy of the French government. Despite our best efforts, Lindsay barely said anything at all. "It'll take time," I assured Ana. "She's been through a hell of a lot."

It was true. Even the children I'd retrieved from their estranged parents often needed years of therapy to help them deal with everything they'd been through.

Ana was still recovering from the gunshot wound. Doctors at the clinic had removed the bullet from the upper left side of her chest rather easily. The storefront window had slowed the bullet down significantly, or else it might have traveled right through her. Marek arranged for Ana to be flown via helicopter directly to a hospital in Warsaw, but Ana of course refused. She wasn't going to Warsaw, she said. She was seeing this through to the end; she was accompanying me to Paris. I didn't bother to argue. Even when she was doped heavily with painkillers, I knew that there was no hope of winning a verbal duel with Anastazja Staszak.

Davignon had Bertrand and another of his men pick us up from Charles de Gaulle and drive us to the cottage in Saint-Maur-des-Fossés, where Davignon was waiting with an ecstatic Lori Sorkin.

Upon seeing her mother, Lindsay sprinted and leaped into Lori's arms. Lori covered her daughter in kisses, then lifted her toward the sky and spun her till they both fell into the tall blades of grass, crying and rolling around like a pair of jubilant toddlers.

After watching the reunion, I asked Ana to follow me upstairs to afford Lori and Lindsay some privacy.

"What happens now?" she said as we entered a large, well-appointed bedroom.

I stared at the king-size bed and wished I could sleep for a month.

"Even if everything Richter told me is true," I said, "I doubt very much the U.S. government will be able to prove Lori's involvement."

Given the fact that Vince Sorkin was still missing, I had little reason to question whether Richter was being honest about Vince's selling weapons technology to Tehran. But then, over the past ten years, I'd learned to question everything. And Vince's guilt would be no exception.

Still, I thought it likely that in her hysteria, Lori had threatened to spill everything in the hopes that it might somehow help get Lindsay back. And that's why Vince Sorkin had run.

"Do you think Vince will ever be found?" she said.

I didn't reply.

Dr. Keith Richter was already in U.S. federal custody in California after being stopped at the Mexican border on his way to Tijuana for what he called a spontaneous vacation. In preparation for said vacation, Keith Richter had bleached his hair and beard blond and stuffed his pockets with wads of cash. He'd left behind his wife and children.

Stephen may well have been the mastermind but he couldn't have done it without his brother. Keith Richter evidently tested hundreds of children, then supplied the information to Stephen for comparison. Lindsay Sorkin was the perfect donor for Mila Richter. Age, weight, blood type O, and, most incredibly, a six-antigen match—the best compatibility possible between a donor and a recipient who aren't identical twins.

Lindsay's heart was Mila's only chance at life. Mila would never have survived a second transplant, so Stephen Richter couldn't afford to try any heart but Lindsay's. A rejection of the heart by Mila's body would have made it all for naught. The Richter girl would have died.

After receiving the data, Stephen had used his significant resources—millions of dollars he'd raised for his Chernobyl charities from people and businesses all over the world—to discover as much about Vince and Lori Sorkin as he possibly could. He hired a private intelligence firm in the States. The firm, aptly named Third Eye, employed only top-notch intelligence vets from American, British, and German intelligence. It didn't take them long to infiltrate Nepturn Technology and discover Vince's plans to sell secrets to Tehran.

Of course, Stephen had justified his actions to me based on Vince's treason, but I doubt that if he'd learned that the Sorkins were model citizens he would have done anything differently. He didn't have time to be choosy; his daughter didn't have time. Once the heart-valve procedure failed, there was a good chance Mila would die. Short of a transplant, nothing would have saved Stephen Richter's little girl.

Davignon tapped on the open door and stepped inside.

"Sorry to disturb you," he said. "But Lori insists on thanking you personally, and of course, she'd like to take her daughter and leave France as soon as possible."

"Did she say where they were going?" I said.

He looked at me strangely. "I assume back to the States."

"Without her husband?"

Davignon took a step toward me, lowered his voice.

"Is there something you are not telling me, Simon?"

I hadn't told anyone. Yet. Before I told anyone anything, I needed to get to the truth.

"Send her in, Lieutenant." I turned to Ana. "If you'll excuse me for a minute, I'd like to speak with Lori alone."

"Of course," she said.

Once Ana returned downstairs with Davignon, I folded my arms across my chest and walked to the window. The sky was gray, just as it had been when Davignon first brought me to this cottage ten days earlier. Strange, I thought, where my mind kept returning during these past twenty-fours hours. Back to Kiev. To that run-down apartment complex in the Podil district, Lower City. To Dorota Wojcik, the young girl who'd led us to the Podrova brothers. Dorota was the only innocent person to have admitted to seeing Lindsay since her parents had put her to bed in Paris. She deserved the credit, not me. Yet, Dorota remained in her unthinkable situation back in Ukraine.

I'd spoken to Martyn Rudnyk from the plane. With the Podrova brothers out of the way, he assured me, his and Kidman's investigation would move forward with alacrity. I had no reason to doubt him. Bad people would be put away. But I couldn't help but wonder what would become of the children. Because the Podrova brothers and their so-called modeling agency weren't the only problems in these kids' lives. Far from it. Fact was, they were surrounded by evil and they had no one in the world to protect them.

"Simon?" Lori's voice remained hoarse but she sounded better than anytime I'd spoken to her over the phone these past several days. "May I come in?"

"Of course," I said.

She stepped in slowly. She was alone; she'd left Lindsay downstairs with Ana and Davignon. I was surprised that she could let her daughter out of her sight so soon, but I supposed it was healthy.

"I really don't know how to begin to thank you," she said.

"Seeing Lindsay safe is thanks enough, I assure you."

Lori walked up to me and put her arms around me and hugged

me with everything she had. I let her rest her head against my chest as I warmly hugged her back.

"Lieutenant Davignon tells me you had an ultrasound," I said, "and that the baby looks great."

I felt her nodding, felt her tears seeping through the cotton of my shirt.

"They saw boy parts," she said.

"Vince must be elated."

She was silent for a few moments, then said, "He doesn't know yet. He left before I told him."

I gently took her by the shoulders and held her away from me so that I could look into her eyes, the eyes that reminded me so much of Tasha's.

"Do you know where your husband went?"

Lori shook her head.

I believed her. He wouldn't have told her. If he was indeed a traitor to the United States, he wouldn't have told anyone. The risk would have been too great.

"Do you expect him back?" I said.

She shook her head ever so slightly again as she cast her eyes on the floor.

Of course, she knew what Vince had been doing. If he hadn't told her outright, she'd have suspected. She wasn't dim; quite the contrary. Her husband would have been constantly nervous and she'd have noticed the changes in him. He could have supplied her with any story he could dream up and she might even have gone along with it, but deep down she would've known. It was why she'd ultimately blamed her husband for their daughter's abduction.

Lori had threatened him; I was sure of it. It was why Vince had run.

Under the law, Lori would be culpable. But Lindsay was innocent. Children weren't held responsible for their parents' crimes, of course. But in the end, the children were usually the ones who suffered the consequences.

"Don't let them take Lindsay from me," Lori said softly as she buried her head in my chest. "I could never live through that again."

Neither could Lindsay, I thought.

Epilogue

Two months after I returned to the States, I found myself back in Europe, searching for someone. I'd been to Lisbon before and had a good relationship with the Portuguese authorities. But this time around I did everything I could to avoid them. For this task, I needed to remain under the radar.

I booked a room at a lovely hotel in Estoril. Every night I was there I walked across the street to a quiet restaurant and ordered a shrimp cocktail and a small but delectable piece of beef. As I sat there, sipping port wine, I considered what I'd do after completing this assignment.

The plan was to rent a car and drive through Spain and France toward London. There, I would do everything I could to locate my sister and mother. Attempts to find Tuesday through the Internet had proved futile. I hoped that meant she had married and changed her name. Of course, I hoped the same would be true of my mother. When my father left her, she'd still been young and very beautiful. Perhaps she'd remarried and lived happily ever after.

After that I'd drive to Germany and pay a visit to Kurt Oster-mann in Berlin. He'd been released in the deaths of Dietrich Braun and Karl Finster after a witness came forward. The witness was a young Turk who'd been good friends with Sidika. His name was Fi-rat and he was the other man we'd seen at Tunnelbar in Kreuzberg with Sidika and Alim. He knew everything, apparently. Including where Alim had been hiding out since he returned to Berlin following his uncle Talik's death in Poland. Alim was now in German custody, awaiting trial for murder.

After seeing Ostermann, I'd head east to Warsaw, where Ana was waiting for me. She wanted to show me more of Poland and feed me pierogi. How could I say no? Of course, I also owed her a trip to Hollywood, but she said that could wait a year. She'd started a new job as a prosecutor. Ana wouldn't be prosecuting her former boss Mikolaj Dabrowski personally, of course. But she *would* have a front-row seat at his trial. In any event, she couldn't take any considerable amount of time off just yet. No worries, I assured her. Whatever else happened in the United States, Hollywood would still be standing.

Once I left Ana, I would return to Ukraine. Specifically, to Lower City in Kiev. Martyn Rudnyk had invited me to meet with him and Kidman to discuss their progress in the worldwide child-pornography investigation. My priority lay in retaining lawyers to use the court system to extract the victims from their present situations—not just from the so-called modeling agency, but from the parents, guardians, older siblings, uncles and aunts who permitted them to be exploited in the first place.

After Ukraine, it would be on to Belarus. The death of Dr. Stephen Richter had left a serious vacuum in the medical services available to the continued victims of the Chernobyl disaster. There were other doctors devoted to the cause, of course, and it was with them that I would start. During my brief time back in the States, I'd driven from my home in D.C. north to Rhode Island. I visited with my father. He was much older than I remembered him, of course, and he seemed broken and lonely. I'd told him all about Lindsay Sorkin and the children of Belarus and asked him for his help in aiding the former Soviet state. I knew he wasn't the type of man who'd ever set foot in Minsk, but he did have a hell of a lot of money.

I didn't expect him to part with it all now, just some. And to revise his will, making the Mila Richter Foundation his primary beneficiary. No one lives forever after all. Not even Alden Fisk.

After dinner on my sixth night in Lisbon I made a call to the U.S. embassy, then hopped into a taxi and asked to be taken to the Alfama district. The Alfama is a quaint area, which is to say that many of its buildings are ancient and in terrible disrepair. As the taxi continued deeper into the quarter, twisting and turning around old churches and crumbling structures, I reached into my jacket and checked my gun. The weapon was small, a .22, nothing like the Glock I'd borrowed from Davignon when I left Paris. But then, I doubted I'd need a weapon at all. I didn't expect much resistance.

When I exited the taxi I took a deep breath, relieved that I could still smell the sea even from deep within the confining structures of the quarter. I walked several blocks until I reached a small cellarlike tavern with no name. I stepped slowly down the stairs and entered.

The tavern looked exactly as it had been described to me. It was a dank, dark place, the kind you always see in crime movies. Only about a half-dozen dark men sat around swilling Sagres cerveza, yet the place still felt cramped, almost claustrophobic. Everyone in the tavern eyeballed me with suspicion, except one man seated at the bar with his back to the door. He was wearing a short brown leather jacket and a fitted baseball cap with the MLB logo stitched in the back. I couldn't tell for sure, but it looked to be Dodger blue.

I stepped up to the bar, a makeshift thing you'd expect to find deep in the belly of a college frat house. It was stained badly with port wine. Behind the bar stood a long-faced old man with little hair and few teeth. He took a long pull off his cigarette and ashed on the floor, then regarded me through the smoke as though I weren't a customer but an intruder.

"*Vinho du porto,*" I said, indicating that one of the two glasses of port should be set in front of the man wearing the baseball cap.

The bartender sluggishly nodded his head, then tossed a worn dishrag over his shoulder and shuffled away to retrieve the glasses.

I sat on an open stool and leaned against the plywood. The man sitting next to me was indeed wearing a Dodgers baseball cap, the royal-blue brim pulled low over his eyes. He didn't bother to glance my way. He'd heard my voice; he knew I was there.

The bartender set two cloudy wineglasses in front of us and poured from a new bottle.

"Obrigado," I said, pushing a handful of euros across the bar.

"How did you find me?" Vince Sorkin said.

"It's what I used to do for a living," I told him. "Hunt down fugitives."

He nodded without looking at me. Pushed his beer aside and picked up his glass of wine.

"How's my family?" he said.

"I talked to your wife recently. She and your daughter are doing fine. Lindsay's still recovering but she's made a lot of progress already."

All I could see was his profile, but I could tell he was smiling sadly. I watched a tear glide down the left side of his face.

"I suppose that's the bright side of you being here," he said.

I didn't have to ask what he meant.

"You should finish your drink," I said.

When he put the glass back to his lips, his hand was shaking.

"I'm scared," he said.

"That's understandable."

Vince finally turned on his stool and looked me in the eyes.

"Thank you for finding my daughter, Simon."

"It was never for you and Lori," I told him. "It was always for the child."

I heard at least two vehicles screeching to a stop outside and I thought of the day not so long ago when Davignon and his cadre of white Peugeots topped with flashing lightbars forced my taxi to the side of the road.

Vince lifted his wineglass and threw back the last of its contents before setting it down and carefully wiping his mouth. He looked nothing like the man I'd met a few months ago. His skin was bronzed and peeling behind the coarse hairs of an incomplete mustache and beard. His eyes were bloodshot and I could tell that this was not the first night he'd been crying. Nor, I suspected, would it be his last.

I heard footfalls tramping down the stairs and everyone in the bar turned their heads to stare at the entrance. Everyone except me and Vince. Only we knew what was coming.

Together we rose from our bar stools.

Vince lifted his hands high in the air just as the door flew open and uniformed men burst into the tavern, raising their weapons and shouting commands.